Bess of the Bees

by

David J. Williamson

From an original 1922 story
by
Don Gray

Published by Firebird (SW) Ltd in 2016

A CIP catalogue record for this book is available from the British Library.

ISBN 978-0-9517512-5-1

Firebird (SW) Ltd, PO Box 107, EX15 9AW, UK

books@firebirdconsultants.co.uk

Also by

David J. Williamson

Belles of the Ball

A Pass Through Time

Foreword

As one of a set of women footballer adventure stories, 'Bess of Blacktown' was unique for its time. Under the pen name Don Gray, it was written by Robert Murray Graydon who, by 1922, had already had success writing a number of the famous Sexton Blake detective series and it is for these that he is best remembered.

1922 was after the infamous ban on women footballers by the English FA and to portray them as heroines and victors was a brave move for any writer; but for me it demonstrates that even in 1922 there was still enough popular interest to warrant the handful of such stories that emerged. It is impossible, however, to be completely sure as to whether such interest was merely an extension of the curiosity in the women's game at the time, rather than full bloodied support of their right to play. It is true to say that the stories 'played it safe' and never wavered from the tried and tested formula of heroes and heroines, good versus evil and courage in the face of danger that the regular readers of such sports serials demanded.

In adapting the story I struggled with the instinct to, on the one hand, replicate exactly an historical example of unique popular fiction; whilst on the other recognising the obvious need to make the tale accessible, enjoyable, and palatable for a modern readership.

A large part of adapting the story was transforming its serialised parts into a single tale with a consistent thread, removing any repetition or constant plot reviews.

Secondly there was the language. Gray chose to include the strong Lancashire accent for the local characters – apart from Bess herself; for example using *thee* and *tha* instead of *you* and *your*. I did not feel this to be essential to understanding the characters or their words, but unnecessary hurdles over which the reader must jump. One or two examples do remain – such as *Ah* for I, as well as some Northern expressions which add colour to the language and the characters.

Finally, I felt it appropriate to delete a number of expressions used – either in descriptive narrative or the words of the characters themselves – that although perfectly acceptable in 1922, would not sit comfortably with the modern views of a more open and inclusive society. In making the changes I make no apology for my intention– to pay tribute to the tale and its author and that even in a more modern form it has lost nothing of its original purpose - a ripping yarn to entertain its readers - and in this I hope I have done Bess and her creator proud.

Robert Murray Graydon died in 1937 aged 47

David J. Williamson

Devon, UK

2016

Bess of the Bees

The Busy Bees

The midday hooter blared out its hoarse, welcome note over the huddled houses and narrow streets of Blacktown, and the whirling, chattering looms in the spinning-room of Henneker's Mill gradually came to a standstill.

Bessie Booth, a pretty dark-eyed girl, with curly, chestnut hair and a slender, upright figure, heaved a little sigh of relief as she stepped back from her silent loom. It was a Saturday, and the mill machinery would not burst into its roaring song again until the following Monday morning.

There was an air of suppressed excitement about the crowd of girls who flocked out of the spinning-room and clattered down the stone stairs.

"Hurrah, at last!" cried Amy Olroyd, a tall, fair girl, as she linked her arm through Bessie's and fell into step behind her.

"I haven't half been looking forward to this afternoon. Seemed as though today would never come. I do hope we win, we must win! We can't let Burton's best us and keep us out of the league."

A murmur of agreement came from the other girls as they swarmed out into the mill-yard. Cheeks were flushed, and eyes sparkling with eager excitement.

"Burton's beat us!" exclaimed Sally Soper, a strongly built lass, with a comical turned-up nose, freckled cheeks, and twinkling, grey eyes.

"Girls, listen to Amy! She's talking about Burton's beating us!"

"Reckon it won't be your fault if they do., Sally. We can trust you to keep your end up 'tween the sticks."

"And our Bess, here. How many goals this afternoon, Bess lass?"

"As many as they'll let me get," laughed Bessie Booth gaily.

Any stranger to Blacktown, overhearing the remarks, would have been hard put to fathom what it was that the eager, chattering mill-girls were talking about.

Football was the topic that filled their minds to the exclusion of everything else. Ever since a few isolated girls' teams had been formed in England and France, speedily to show that they possessed a natural aptitude for the great winter game that hitherto had been monopolised by members of the opposite sex, football for girls had swept through Lancashire and Yorkshire like a wave.

Teams sprang up in all districts, clubs were formed one after the other, and such an enthusiasm was shown as amazed and bewildered even the great F.A. itself.

The girls of Henneker's Mill, ably led by pretty Bessie Booth, were some of the first to form a club of their own. Out of the hundreds employed at the mill, many were actively interested, whilst others gave their support, so that a strong team was eventually placed in the field.

This had been the latter end of the previous season, when Bessie Booth's eleven – the Busy Bees, as they called themselves – had played half a dozen matches, with other girls teams in the district, and showed a superiority that more than repaid them for their pains.

And the girl's interest in football had not waned during the summer months. Active organisation had resulted in the formation of a girl's football league that embraced twenty industrial towns within a fifty-mile radius of Blacktown.

But so speedily had the craze spread that the promoters of the league found themselves faced with the difficulty of selecting one representative club from each of the twenty towns.

Eventually it was decided to institute a knock-out competition amongst the clubs in each town, the survivor in every case to become members of the league.

In Blacktown itself, as it happened, there were only two teams – the Busy Bees, and an eleven that had been formed by the girl-employees of Burton's Iron Works.

Therefore it was left to these two teams to meet and fight it out as to which should win a place in the newly formed Girl's Football League.

And the all-important match was to take place that afternoon, hence the eager excitement of Bessie Booth and her companions as the hooter sounded its welcome note and they swarmed down into the recreation-room.

"One thing, girls, we've got the advantage of playing on our own ground, such as it is," said Amy Olroyd. "An' we beat Burton's easily in a friendly last season, so we ought to be able to whack 'em again."

"They've got a much better team than they had last year," said Bessie Booth cautiously. "And they've been training hard to beat us and get a place in the league."

"Ay, Ah've heard all about it," broke in Sally Soper, who played in goal for the Busy Bees. "Peg Davis, the captain of Burton's, her brother, he's a professional footballer, and he's been coaching them this past fortnight. That don't seem fair to me; yet I suppose it must be, else they wouldn't do it."

Bessie Booth nodded her head as she pinned a sheet of paper on to the baize-covered notice-board in the recreation-room.

"Never mind their coaching," she said confidently. "There's the team they've got to meet this afternoon, and if they can beat it they'll deserve their place in the league."

" Ay, that they will!" agreed Sally, glancing down the composition of the eleven, which showed, amongst others, herself in goal, Amy Olroyd and Enid Foster, backs, and Bessie in her usual position at centre-forward.

"But we mustn't let 'em beat us. This match means everything to us girls, Bess. If we don't get a place in the league, we might just as well give up the game."

"You're right, Sally," replied Bessie gravely. "This is the most important match we have ever played, and the whole future of our club depends upon our winning it."

Meanwhile, in his private office at the other end of the building, Peter Henneker, the sole proprietor of Henneker's Mill, closed down his desk and rose to his feet. Henneker was a tall, thin man, with a sallow complexion, jet-black hair, and a thin-lipped mouth that seemed set in a perpetual sneer of superiority.

Five years before, such a person as Peter Henneker had not been known in Blacktown. Then, on one well-remembered day, he had suddenly descended upon the town and entered into proprietorship of what had previously been known as Lydall's Mill.

And Henneker soon proceeded to make his presence felt. There were only two mills in Blacktown – the one he had bought, and Browell's Mill, owned by old Joshua Browell, a dour, crusty individual.

Henneker had immediately entered into active competition with Josh Browell. Evidently he had plenty of capital behind him, for he proceeded to cut prices, and gradually lured all his rival's best workmen away from him with the tempting bait of much-increased wages.

Josh Browell had set his teeth and held firm. He refused to reduce his prices or increase the fair standard of that he had always paid.

In less than a couple of years Browell was running his mill at a loss. There was not enough work to keep occupied the few employees who has remained loyal to him, and finally he had suddenly closed his mill down and registered a public vow that he would never open it up again so long as Peter Henneker remained in Blacktown, nor would he sell or allow anyone else to run it.

Everyone in Blacktown knew that Josh Browell would remain faithful to his vow. Once convinced on his point, Peter Henneker showed his true hand at last. Up went his prices with a jump, and down came his wage with a run.

"Take 'em or leave 'em," he as good as said to his indignant employees. "Mine's the only mill in Blacktown. If you won't work for me at my rate of pay, who else are you going to work for?"

It was a question to which the Blacktown folk could find no answer, and they had to knuckle under to Henneker's staggering edict. He was right – he had them in a cleft-stick, and they had placed themselves there by playing up to his cunning propaganda. If they did not work for him they were likely to starve, for there was no other employment to be found in Blacktown.

When old Josh Browell heard the news, he chuckled grimly. A deputation sent to try to open his mill again was sent away with a very emphatic negative

"Serve 'em right!" declared the old man. "They brought it on themselves. My mill's closed, and it's going to remain closed."

And it did. That had been three years ago. Browell's Mill still reared itself up stark and desolate – engines and looms as silent as the dead, weeds growing in the yard, and layers of dust and grime encrusting the gaping, empty windows.

And Henneker's Mill was a busy, flourishing concern, employing several thousand hands, and free from any competition so far as Blacktown was concerned.

Bessie Booth and most of the other mill-girls had started with Henneker's during the past two years, so that they played no part in the rivalry between their employer and Josh Browell. They simply sought employment with Henneker because he was the only mill in Blacktown.

Peter Henneker's dark eyes glittered as he gazed out of his office window at the swarms of men and women, lads and girls, bustling through the gates amid the clatter of clogs and buzz of voices.

"Sheep – a lot of sheep," he muttered scornfully, under his breath. "But I'm getting a lot of wool off of them. And I was the sheep-dog who rounded them up. What a fool Browell was! But it's a good thing for me he's kept his vow and refused to open his again. I couldn't have lasted out much longer, the money I was losing by under-cutting him."

With a chuckle of satisfaction, Henneker donned his overcoat and black bowler-hat and left the office. Half-way across the paved yard he halted, attracted by the shrill clamour of excited voices that came through an open window a few yards away. Henneker knew that it was the window of the recreation room, set aside for use of the mill girls.

"Good old Bess! That's the way to talk, lass!"

"We'll lick Burton's alright!"

"It's up to you to score the goals, Bess."

"An' Sally – Sally's got her bit to do 'tween the posts!"

Peter Henneker scowled, and beckoned to a man who had just emerged from the mill. Ned Bromley was his head overlooker – a stalwart, somewhat clumsy-looking young man, with fair hair and mild blue eyes, and a sheepish expression. But Ned Bromley was a splendid workman, and a sterling fellow in every way – good-natured, generous, and with a heart of gold.

"What's the matter with those girls, Bromley?" asked Henneker sharply. "Why haven't they gone home, instead of making all that noise in there? They're usually eager enough to clear off as soon as the hooter has sounded."

"Ah reckon it's the football, gaffer," replied the overlooker politely. "Just talking over the match the lasses are playing this afternoon."

"Football!" echoed the mill-owner, with a sneer. "Of all the confounded nonsense! You mean to say those fools of girls are still trying to play football?"

Ned Bromley flushed hotly, and for an instant an angry gleam crept into his mild, blue eyes.

"Ay, an' playing mighty well, gaffer!" he blurted, with a faint show of indignation. "As good as some men – and better. It's a great team them lasses make, what with Bess Booth, an' Sally Soper, an' little Connie Tree-......."

"Football!" Henneker sneered again, showing a faint trace of his scorn of healthy sport. "I don't approve of the game for me, let alone for a pack of stupid, gawky girls!"

Ned Bromley's lips tightened as he choked back the angry words that rose in his throat.

"Football's a great game, gaffer!" he said staunchly. "An' why shouldn't a lassie play it as well as a man? Britain ought to be danged proud o' our sporting gals. They can keep their end up at hockey, an' golf, an' swimming, an' tennis, so why shouldn't they play Soccer? Is Soccer any more risky than hunting to hounds? No; but it's a danged sight cheaper, and if the rich women can have their sports, why shouldn't our mill-lasses?"

"They seem to have a staunch supporter in you, at any rate!" snapped Peter Henneker. "If they want to take men's places, why don't they join the Army and fight......?"

Ned Bromley's eyes positively blazed.

"Fight!" he echoed. "Why, them lasses did men's work right through the war, an' well the Kaiser knew it!"

Henneker started as though stung, and his sallow cheeks crimsoned. Bromley's words seemed to have touched upon a raw spot.

"I don't want to enter into a discussion with you on such an idiotic subject, Bromley," he said thickly. "By the way, where do these girls of mine play – or attempt to play?"

Ned Bromley ignored the repeated sneer.

"On the bit o' waste ground in Hagg's Lane," he replied a trifle hesitantly.

"What, on my land?" exclaimed Henneker angrily. "And who the Dickens gave 'em permission to play there?"

"Well, Ah... Ah told 'em as they might," admitted Bromley uncertainly. "Ah didn't think you would mind, gaffer. The lasses are doing no harm, and....."

"And who gave you leave to grant them the use of my land?" snapped the mill-owner. "Are you the boss here, or am I? This has got to stop. You can just tell the girls from me that from this minute the use of that ground is forbidden!"

Ned Bromley's face fell, and a look of dismay crept into his eyes.

"Gaffer, don't do that," he said huskily, "Ah'm sorry if Ah've done wrong, but leave the girls alone. Just let 'em play their match to-day-----"

Peter Henneker hesitated. He felt in a spiteful mood, but his natural caution – or cunning – warned him not to act hastily.

"I'll think it over," he conceded angrily. "I don't approve of girls playing football. I'm going to put a stop to it; but I'll think the matter over first."

He turned on his heel and went striding away across the yard, whilst New Bromley stood staring after him, his big fists clenched in his pockets.

"The mean skunk!" he muttered indignantly. "What difference does it make to him if the lasses play football, or use his dirty old bit of waste ground? Ah wonder if he means what he says?"

The young overlooker suddenly flushed up self-consciously as he caught sight of Bessie Booth, trim and pretty, emerging from the mill, and he hastened to her side. There was a light of almost dog-like devotion in Ned's eyes as clumsily he raised his cap. Ned made no secret of the fact that he loved Bessie Booth – adored the very ground she walked on; but he sadly aware that he was never likely to win the girl for his wife.

Bessie liked and admired the big, honest fellow, and she valued his friendship more than that of anyone else she knew; but she realised that she could never love him in the same way that he loved her.

Ned Bromley never despaired, however. He stuck doggedly to his guns. If Bessie Booth did not love him, at least he would go on loving her, until some lucky chap robbed him of even that privilege.

Their ways into town lay the same. Ned Bromley always waited until the girl left the mill, and now he fell into step by her side.

"Well, Bess lass," he said a trifle huskily. "Ah hopes you puts it across the Burton girls this afternoon! It'll be a great day for Blacktown of you get the league."

"Won't it be splendid Ned?" cried Bessie enthusiastically. "I feel so excited. I scarcely know what I'm doing! Just think if we win! We'll have a match to play every Saturday afternoon – a real league match, and we'll have to go to Loomton, and Oldcastle; and Righam, and Keston, and all those places. Oh, we must win!"

"That's the spirit lass!" encouraged the young man. "Make your mind up to win, an' that's half the battle."

"And if we *do* win," said Bessie eagerly. "I mean to go to the gaffer – Mr Henneker – and ask him if he'll advance a bit of money to do our ground up. Fix up a proper dressing room... and some banking and....."

Ned Bromley stopped short, and Bessie Booth stared in surprise at his flushed, rueful countenance.

"Reckon you'd best leave the gaffer out of it, lass," said the young overlooker gravely. "You'll get no brass out of such as him for football. Why even now he's talking of forbidding you to play on the old waste piece of ground."

Bessie's brown eyes widened, and she uttered a little gasp of dismay.

"Why, Ned!" she exclaimed. "When did you hear this? Surely he can't mean it?"

"He told me with his own lips, lass. He don't approve of gals playing football, and he proper tore me up for allowing you to use the waste ground. He wanted to stop you playing this afternoon, only Ah persuaded him to think it over."

"Surely he wouldn't be such a beast as to refuse" cried the girl hotly. "He wouldn't dare!"

"Well, reckon we'll hope the best," muttered Ned Bromley lamely, though in his heart he had scant hopes indeed. "You'd best hurry off, Bess. Ah'll be up on the ground to give a cheer!"

The Great Match

Bessie's thoughts were anxious ones as she hurried along to the little cottage in Chapel Lane, where she lived with her aunt. Ned Bromley's disquieting news could not have come at a worse moment – within an hour of the kick-off of the all-important match that was to settle the future of the Busy Bees.

Election to the league would be a barren triumph if the club was to have no ground on which to play future home fixtures.

The girl snatched a light lunch, washed, and combed and brushed her bobbed hair. Then, grabbing the bag containing her football kit, she hastened off to join her companions.

The ground that Peter Henneker threatened to take away from the mill-girls was by no means an ideal one. It was uneven and patchy, but there was plenty of room, and it was marked out correctly, and complete with posts, nets, and corner-flags that they had bought cheap from a football club to which Amy Olroyd's brother belonged.

The dressing accommodation was a big canvas tent divided by a partition, and here Bessie found Sally Soper and the rest of the girls eagerly discussing their chances of a victory over their rivals for a place in the Girl's Football League – Northern Section.

Bess had already decided not to acquaint her companions with the unpleasant news that Ned Bromley had told her.

'It can wait till after the match, whatever the result,' she had thought. 'It would only upset them, and put them off their game.'

A noisy chattering on the other side of the canvas partition made it very evident that the Burton Iron works team had arrived.

"Just listen to 'em," chuckled Sally Soper, as she hopped around the tent on one leg, trying to get a disobedient boot on to her foot, "talking about what they're goin' to do when they get into the league!"

"We'll give them something to talk about later on!" declared Amy Olroyd. "They'll have a different song to sing when the Busy Bees have stung 'em several times!"

"My word, girls, Ah'm beginning to feel quite nervous!" said Mary Bonny, a half-back, as she peered through the flap of the tent (Mary Bonny, commonly called "Bony Mary," was a tall, thin, strong girl, who was frightened of nothing on earth). "Just look at the folk round the ground, and they be still tramping up Hagg's Lane like an army of soldiers."

Mary was right. The match between the girls of Henneker's Mill and Burton's Iron Workers had evidently excited the interest of the good people of Blacktown, for already there were several hundred ranged around the touch-line, and more were still streaming in, in batches.

"There's the referee, talking to Ned Bromley, an' a good-looking young fellow he is, too!" whispered Connie Tree, a slim fair-haired wisp of a girl who played at outside-right. "If we look like getting beaten, you'd best set yer cap at him, Sally, while we score a few goals."

The referee, who had been appointed by the league, was none other than Dick Lawson, who played centre-half for Blacktown Rovers, a professional club in the Northern Section of Division III of the English League. He was a big, cheerful, powerful fellow, and he looked very business-like as he glanced at his watch and then in the direction of the tent, as much as to say: 'Now, then you girls – step lively!'

"Come on, the Bees!" cried Bessie Booth excitedly and, snatching up a practice ball, she whipped open the tent-flap and led her trim team out on to the field.

She almost stopped dead in surprise at the cheer of welcome that greeted them.

"Here they come! Bravo, the Bees!"

"Up and at 'em, Henneker's!"

Very smart and workman-like the girls looked in their green-and-white striped jerseys and white knickers, and the smooth, deft manner in which they swung the ball about elicited a shout of admiration.

A moment later the Burton team, in red and white, made their appearance, and it was evident that they, too, had their supporters in force on the ground.

The referee placed a brand-new ball on the centre-mark, and first Bessie Booth and then Peg Davis, the Burton captain, went forward to shake him by the hand, and then greeted each other with a hearty kiss.

"What about the ref? Don't he deserve one?" roared a voice, amid a ripple of laughter.

Dick Lawson flushed and laughed, as a coin was spun in the air. Bessie called correctly and smiled happily as she pointed to the goal that gave her team the advantage of a slight breeze.

The two elevens lined up, and Peg Davis set the ball in motion. For the first few minutes nerves had the upper hand over skill, and the play was ragged and aimless. Both sides were a trifle overcome by the importance of the occasion, and there was little combination. The ball sped erratically from player to player until Mary Bonny, the Bees' centre-half, nipped in, dribbled well down the field, and transferred smartly to Connie Tree on the right wing.

The little mill-girl went off at a pace that brought a roar of delight from the crowd. Swerving around the opposing back, she centred with a neat, accurate pass and, coming up on the run, Bess got her boot to the ball with a first-time shot that sent it whizzing into goal like a stone from a sling. In vain the goalie flung herself headlong, with stretching arms and straining fingers.

"Goal!"

Ned Bromley's lusty voice boomed across the field like a thunderclap. The ball was in the net, and already Bessie Booth had given her side the lead. Surrounded by her flushed and radiant companions, she ran back to the centre of the field, and the dejected Burton team kicked-off again.

Both elevens had now settled thoroughly into their stride – the one stung by their reverse; the other stimulated by their success. It was a fast, skilful, clean game, and for the next half-hour neither side showed any marked superiority over the other.

Then within a few minutes of half-time, the Burton team forwards broke away, and a hot shot forced Sally Soper to concede a corner. The kick was a well-placed one – a scramble right in the goal-mouth, a bobbing head, and the scores were level! It was a fitting finish to a well fought first half, and Mary Bonny's shrewd eyes gleamed with satisfaction as they repaired to the dressing-tent.

"We've got 'em beat, girls," she said confidently.

But the Burton girls were a long way from being beaten yet. They did not mean to lose their chance of a place in the league if they could help it.

"Buck up, the Bees!" roared Ned Bromley encouragingly, and then the young overlooker's heart gave a great leap of dismay as he caught sight of a well-known figure forcing his way through the crowd. It was Peter Henneker, his sallow cheeks crimson, his dark eyes glittering with anger.

"Get away from here – get off my ground!" he roared. "You're trespassing – ruining my property! Who gave you leave to trample all over my field? Stop the game!"

The people scattered to right and left in surprised alarm, and Peter Henneker dashed out into the centre of the field, waving his arms frantically above his head. It was just at that moment that Mary Bonny got her foot to the ball in a mighty kick that would have lifted it right down into the opposing goal-mouth.

But there was another mouth in the way – Henneker's mouth, to be precise! The muddy ball struck him full in the face with a dull thud, and sent him sprawling full-length.

Bessie Booth's pretty countenance was pale with dismay as the referee blew his whistle and ran forward just as the mill-owner rose, spluttering and foaming, to his feet.

"Now, then, my man! What do you mean by interrupting this game?" cried Dick Lawson. "Leave the field at once!"

"You impertinent fool!" raved Henneker. "This is my field! I order you to stop this game and clear off my property! My name is Henneker!"

"I don't care if your name is Henneker, Hen-coop, or Hullaballoo!" snapped the referee angrily. "Or if you own all Blacktown! There are only five minutes to go, and I mean to see this game finished. You can speak to me afterwards, if you like. Now clear off!"

The muddy ball struck the angry Henneker full in the face, and sent him sprawling full length.

"I'll have the police on you!" Henneker snarled. "And those girls! By thunder, I'll teach them who their boss is! Just you wait till Monday!"

Amy Olroyd stared at Bessie Booth in bewilderment.

"The gaffer!" she gasped. "What does it all mean, Bess?"

"Finish the game first, and you'll hear all about it," cried Bessie Booth anxiously. "But we must finish the game. Play up, girls – one more goal!"

The referee threw the ball down, and from the ensuing scramble it came to Mary Bonny, who flashed it out to Connie Tree. But the little outside-right was closely shadowed and forced over the line, though not before she had managed to transfer to the opposite wing.

The Burton right-back miss kicked in an attempt to clear, and the leather came straight to Bessie Booth. She caught it breast-high, trapped it, and was off like a flash. She had the heels of everyone else on the field, and she knew that it was now or never – her last chance to score.

The goalkeeper came rushing out. There was a hazy whirl of intermingling colours – green, red and white – then two figures lay outstretched on the turf; but the ball was spinning at the back of the net, and the Busy Bees had taken the lead! It was the winning goal, the referee's whistle shrilled loud and long, and Bessie Booth and her team of mill-girls had won their place in the big league!

"So now you know all about it, girls," said Bessie Booth, five minutes later, as she stood facing her bewildered companions in the dressing-tent. "We've won our place in the league, but it looks as if we've lost our ground. Gaffer Henneker's forbidden us to play here anymore! He told Ned Bromley that he would see us on Monday. It means trouble for us, girls, but never mind! If we stick together, we'll pull through, and if he won't let us have the use of this ground, we'll have to find another."

"Hear, hear!" cried Sally Soper. "We've won our place in the league, and, by gum, we've got to keep it!"

Bessie Booth led the rousing cheer that followed. She little dreamed of the amazing adventures, tribulations, and triumphs that the near future held in store for the Busy Bees of Blacktown!

Facing the Music

By their well-earned victory over Burton's XI, a team of girls representing Henneker's Mill and styling themselves the "Busy Bees," qualified for one of the twenty places in the newly formed Girl's Football League. It was a well-contested game, and victory was principally due to the clever play of Bessie Booth, the centre-forward and captain of the "Bees," who scored both goals and proved herself a capable leader.

Football for girls is indeed booming, and in the "Bees" Blacktown possesses a team that should ably represent them in the league.

This paragraph appeared in the Monday morning issue of the "Blacktown Chronicle," and Bessie Booth's brown eyes gleamed proudly as she read it through.

"Well, I think they might have mentioned Sally Soper in goal, and the way Mary Bonny played at centre-half!" she said indignantly. "And Connie Tree on the right wing. Neither of our goals would have been scored but for her. It's a shame! I did practically nothing save just turn the ball into the net."

Bessie glanced at the cheap clock on the mantelpiece, and, snatching up her shawl, wrapped it around her head as she hastened out into the cold, narrow streets of Blacktown. It was early morning, and from all sides resounded the clatter of clogs as the workpeople converged on their way up the hill to the gaunt, grey building that bore the name, "Henneker's Mill."

Bessie Booth, the pretty, brown-haired girl of eighteen, who worked at the mill was also the captain of the football team and now they had won a place in the Girls' League, there would be an interesting programme of home and away fixtures, with a silver cup and medals for the team with the best record at the end of the season.

"Morning, Bess lass!"

"Good morning, Ned!" Bessie Booth nodded a greeting to the big, broad-shouldered young man with the somewhat heavy face and mild blue eyes, who had obviously been waiting for her at the corner, and now fell into step by her side.

It was transparent to everyone that he was in love with pretty Bessie Booth. But Bessie did not return Ned's love.

"Bess, Ah reckon you and the rest of the football team are in for a hot time this morning" said the young man anxiously. "You'll have to go before the gaffer."

Bessie nodded, and her lips tightened. She wasn't altogether relishing the prospect of the interview that lay before her within the next hour or so. The interview was to be with Peter Henneker, the owner of the mill – her employer – and, as Ned Bromley had hinted, it would probably be a stormy one after the recent match; using his ground without permission and being struck in the face with the ball had left the mill owner humiliated and angry.

"We'll have to find another ground," said the pretty captain of the "Busy Bees" hopefully. "We've won our place in the league, and we mean to keep it. We've got a whole fortnight in which to secure a ground, Ned, for our first league fixture, fortunately, is an away one."

Ned Bromley shrugged his shoulders. He knew very well that it would be no easy task to find a fresh football pitch anywhere in the district of Blacktown.

The hoarse note of the hooter was blaring over the town as Bessie hurried through the mill gates, checked in with the timekeeper, and clattered up the stone steps to where she worked. Here she was greeted by her fellow-members of the football team – Amy Olroyd, big, stalwart Mary Bonny, the centre half, Sally Soper, the goalkeeper, and Connie Tree, a fair-haired wisp of a girl who played at outside-right, and who combined the speed of a hare with the slipperiness of an eel.

"Come to take your medicine, Bess?" greeted Sally, with a meaning wink. "Wonder what the gaffer'll have to say to us? Best take some smelling-salts for Mary; she's nervous, like."

"Nervous!" snorted Mary Bonny – commonly known as "Bony Mary" – setting her muscular red arms akimbo, with a scornful gleam in her eyes. "If the gaffer has much to say to me Ah'll put him across my knee and spank him – the long, mean gawk!"

There was a roar as the engines swung into their stride, and Bessie Booth soon found herself fully occupied with looms she had to attend to. Bessie was a deft, clever weaver, and earned good money.

At eleven o'clock the machinery ceased again, and it was Ned Bromley who brought the anticipated summons to the presence of Peter Henneker.

A moment later the girls found themselves in the mill-owner's private office, ranged in a row before Henneker's big desk.

"Well, and what have you girls got to say?" Henneker snapped viciously, sweeping them with his close-set dark eyes. "I suppose you are responsible for the disgraceful scene on my ground on Saturday? Did I give you permission to play there, and invite all your hobbledehoy friends to come and trample down my hedges and ruin my property?"

"No one was doing any harm, gaffer," said Bessie Booth clearly, stepping forward. "It was just an ordinary game of football….."

"Football! I don't approve of football …especially for girls," sneered Henneker. "You ought to be ashamed of yourselves, making a public exhibition by kicking a muddy ball about ….."

"And why shouldn't we girls play football?" flashed Bessie indignantly. "It's a clean, healthy sport, and there's no reason why the men should think that they're the only ones who can….."

"I am not opening a discussion on the subject," interrupted the mill-owner, though there was a look of grudging admiration in his dark eyes as he gazed into the pretty, flushed face of Bessie Booth. "I simply say here and now that I won't have you playing football on my land. You understand? There must be no more football on my ground."

The faces of the mill-girls fell, and they stared at one another in silent dismay. The dreaded blow had fallen!

"Gaffer, you're not fair!" cried Bessie boldly. "Why should you grudge us our bit of sport, and the use of the old field in Hagg's Lane? It hasn't been used for years. We cleared it ourselves, levelled it, cut the grass, and mended the fence. And by winning our match on Saturday we've got into the new Girl's Football League. We're to be known as Henneker's Busy Bees, and if you were a man and a sport you'd give us the support we need."

"That'll do; I don't want to argue with you!" rasped Peter Henneker furiously.

Bessie Booth bit her lip, a spot of colour in each cheek.

"So you won't let us have the use of the old piece of waste land in Hagg's Lane?" she said in a low voice.

"Most decidedly not. You have had my answer."

"Then – then we'll have to find another ground, that's all," declared the girl, turning towards the door.

"Steady on, there – you don't seem to catch my meaning," rapped Henneker sharply. "I won't have any girls' football club run in connection with my mill! Is that clear enough?"

There was a simultaneous gasp of surprise, dismay, and Bess stared incredulously at the mill-owner.

"You.....you mean that we have got to give up our football?" she said slowly.

"So long as you remain in my employ, yes."

"Why, you must be crazy!" burst out Mary Bonny, unable to control her feelings any longer. "What right have you got to forbid us playing the game? It's nothing to you what we do with our spare time!"

Henneker glared balefully at the big, raw-boned girl, and dropped his eyes again beneath Mary's steady gaze.

"What I say I mean!" he cried, thumping the top of his desk. "I forbid anyone in my employ to run a girls' football team!"

"You can't ....you can't prevent us!" declared Bessie.

Peter Henneker sprang to his feet.

"You have your choice!" he snapped maliciously. "Either you give up your rubbishy football, or you leave my employ! Now, is that plain enough?"

It was only too plain. White-faced and wide-eyed, Bess and her companions stared ruefully at one another. What were they to do?

"It...it's not fair!" gulped Connie Tree.

Peter Henneker sprang to his feet. "You have your choice!" he snapped maliciously. "Either you give up your rubbishy football, or you leave my employ!"

Peter Henneker sat back with a cold sneer on his sallow face.

"I am the best judge of that. You have your choice."

There was a moment's silence. Mary Bonny breathed heavily as she clenched and unclenched her big hands.

"Yes or no?" rapped Henneker, glancing at his watch. "I can't waste any more time on you!"

Bessie Booth turned slowly to her companions.

"No!" burst from Mary Bonny and every voice echoed her. "We'll see you hanged first, gaffer!"

"Ay... that we will! You've no right to interfere with our sport. We don't play in your time."

Peter Henneker stared at the girls in surprise. He had not expected that they would defy him in this manner, and at heart he didn't want to lose them. Good operatives were scarce; but he couldn't climb down now.

"Very well," he said harshly. "You can all take a week's notice!"

An awed silence hung over the little group of mill-girls as they made their way to the recreation-room. It was several minutes before they realised the full seriousness of the step they had taken.

"My word, girls, we've done it this time!" exclaimed Sally Soper gravely. "We're sacked! We'll be out o' work after the end o' this week! And where are we going to find other jobs in Blacktown? But I don't care. I'd rather starve than knuckle down!"

"That's just how I feel," declared Bessie Booth. "Surely he must realise that it's not his business to interfere with our football, which is played in our own time! Perhaps.... he'll have changed his mind by the end of this week."

"More likely he'll be looking for us to have changed ours," said Mary Bonny. "But not me! Ah wouldn't give in to the gawk!"

"Nor I!" chorused the others; and they meant it!

The First League Match

The days that followed were fraught with anxiety and uncertainty for Bessie Booth and her companions. Once they left Henneker's, what was to become of them? Where were they to get any other employment, unless they left Blacktown? For there was no other mill in the place save Henneker's.

On the Tuesday came a written confirmation of their election to the Girls' League and a copy of their fixture-list for the season. On the coming Saturday they were to play away against Oldcastle Rovers. Would the match be played?

"It.....it don't seem fair to the league for us to play only the one match, and then have to resign because we'll have no ground to play our home fixtures on," said Sally Soper gloomily. "If we've got to resign, we ought to resign at once, and give the league a chance to get another club to take our place."

Bessie Booth's cheeks were flushed as she sprang to her feet.

"There must be no talk of resignation from the league!" she said firmly. "Why, we've as good as lost our jobs here because we refused to give up our football! We've got to buck up, girls, and find a new ground. Perhaps the Burton team will lend us theirs for a couple o' weeks. In any case, we're going to play our match with Oldcastle on Saturday, no matter what happens!"

Saturday morning came at last. It was with mingled feelings that Bessie Booth and her companions bent over looms for what was to be the last time. They were bubbling over with excitement at the prospect of their journey to Oldcastle to play the Rovers, but their high spirits were overshadowed by the knowledge that the following week would find them out of employment.

Just before the hooter blew at twelve o'clock one of the clerks from the general office approached Bessie Booth.

"Mr Henneker wants to see you in his office at once," was the message he brought. Bess's heart leaped as she stopped her looms and hurried away. Perhaps Peter Henneker had changed his mind!

But Bessie's hopes were very far from the truth. Peter Henneker rose from his chair as the pretty, brown-eyed mill-girl entered his office, and there was a look of admiration on his sallow face.

"Come in, Miss Booth," he said suavely. "You don't want to lose your job, do you?"

"Lose...lose it? Of course I don't!" stammered the surprised girl. "But...."

"Then you needn't, if you're sensible," said Henneker, coming closer, an ingratiating leer on his thin lips. "Those other fools of girls *must* go, but you may stay on."

Bessie stared at the man, an inkling of the truth gradually filtering into her mind.

"They must go – I may stay on?" she echoed.

"Yes, my dear; I'm willing to keep you on," smiled Henneker, thinking the girl was overcome with delight. "You're one of my best weavers – and you're a dashed good looker. In fact, I've taken quite a fancy to you. I can give you a better time than you'd get playing football, or looking for work! What about a theatre tonight, or a run into Manchester in my car......"

Bessie's heart was throbbing as though it would burst. Peter Henneker was right beside her now; one arm closed around her slender waist, and his flushed, sallow face was very close to her own.

The next instant the mill-owner received the surprise of his life. A firm palm was planted beneath his chin, and at the same instant a deft back-heel threw him off his balance and sent him crashing into a far corner of the room.

"You cad – you low beast!" cried Bessie, her eyes flashing, her breast heaving with indignation. "Why, I wouldn't stay and work for you for all the money in the world after this! Want me to turn my chums down, do you – leave them in the lurch and toady to you? You despicable rotter!"

Henneker staggered to his feet, stuttering and stammering with fury as he rubbed his aching head.

"You vixen! By heavens, I'll get my own back on you for this!" he snarled thickly. "I'll see you in the gutter before I've finished with you! I'll drive you out of Blacktown – you and your precious girl footballers!"

Bessie Booth did not wait to hear any more. With a final scornful glance at the raving mill-owner she darted from the room, tears of mortification and anger in her eyes.

In asking her to desert Sally Soper, Mary Bonny and the rest, Henneker could not have offered her a greater insult. She halted for a moment to get her outraged feelings under control, and made her way back, deciding not to worry them with the story of her interview with Henneker.

A few minutes later the little band of mill-girls drew their money for the last time at the pay-office, and passed out through the mill gates.

White-faced and agitated, Ned Bromley came hurrying up, and drew Bessie to one side.

"Bess, lass, is it true?" he gulped. "You've left the mill for good? That dirty skunk Henneker's sacked you an' the rest of the team?"

Bessie nodded her curly head.

"Yes, it's quite right, Ned"

"But what are you going to do, lass?"

"Find another job, of course, Ned," replied the girl confidently.

Ned Bromley frowned reprovingly.

"There's no other jobs in Blacktown, an' you know it," he said grimly. "Bess, Ah've asked you before, and Ah ask you again. You'd best marry me. You know Ah just worship you. Ah've got a bit of brass put by, an' a good job....."

"Ned, you're an old darling!" Bessie's eyes were suspiciously moist as she spoke. "You're the best friend I've got. I love you in that way, but I could never marry you. I've told you before, but you simply won't take 'No' for an answer."

"Well, promise me this, Bess – if you ever want any help you'll come to me?"

The girl readily gave this assurance, and hurried away home to get her football kit, and then meet the rest of the team at the station, to catch a train to Oldcastle.

The mill-girls' troubles were temporarily forgotten as they stood grouped on the platform, eagerly chatting over the prospect of their defeating Oldcastle, and thus registering their first victory in the new league.

Their train was due in a few minutes' time, on the right-hand side of the platform, and as Bess stepped across to extract a piece of chocolate from an automatic machine, another train came roaring in on the left.

Within a few yards of her stood an old, white-haired man, attired in well-worn clothes and a dusty pot-hat. He was supporting himself on two sticks and, startled by the thunder of the approaching train, he swung round sharply.

One of his sticks slipped on the smooth asphalt; he stumbled, and in another instant would have toppled off the platform, to be dashed to fragments beneath the wheels of the train as it swept past. How she managed it Bessie Booth never knew, but she sprang forward like a flash of lightning, and in the nick of time grabbed him back from certain death.

The man's face was as white as his hair, and beads of perspiration stood out on his forehead as he propped himself up on his sticks and turned, amazed to find that it was a slim, pretty girl who had so providentially come to his aid.

"Lass, that was a brave deed!" he said huskily. "You saved my life! If you hadn't pulled me back I'd been down on the line!"

"I'm glad I happened to be near. It was nothing – I just put my hand out….."

"Nothing? I don't reckon my life as nothing!" said the old man, with a grim smile. "And I want…."

Bessie suddenly heard the voice of Sally Soper screaming her name, and she had just time to spring across the platform and leap into the moving train that was carrying her friends away to Oldcastle.

The old man stood staring after the train until it had vanished from sight, and then he turned to a porter who stood close by.

"Say, lad, who was that lass with the red tammy hat?" he queried eagerly. "Do you know her?"

"Ay; that's Bessie Booth, the girl footballer," replied the porter enthusiastically. "An' a rattling fine player she is, too. Ah saw her play last Saturday, when her team beat Burton's girls; an' now they're off….."

The old man did not wait to hear anymore, but hobbled off towards the exit from the station.

"Bessie Booth!" he muttered under his breath. "Reckon I won't forget that name, an' I'll soon find out where the lass lives. She's a brave lass, an' she saved my life, right enough!"

Roar upon roar of cheering swept around the touchlines of the Oldcastle Rovers' cosy little ground. The two or three thousand people assembled there had no reason to be dissatisfied with the football fare that was being served up to them by the twenty-two darting figures in the green-and-white and black-and-white jerseys.

"Go it, the Rovers! Play up, Oldcastle!"

"What about the Bees? Good old Blacktown!"

"Now then Bess! Pull your socks up, Mary!"

Half-time had come and gone, and the scores were level. Bessie Booth had scored a brilliant goal for her side ten minutes from the commencement of the game; but the Rovers had succeeded in equalising just prior to the interval, and now each team was striving might and main to snatch a winning goal.

And three minutes from full time it came. It was Mary Bonny, the Bess' centre-half, who started the movement and sent her forwards away. From wing to wing the leather was transferred with long, swinging passes. Now Connie Tree had the ball, and was tearing down the touchline with the opposing left-half panting at her heels.

"Centre, lass...centre!"

"Now's the chance! In with it!"

But Connie didn't centre. She passed obliquely back to her inside partner, Millie Royd, and Millie just flicked the ball with her boot, deflecting it neatly to Bessie Booth's toe.

Bessie took three strides, dodged a charging back who went sprawling from her own impetus, and with a lightning, twirling shot flashed the leather into the net.

"Goal! Bravo Bess! Good old Bess!"

It was Ned Bromley's stentorian voice that boomed across the field, and he was still cheering when the final whistle blew and the victorious Bees ran from the ground, hugging Bessie Booth joyously in their midst.

All their troubles were forgotten in the happy realisation that they had played and won their first match in the Girl's Football League.

It was past nine o'clock when Bessie Booth returned to the little cottage in Chapel Lane where she lived with her aunt. Good-hearted Ned Bromley had insisted on treating the entire team of girls to a fish supper, in order to celebrate their brilliant victory over Oldcastle Rovers, and Bessie now felt thoroughly tired out as she sank into a chair.

The double journey to Oldcastle and the strenuous game with the Rovers, on the top of a half-day's work at the mill, was sufficient to tire out a grown man, let alone a girl of eighteen. Just as Bessie was about to turn out the light she caught sight of something white propped up against the clock on the mantelpiece.

It was a letter addressed to her, and it had evidently been delivered by hand, for it bore no stamp or postmark. The girl's smooth forehead puckered in a perplexed frown as she tore the envelope open and glanced at the note within.

'Dear Miss Booth' – it ran – *'Please accept an old man's heartfelt thanks and gratitude for the invaluable service you rendered him this afternoon. Though old, I still place a considerable value on my life, which now rightfully belongs to you. If at any time there is anything that I can do for you, to show my sincere appreciation of your bravery, you have only to apply to* JOSHUA BROWELL'

"I wonder how he found out my name, and where I live?" muttered the girl. "Joshua Browell!" why, goodness me, that shabby old man.... Josh Browell!"

Bessie's eyes opened wide at the thought that she had saved the life of one of the wealthiest men in Blacktown. And evidently he was really grateful. What was it he wrote? 'If at any time there is anything that I can do for you . . . you have only to apply to Joshua Browell.'

Bessie Booth suddenly sprang to her feet, a gleam of excitement lighting her brown eyes. This note in her hand – why shouldn't it hold the solution to all the doubts and perplexities that had been worrying her all that week?

Amy Olroyd and all the other members of the football team were out of work and in need of employment. And the Busy Bees needed a new ground on which to play their league fixtures at home.

And here was a rich old man who....

"I'll do it!" declared Bessie Booth aloud and very emphatically. "I'll do it! I'll go and see him tomorrow! Yes, I will!"

And she marched hopefully upstairs to bed.

Bess Gets Busy

From the top, back window of the little, red-brick house in Chapel Lane, where she lived with her aunt, Bessie Booth could gaze down right into the heart of Blacktown – a vista of narrow, twisting streets, and cluster upon cluster of chimneypots – a whole army of chimney-pots, each belching out its quota of black smoke to add to the sable pall that forever hung over the town and the adjacent countryside.

And dotting the horizon were various other lowering black clouds, each one denoting a separate town devoted to the cotton industry – Loomton, Oldcastle, Rigan, Keston, and Barton, to name only a few.

It was not a particularly beautiful view; but Bessie Booth had been born and bred in the Lancashire borough of Blacktown, and therefore did not realise its drab ugliness. Besides, she was thinking of something quite different as she leant out of the window of her little bedroom, a thoughtful look in her pretty brown eyes.

The harsh note of a hooter came screaming over the silent town, and Blacktown seemed to awake like a camp of soldiers to the trumpet-call.

Browell's Mill stood silent and aloof, like a grim, rugged-faced old man. The gates were closed, the windows thick with dust – the dust of three long years – and the looms and engines motionless. The chimney –stacks did not smoke. They had long since ceased to smoke. Three years of seasonable rain and snow and sleet had washed the last flavour of smoke out of their throats.

Bessie Booth sighed as she tucked her dressing gown around her pink toes and gazed at the streams of people filing like ants up the slope to Henneker's Mill. With careful nicety she judged the exact spot where she herself would have been a week back complete with clogs and shawl and the prospect of a day's work in front of her. But not now.

Bessie Booth rested her round, dimpled chin on her folded arms as she allowed her mind to run back over the events of the past eight or nine days.

But when it came down to hard facts, Bessie Booth and her girl footballers realised that they were in a dismal quandary. They were all out of work, and the possibility of finding fresh employment in Blacktown was almost a minus quantity. And on top of that they had no ground ton which to play their home league matches. And at the end of that week they were expecting a visit from the Rigan Rangers.

The position seemed hopeless. Unless they could find a fresh ground they would have to resign from the league. And they would have to find work – else how could they afford to pay for their travelling expenses for their away matches?

It seemed that they had burnt their boats behind them. They might just as well have resigned from the league in the first place and kept their jobs at Henneker's Mill.

What were they to do?

There was an answer to the question in Bessie Booth's curly head as she leaned on the window-sill and stared long and earnestly, not at Henneker's Mill, but at the grimy, gaunt, towering bulk of Browell's long-silent mill.

Then she drew a crumpled sheet of paper from her pocket, smoothed it out, and read with eager, glistening eyes the words written upon it.

"Dear Miss Booth" – it ran – *"Please accept an old man's heartfelt thanks and gratitude for the*

invaluable service you rendered him this afternoon. Though old, I still place a considerable value on my life, which now, rightfully, belongs to you.

If at any time there is anything that I can do to show my sincere appreciation of your bravery, you have only to -

Bessie Booth turned her thoughtful gaze out of the window again.

At the foot was the signature,, " Joshua Browell."

The old man whose life she had saved was none other than Josh Browell, the wealthy, crusty proprietor of Browell's Mill, which had been closed for the past three years!

And he was grateful to her; he did not attempt to conceal the fact. Here it was in black and white.

"If at any time I can do anything for you...you have only to apply to Joshua Browell."

Bessie Booth suddenly sprang to her feet. There was a bright gleam of determination in her brown eyes as she quickly proceeded to dress and ran downstairs.

A few minutes later she was walking through the town, and at the corner of the High Street ran full tilt into Amy Olroyd and Sally Soper. Both looked moody and depressed, but they made a feeble attempt to assume a cheerful expression as they caught sight of Bessie.

"Hello, Bess, where are you off to?" greeted Amy Olroyd. "The same way as us I suppose – looking for a job? There's nothing doing, lass. We've been tramping round this past two hours. There's no work in Blacktown – save up at Henneker's Mill."

"Then we must make work," smiled Bessie.

"Make work?" echoed sally Soper. "What do you mean, lass?"

"I'll tell you later on," replied Bessie Booth. "I'm off on a secret mission of my own. If I succeed there'll be work for all of us – and a new football ground as well. If I don't succeed we'll be no worse off than we are now."

And leaving the two girls staring blankly after her, Bessie proceeded on her way. Ten minutes' walk brought her to the better-class, residential part of the town. She referred to the letter in her pocket, and finally passed through the gateway of a big house standing in its own grounds, and marched straight up the drive to the front door, on which she beat a lively rat-a-tat.

After a long wait a stoop-shouldered, bald-headed old manservant shuffled into view and blinked in surprise at the pretty, neatly clad young girl.

"Did...did you knock?" He asked, as though such a thing had never been known to happen before.

"Why, yes. I'd almost forgotten it was such a long time ago," replied Bess, with a sly twinkle in her brown eyes. "I want to see Mr. Browell."

"You want to see Mr. Browell?" echoed the manservant. "Bless my soul! You want to see Mr. Browell? But you can't. He doesn't receive visitors – especially at this time of day."

"But I want to see him. I must see him!"

"Have you an appointment?"

"Yes – at least, I have a letter," explained Bessie "Will you tell Mr. Browell that Bessie Booth would like to see him?"

The old man cautiously put the chain on the door, and shuffled away, mumbling and shaking his head.

Joshua Browell was seated in a bright room overlooking a cheerful garden, reading the morning paper. He wore a dressing gown, carpet-slippers, and a black silk skull-cap.

"There's a young lady called to see you, sir" announced the servant severely.

"A young lady!" Josh Browell sat up so sharply that his spectacles leaped high in the air. "A young lady....to see me? Don't talk daft, Boggins. Ah know no young lady in Blacktown – 'cepting Mrs. Diggett, the parson's wife, and I'm danged if she's any younger than sixty-five."

"I said a young lady, sir" repeated the servant. "A wee limb of a girl with a pert tongue, and she says her name's Booth – Bessie Booth."

Josh Browell started, and sighed.

"Bessie Booth – the lass Ah wrote to," he muttered. "Ah'm sorry, danged sorry. Ah like the look o' the lass; but it seems she's just like all the rest. Save my life, and now she's after the brass, Ah suppose. Show her in, Boggins."

"Sit down, lass," he said curtly, as Bessie entered the room a moment later. "So you'll come to see the old man – eh?"

Bessie Booth perched herself nervously on the edge of a chair.

"Yes. I got your letter, sir," she said hesitantly, "and I – I've come to ask you a favour."

Josh Browell's lips tightened, and he nodded his head.

"You see, you said in your letter," stammered the girl, "that if there was anything you could do at any time – "

"That's so," said the old man more coldly than ever. "You saved my life sure enough, and you want summat a bit more substantial than just a letter o' thanks. Well..."

A spot of colour flamed in Bessie's cheeks, and she half rose from her chair.

"I haven't come to ask you for money," she cried indignantly, "You.......you misunderstand me."

"Lass I'm sorry. Ah begs your pardon!" cried old Josh Browell contritely, realising at once that he had been too hasty in his judgement. "Just you sit down, my lass, an' tell me all about it. If Ah can help you, then it's mighty glad Ah'll be. What's you trouble?"

Bessie Booth did not beat about the bush. In a low voice she quickly told the old man exactly who she was; that she had been employed at Henneker's Mill – the mention of whose name brought a hard glint to Josh Browell's blue eyes – and the exact circumstances in which she and her companions had been dismissed.

"It....it's not myself I'm thinking of," finished up the girl shakily. "There's Sally Soper and Millie Royd and all the rest of them out of work, and no prospect of getting any."

Josh Browell leaned back and stared, puzzled at the girl.

"So Henneker sacked the lot of you because you would play this game of football?" he muttered. "Ah know nothing about that – the lasses o' today are different from what they were when Ah was a lad. But, lass, you put a stiffish problem to me. How can Ah help you an' your friends? If it's a bit o' brass you wants ... "

"No, I don't want money," declared Bess vehemently. "All we want is work."

Josh Browell blinked his blue eyes in bewilderment.

Why; that's a danged sight worse than ever!" he exclaimed. "Ah can't find you work, lass – "

"Oh, you can – you can if you want to!"

"What! Ah can? An' how?

"By opening your mill again!"

Old Josh Browell gasped, gulped, and sank back in his chair. It was as if Bessie Booth had thrown a gas bomb at his feet. His face hardened, and he shook his head gravely but determinedly.

"Open the mill again!" he said slowly. "Lass, what you ask is impossible. I made a vow three years ago that I'd not open my mill so long as Peter Henneker remained in Blacktown. And Ah've never broken my word yet!"

"But I don't mean that you should open it," cried Bessie eagerly. "Why should it stand idle all this time, going to rack and ruin. You are only playing into Henneker's hands – doing just what he wants you to do. Let someone else open the mill, and beat Henneker at his own game!"

"In the name of .... But who?"

"Why, myself and my chums .... Sally Soper, Mary Bonny, all – all the rest of them. All skilled workers. We don't want big wages – we could run the mill on a profit-sharing basis, and undercut Henneker every time. And we'd pay you rent for the mill, and..."

"Dang it, lass!" exploded old Josh Browell. "Art daft? Dost think you can run my mill with a pack o' gals – eleven or twelve of you. You want engineers, mechanics, packers, dispatchers, overlookers..."

"We can get them."

"Where?"

"Why, from Henneker's, of course," smiled Bess excitedly. "They'd come like a shot – the profit-sharing basis would appeal to them. They haven't forgotten the dirty trick Henneker played them by reducing their wages as soon as he knew you'd closed your mill for good. Oh, can't you see how easily it would work? It's bound to succeed."

Josh Browell carefully set his spectacles on his nose and stared open-mouthed at Bessie Booth for several long minutes. Then a slow smile broke across his face, a great chuckle welled up in his throat, and the old manservant nearly fainted dead away in the hall as he heard a great bellow of laughter boom from the other side of the closed door.

"Lass, that's champion –you're a real gradely top-notcher!" roared Josh Browell, rocking backwards and forwards in his chair. "Here Ah've been puzzling three long years how to get my own back on that skunk Henneker, and you've hit the nail on the head first time off!"

"You – you'll do it? You'll let us have the mill?"

"Do it! Ay, take the mill! Do as you like with it, lass so long as my name's not mentioned in connection with it. It's nothing to do with me, mind you! Ah want nothing out of it so long as you pay the ground rent an' taxes, and give that skunk Henneker a shaking up such as he gave me five years ago."

"And you'll be able to do it right enough. There's twenty thousand bales o' cotton packed away in the factory. Ah bought it at half the price you could get it at now, so you can undercut Henneker by fifty per cent, and still make a profit. You can have the cotton on six months' credit, and Ah'll pay to have the mill put in working order. There's nothing much wrong with it save a bit o' dirt. Why, dang it, you're weeping, lass!"

But they were tears of joy and relief that were streaming down Bessie Booth's cheeks as she bent across and positively hugged Josh Browell in her arms, to the horror and consternation of Boggins, the manservant, who happened to open the door at that moment.

There were tears of joy streaming down Bessie's cheeks as she positively hugged Josh Browell.

"And at his age, too!" muttered the latter, as he made a hasty departure. "He ought to be ashamed of himself, carrying on with a young girl – him with one foot in the grave and gout in the other, not to speak of lumbago and an occasional touch of sciatica!"

A Surprise for Blacktown

It was two days later that a certain discovery was made that burst upon Blacktown like a bolt from the blue. The town seethed and hummed like a disturbed nest of hornets. People peered from windows and doors, and the public-house emptied with a rapidity that had never been known before.

Like wildfire the news ran from mouth to mouth.

Smoke was issuing from the chimney-stacks of Browell's Mill! Soon authentic information commenced to drift in. The mill was opening up again after three long years! The gates had been repainted; the windows cleaned. The furnaces were alight – the engines running - and the looms clicking and whirring as of old!

What did it mean? Had old Josh Browell broken his word, or had he sold his mill, as so many people had unsuccessfully begged him to do?

The news was brought to Peter Henneker in his office, but he flatly refused to believe it. Finally, he went into the yard with an incredulous scowl, and saw for himself the great, billowy column of black smoke spreading up from the long-cold chimneys of Browell's Mill.

Then he put on his hat and coat and set out on a voyage of discovery. What he discovered brought a curse of savage fury to his lips. There was not the slightest doubt that the mill was opening up again. The open gates glistened with a coat of new paint, the newly cleaned windows winked like diamonds, the yard had been swept and tidied, and from within came a busy hammering and the purr of the engines.

A trim figure in overalls came striding across the yard, and Henneker's jaw sagged as he found himself staring into the steady brown eyes of Bessie Booth.

"You.....you!" he gulped huskily. "What are you doing here?"

"Minding my own business, Gaffer Henneker, and not trespassing, as you are doing!" replied Bessie coolly.

"So you're working for old Browell, are you?" snarled Henneker. "By thunder, I'll soon have you out of here! I'll smash him to a pulp this time!"

"Look out we don't smash you, gaffer!" replied the girl meaningfully. "There's two can play at your game, you know."

Peter Henneker hurried away, speechless with fury.

"It's that vixen of a girl!" he decided. "She's got around that old fool Browell and persuaded him to start his mill again."

As he passed through the gates of his own mill, Ned Bromley, the head overlooker, followed by a crowd of men and girls, stepped briskly out.

"Here, where the dickens are you going?" demanded Henneker harshly. "It's not twelve o'clock yet."

"No; we're just going," replied Ned Bromley calmly.

"Going?"

"Yes, gaffer, going. We've left a week's money with the cashier in lieu of notice, and we're off!"

Peter Henneker almost exploded with fury and chagrin as he realised where his employees were "off" to. He dashed into his office like a madman, seized the telephone, and gave the number of old Josh Browell's private house. A moment later Browell's broad drawl answered him.

"You crazy old fool!" snarled Henneker into the instrument. "Think you can beat me at my own game, do you? By heavens, I'll break you for this, Browell! I knew you wouldn't keep to your vow – the vow you made three years ago! Is that a sample of a gentleman's word – eh?"

Henneker listened for the reply. His face purpled, and he slammed the receiver down with a crash that shattered it. Josh Browell had been rude to him and Henneker swore viciously as he threw himself into his chair.

"I'll break him – I'll break him if it costs me every penny I've got!" he vowed. "And that girl – I'll bring her to her knees before she's many days older. I've got her to thank for this!"

Later that day he learned the truth – that old Josh Browell had not broken his vow, that he had no interest in the re-opening of his mill, beyond the fact that the premises and freehold were still his property.

"I can't make it out," said John Smith, Henneker's manager, bluntly. "It seems that the place is being run by a pack of girls, with Bessie Booth at the head of them. How on earth she managed to get around old Josh Browell..."

"Never mind! I'll soon settle her!" snarled Peter Henneker, pounding up and down the floor of his office. "I'll find a way to break her before I'm many days older. I'll not allow a chit of a girl to stand in my way, and steal all my best workers away!"

All the evil in Peter Henneker's nature was aroused. So far as he was capable of love he loved Bessie Booth, self admittedly, but he hated her at the same time for the manner in which she had turned the tables on him.

So far as open business was concerned he had never feared old Josh Browell, but he had vague misgivings as to the near future now that Bessie Booth had once again set in motion the long-silent looms of the mill he thought he had closed forever.

"The Bee-Hive", chuckled Ned Bromley, glancing up at the letters painted across the front of the mill that no longer bore the name of "Browell". "Ah reckon that's a mighty good name, Bess lass. Hark at the old engines humming! Look at the lads and lasses swarming in!"

Bessie Booth, trim and neat in spotless overalls nodded her curly head. Four days had worked a wonderful difference both inside and out of the old mill that had lain quiet for so long. It was her suggestion that the mill should be named the Bee-Hive – partly from the suggestion of industry that it conveyed, and the connection with her football team, the Busy Bees.

And they *were* busy bees. Already half the available looms were in working order, and there was no lack of orders and contracts. Nor was there any lack of hands. The profit-sharing scheme was an instant success – an attraction that robbed Peter Henneker of a good forty per cent of his working staff. Minders, piercers, clerks, mechanics and weavers flocked to the banner that Bessie Booth had raised. Blacktown had never forgotten the dirty trick Peter Henneker had played them three years before, and they were not slow in seizing the opportunity to get their own back on the rascally mill owner.

"We don't want to be too confident and count our chickens before they're hatched, Ned," said Bessie gravely. "It's up to gaffer Henneker to make the next move, and you may be sure he's got something up his sleeve".

"So long as we hang together we're bound to win through," declared Ned Bromley emphatically. "Bess, lass, you....you're a knockout! No wonder you wouldn't marry a silly boob like me! You've got more brains in your little finger than I've got in my great thick head!"

"But I couldn't do without you, Ned," said Bessie sincerely. "I couldn't have done half of what I have done if I didn't know I had you behind me....a sturdy staff to lean on, old friend".

Ned Bromley blushed all over his plain, honest face, and squared his broad shoulders.

"The more you lean on me the better I like it, lass," he said heartily. "I only wish...."

The overlooker broke off with a sigh of resignation. He had been on the point of asking Bessie Booth to marry him for the hundred-and-first time, but he knew that it would only mean his receiving his hundred-and-first refusal.

He followed meekly by Bessie's side as she made her way to the back of the mill. Here was a spacious piece of waste ground that had been fenced in, cleared and levelled. The turf was in good condition; it had been accurately marked out for football, and the goal posts and nets were already in position.

"Ay, it's not a bad ground," said Ned Bromley sagely. "A sight better'n the one back at Henneker's."

Bessie Booth nodded happily. Here was the ground on which the Busy Bees would play all their home fixtures. In fact, they were to play their first home match on the following afternoon, when they were due to receive a visit from Rigan Rangers.

The girl's gaze mechanically moved to the south, where the chimney-stacks of Henneker's Mill were belching forth clouds of dense, black smoke, and a vague twinge of misgiving ran through her slender frame.

Something seemed to tell her that, in Peter Henneker, she had made an enemy who would stop at nothing to shatter the daring enterprise on which she and her team of mill-girl footballers had embarked.

Henneker's Revenge

There was a time when Peter Henneker had fancied that Blacktown, more or less, had belonged to him. Fifty per cent of the small Lancashire town had been dependent upon him for their means of livelihood, by virtue of the fact that Henneker's Mill – *his* mill – had been the sole industry in Blacktown.

If people didn't choose to work for Peter Henneker then they had had no alternative, save to remain out of work or seek employment in some other part of the country. Having driven his rival out of business in a price war it had been a case of 'take it or leave it' and for three years he had chuckled to himself over the manner in which he had cornered the sole industry of the town and held total sway over the disillusioned work folk of Blacktown.

But Peter Henneker was not chuckling now as her sat in his private office, drumming his fingers on the edge of his desk and scowling blackly out of the window. From where he sat the giant bulk of Browell's Mill was in plain view. For three years it had been a silent, desolate structure but now, within a week, everything was strangely altered. Browell's Mill had opened up again and was now throbbing with reawakened industry. Peter Henneker almost fancied he could hear the thump of the machinery and the click of the busy looms from where he sat. Smoke billowed from the tall chimney-stacks; tiny figures swarmed in and out of the big gates.

Peter Henneker cursed viciously under his breath. He had always boasted that he feared no other man in business. But it was a mere slip of a girl who had given his this rude shock, throwing open the gates of Browell's Mill and challenging his claim to be emperor of industry so far as Blacktown was concerned.

Bessie Booth, a girl of eighteen, until recently a weaver in his employ!

Henneker cursed again, aware that his present predicament was partly his own doing. Henneker detested football, or any sport for that matter, especially for women. By forbidding Bess and her friends to play he thought he had called their bluff, confident they had nowhere else to go; but that had been a mistake. To his amazement the mill girls had defied him. Bessie Booth was only a girl of eighteen, but she had a wise head on her young shoulders and persuading Josh Browell to give her the use of his mill had been a stroke of genius.

As he continued to stare out of the window Peter Henneker realised he was back to square one. His prices were being undercut; his employees were steadily leaving him and throwing in their lot with Bessie Booth and her profit-sharing scheme. Henneker snarled a curse.

"Come in!" he shouted as someone knocked on the door of his office. It was his manager, John Smith, a squat, heavy-featured man, who entered the room.

"Something will have to be done, Mr Henneker" said the latter seriously. "Another thirty hands gave notice this morning. We shan't have any left at this rate, and several contracts must be fulfilled this week."

Peter Henneker threw himself back into his chair with a vicious oath.

"Offer them double the wages to stay on!" he said grimly.

John Smith shrugged his shoulders.

"I don't think they would stay on if you offered them treble wages," he replied bluntly. "They say they'd rather work for this Booth girl for nothing than...."

"Confound them! Let them go, then!" rasped Henneker savagely. "I'll soon fill their places, if I have to send to Belgium for weavers. Advertise in all the Lancashire papers for hands."

"There's another point," said his manager meaningfully. "We're losing a lot of our custom, Mr Henneker. Menzies and Jackson have cancelled their order, and so have Barratt and Yeoman. And I know they've placed them with this Booth girl."

Peter Henneker's sallow cheeks crimsoned with fury.

"It can't last! We'll beat them in the end, Smith," he declared hoarsely. "I'll smash that girl, if it costs me every penny I possess. I'll grind her to dust! I'll see her in the gutter! Send out a circular letter to all our customers. Quote them a thirty-five percent reduction in all prices."

The manager pursed his thick lips.

"Can it be done?"

"It'll have to be done. I'm not out for profit now. I'm out to close that mill down again."

Smith retired, and Peter Henneker rose and crossed to the window. Here he stood for several minutes, his clenched fists jammed in his trouser pockets, his dark eyes fixed moodily on the smoke belching chimneys of old Josh Browell's mill. Finally, with a fierce gesture of determination, he grabbed his coat and hat and left the building. Ten minutes walk brought him to the scene of Bessie Booth's shrewd activities. The name 'Joshua Browell' was no longer painted across the front of the mill. Instead it bore the words 'The Bee-Hive' and Henneker knew this was a direct reference to Bessie Booth's football team – The Busy Bees- the very team that was at the centre of all his problems.

Henneker ground his teeth viciously as he passed through the mill gates. The place was a veritable hive of industry, and nine persons out of every ten had lately been in his employ

He beckoned authoritatively to a big, broad-shouldered young man, with fair hair and mild, blue eyes. Ned Bromley looked his former employer straight in the eye.

"Who's running this show, Bromley?" demanded the mill owner curtly.

"We are," replied the young man bluntly.

"Yes...but who's the real boss? Who's at the head of affairs?"

"Our Bess....that is, Miss Booth. I reckon she's the one who's running the show," replied the head overlooker.

"Well, I want to see Miss Booth," said Henneker with a veiled sneer. "Just tell her that I want a few words with her."

Ned hesitated and glanced suspiciously at the mill owner out of the corner of his mild, blue eyes.

"You'd best wait here and Ah'll find out if Bess'll see you," he replied cautiously, and ran up the stone steps and through the swinging doors into the mill.

Almost the first person he ran into was Bessie Booth herself, and for a second Ned was transfixed by the slim pretty girl with dark eyes and curly chestnut hair.

"Just the person I was looking for, Ned!" she said briskly. "You're wanted in the spinning room. There's something gone wrong with number five loom."

"Ah'll tend to that in a minute, lass," replied the overlooker. "There's a visitor waiting to see you."

"A visitor?" echoed the girl in surprise. "Who?"

"You'll never guess!" declared Ned Bromley. "'Tis Gaffer Henneker. He's waiting outside."

Bessie Booth stared incredulously at the young man, and a glint of perplexity crept into her dark eyes as, through the glass panels of the swing door, she caught a glimpse of the tall figure of Peter Henneker, her late employer.

"Henneker....here!" she breathed, "What does he want?"

"That's more than Ah know," grunted Ned. "He just said he wanted to see you, Bess. Shall Ah send him packing, with a flea in his ear?"

Bessie hesitated for a moment.

"No, I'd better see him," she decided. "Send him into the office."

An instant later Peter Henneker was ushered into a plainly furnished office, where Bessie Booth stood confronting him across a flat topped desk. She looked particularly dainty and desirable at that moment, he thought, and a glint of admiration leaped into Henneker's black eyes.

"You want to see me?" said the girl crisply and coolly.

Peter Henneker showed his long teeth, in a would-be ingratiating smile.

"I have come in a magnanimous mood," he said pleasantly. "I am even willing to admit that perhaps I made an error of judgement in putting my foot down on your football team."

Bessie Booth stared at him in amazement.

"I don't understand," she said slowly. "I don't know what you mean. Are you suggesting......"

"I am suggesting you throw this silly notion up, before you burn your fingers, and come back to my mill," said Peter Henneker suavely. "I shall raise no further objections to your football team. In fact, I will have the ground properly fitted up for you. And......"

"What you suggest is impossible, Mr Henneker!" cut in Bessie Booth sharply. "Neither I nor anyone else would dream of returning to your employ. We are perfectly happy and satisfied where we are. You are only wasting your time in......"

"You mean to say you refuse my offer?" snapped the mill owner. "Why, you must be crazy, girl! Do you think you can stand up in business and competition with me? Why, I've only got to raise my little finger to crush you like I would......."

"Why don't you do it, then, instead of coming here, and trying to get us to close down and come back to your mill?" said Bessie scornfully. "Why, there's not one of us would come back to you if you offered us twenty pounds a week each!"

Two spots of anger rose into Henneker's sallow cheeks, and he bit his lip in silent chagrin.

"You...you'll be sorry for adopting this attitude!" he said with meaning. "I closed this mill up once before, and I'll close it up again. You've no capital to fight me. I'll undersell you...."

Bessie Booth laughed confidently.

"Undersell us?" she echoed. "Why, do you know what price we are quoting now?"

"No, I don't. But...."

The girl told him, and Peter Henneker uttered a gasp of dismay. The price was just fifty percent below his own, and one he couldn't sell at, except at a dead loss!

"You can't do it!" he snarled. "Where does your profit come in?"

"That's our business," replied the girl footballer. "But I can assure you that we shall get quite a satisfactory profit out of it at that figure. And now, if you'll excuse me....."

Henneker snatched up his hat. His face was twitching with rage and chagrin.

"Very well, this means war to the knife!" he said thickly. "I was inclined to be lenient, but I shan't spare you now. You and your confounded rubbishy team of footballers! By thunder I'll make you pay for this! I'll smash you! I'll bring you to your knees!"

Henneker uttered a yell of pain and surprise as a vice-like grip closed over his wrist and he found himself being propelled gently but firmly towards the door. It was Ned Bromley, who had entered the room and calmly taken upon himself the office of 'chucker-out'. Spluttering and panting, Henneker found himself out in the open air.

"Take your filthy hands off me you lout!" he snarled. "How dare you maul me about! I'll have the law on you for this!"

"When you know how to address a lady you can come back again," said Ned Bromley imperturbably.

"A lady?" sneered Henneker. "What, that low-down hussy...."

The next sixty seconds or so were rather confusing to Peter Henneker. A hundred strong hands seemed to seize him at once, all tugging in a different direction. The sky revolved, the earth came up and hit him, and he found himself sitting in the middle of the dusty road, with his hat over one eye and his tie draped negligently over one shoulder.

"All right, you hound!" he snarled, shaking his clenched fist after the retreating figure of Ned Bromley. "By heavens you'll have to pay a price for this before you're very much older. I'll get my own back on you, and on that confounded brat of a girl!"

Peter Henneker did not go straight home. For half an hour or more he prowled around the busy mill, revolving various schemes of revenge in his head. Two particular things attracted his attention. One was the well-laid-out football pitch at the back of the mill, and the second the enormous iron tank, holding many thousands of gallons of water, that surmounted the roof of the building.

Finally, he came across a bill, pasted onto the gate leading to the football ground, which announced that on the following afternoon would be played the league match between Bessie Booth's team, the Busy Bees, and Rigan Rovers.

This announcement seemed to interest Peter Henneker, and he turned towards home with an unpleasant gleam of excitement in his close-set eyes.

Meanwhile, having delivered her ultimatum to Henneker, Bessie Booth made her way, up the stone stairs, to the big spinning-room. Here she took her place at the whirling, clacking looms, and worked deftly and rapidly until the midday hooter went.

"Girls, I had a visitor this morning. Who do you think it was?" she asked, as they all clattered in the direction of the food canteen.

"Old Josh Browell?" suggested Mary Bonny, the tall centre half of the team.

"Someone from the football league!" declared Sally Soper, the merry-eyed, freckle-faced goalkeeper.

"Wrong, wrong! You're nowhere near the mark!" smiled Bess, with a shake of her head.

"I know who it was!" exclaimed dainty Connie Tree, the skilful outside-right of the Busy Bees. "'Twas Gaffer Henneker."

"That's just who it was," admitted Bessie Booth. "He came to ask us all to go back and work for him again. Said he wouldn't object to us playing football....that we could have our proper ground, and that he'd put it in order for us."

"Well, of all the blessed cheek!" snapped Mary Bonny. "Fancy the gaffer having the nerve to come and ask you that! The slimy cad! It just shows which way the wind's blowing, girls. We're beginning to hit him pretty hard."

"Of course we are!" said Bessie, with a business-like shake of her curly head. "We've taken twenty-five percent of his trade away already, and he can't compete at the same price as us, thanks to the fact that Mr Browell had a big stock of cotton in hand which he bought when it was half the price it is now."

There was a girl on the outskirts of the crowd, with red hair and little green eyes, who made a mental note of the fact that it was the big stock of cheap cotton they had on hand that enabled the new Bee-Hive Mill to cut their prices so severely.

Later, this piece of information would be transmitted to Peter Henneker for Ada Miller, the carroty-haired girl, was a spy in the mill owner's employ, and a traitor to the plucky band of girls she worked with.

The day of days dawned at last! The Busy Bees were to play their first home fixture in the Lancashire Girls' League, and the visiting club was Rigan, a team of mill girls from a neighbouring town.

Bessie and the girls were in high feather when the hooter announced a cessation of work until the following Monday morning, and the mill closed down for the week-end. They had high hopes of gaining another couple of league points at the expense of the Rigan team, after the ready manner in which they had defeated Oldcastle Rovers the previous Saturday.

It was evident that Blacktown meant to support the plucky team of girl footballers who had set up in opposition to Peter Henneker. They came flocking up from the town in a never-ending stream, and willingly paid the three pence gate money that was charged for admission to the ground.

There was plenty of room for all to see, for there was natural banking on one side of the pitch, and some rough tiers of wooden steps had been fixed up at the other by Ned Bromley and a few energetic enthusiasts.

And the girls had a real clubhouse, in the shape of a portable hut, that contained a couple of dressing-rooms, and another room set aside for meetings and secretarial work.

Here was where they changed in preparation for their match with Rigan, donning the yellow and black jerseys and black knickers that had been decided upon as their new colours.

The visiting team had driven up from the station in a horse-wagonette, and the referee was an official appointed by the League.

Five minutes from the kick-off there must have been quite four thousand people present on the ground, and Ned Bromley led the rousing cheer of delight that greeted the Busy Bees as they came filing out on to the field, pretty, bright-eyed Bessie Booth in front.

Another enthusiastic roar was accorded the visitors, in their blue and white quartered shirts. They won the toss and without any delay Bessie set the ball in motion.

"Now then, the Bees!"

"Come along Bess! That's the style, lass!"

"Play up, Bony Mary!"

But Rigan was the first to attack. Swinging the ball from wing to wing, they made a determined raid on the home goal and Sally Soper was called upon to clear within a minute of the commencement of the game.

Then it was the Bees' turn. Mary Bonny sent her forwards away with a well-judged pass, and delightful combination between Bessie Booth and her inside 'men' ended in a first-time shot that just grazed the post and went behind.

It was a ding-dong struggle for first honours, and, as luck would have it, Rigan was the first to take the lead. It was a somewhat fluky, long-range shot that found Sally Soper unsighted, and the ball went into the net without her having as much as seen it.

And Rigan managed to retain their lead until the interval came.

"Never say die, girls!" grunted Mary Bonny grimly, as she made a raid on the slices of lemon. "We'll run 'em off their feet this half!"

On the slope of a wooded hill, a hundred yards away from the football ground, which lay in a kind of hollow beneath him, Peter Henneker stood, peering keenly through powerful field-glasses. But he was not following the course of the match in progress. Occasionally he did shoot a sneering glance at the busy figures in the blue-and-white and yellow-and-black jerseys, but mostly the glasses were levelled at the enormous water tank that loomed up on the roof of Browell's mill. He alone saw the figure of a man who appeared for a few brief seconds silhouetted against the sky, and it was ten minutes later that he placed his glasses in his pocket, and went forward to greet the furtive-eyed, hang-dog-looking man who came slinking towards him.

"Well, Cully, did you manage it?" Henneker asked eagerly.

"Easy as kiss yer 'and," replied the man. "Not a soul about the mill. They're all 'aving a decko at the match, I suppose. It can't fail, guv'nor. What about the brass?"

Peter Henneker handed over a bundle of notes.

"You'll get the other half when it's all over," he said menacingly. "I'm not buying a pig in a poke."

Meanwhile the second half of the football match was well under way, but it was twenty minutes before Bessie Booth scored, with a neat, left-footed shot that put the Bees on level terms. The game was being fought out at a tremendous pace, and several times the Rovers came within an ace or regaining the lead. But, barely five minutes from time, Mary Bonny gave Bessie a pass that she had no difficulty in turning into the net.

As the teams were lining up again, a queer, muffled report, and then a loud, rending sound caused the players and spectators to stare, puzzled, at one another.

Then a yell of horror and dismay went up from someone in the crowd.

"By gum, look! It's the water tank on the roof! It's burst!"

Bessie Booth glanced up, just in time to see the side of the big tank on the mill roof topple outwards, and, with a sound like thunder, the thousands of gallons of released water cascaded down from a height of sixty feet.

The ground positively trembled with the contact. A wall of water, three feet high, swept across the football field, and as Bessie turned to run, she was tossed up like a cork and swept violently along.

The next thing she knew she was seated on the high bank on one side of the ground with her head in Mary Bonny's lap. The football pitch was six inches deep in water, nets and posts

The wall of water swept across the football field, and as Bessie turned to run she was tossed up like a cork and swept violently along had been swept away, and even the clubhouse had been carried bodily a matter of twenty yards or so.

"It's all right, Bess, lass," assured Mary Bonny gravely. "There's nobody been hurt, but Ah reckon there's not many got off with dry clothes. Fancy the old tank bursting like that! It's dashed bad luck for us. The referee will abandon the match and we'll have to replay it some other time."

Bessie sighed in disappointment. It was certainly a piece of very bad luck for the Busy Bees. They had been a goal ahead, with only three minutes to go, when the tank had burst and swept their chance of victory away.

Up on the hill Peter Henneker lowered his glasses with a chuckle of delight.

"Splendid……splendid!" he muttered. "I reckon that puts an end to their football for a time. And I haven't finished with them yet. Just wait till next week, Miss Bessie Booth! I'll make you rue the day you ever put yourself up against me!"

There was certainly an anxious time coming for Bess of Blacktown and her team of Busy Bees

Foul Play

"Well, lass, and how are things going? Are you making good or have you found you've bitten off more than you can manage at one mouthful?"

Old Joshua Browell leaned back in what had once been his own private office chair, and stared quizzically into the pretty face of Bessie Booth.

The mill had only been opened just over a week and old Josh Browell was paying his first visit. His eyes glistened reminiscently as he listened to the roar and clatter of the looms and gazed admiringly into the pretty face of Bessie Booth, neat as new pin, in spotless overalls.

"You've got all the looms working, lass?" said the old mill owner incredulously.

"Every one of them!" replied the girl proudly. "We've got all the work in hand that we can cope with, Mr Browell, and forty per cent of it used to be done by Henneker's Mill."

Old Josh Browell chuckled delightedly.

"And what has Peter Henneker got to say about that?" he queried.

"Well, he had a great deal to say last time I saw him, which was Friday last," replied Bessie slowly. "He realises we're bound to beat him in the end, Mr Browell. He wanted us to shut down and go back to him at an increased wage."

"The cunning hound! I hope you sent him away with a flea in his ear?"

"Well....he had the assistance of Ned Bromley's boot," smiled the girl.

"Well, well lass, you've amazed me," admitted old Josh Browell with a vague shake of his white head. "You're doing now what I should have done years ago...set about Peter Henneker and turn the tables on him. But you want to be careful. He's a dangerous man. He's as vicious as a rat, and a cornered rat is not a nice thing to tackle. I wouldn't trust the fellow any farther than I could see him. And how's this here football team of yours getting on? Did you win last Saturday?"

"We should have done," replied Bess a trifle ruefully. "We were leading by two goals to one a few minutes from time, when the big water tank on the roof of the mill burst and flooded the ground. The match had to be abandoned."

"Well I'll be danged!" exclaimed old Josh Browell. "The water tank? How the dickens did that happen?"

A serious look crept into Bessie Booth's brown eyes.

"That's just what we girls would like to know, gaffer," she said meaningly. "The work men came this morning, and they say that it looks very much as if one of the uprights supporting the water tank had been cut through with a file!"

The old mill owner stroked his bristly chin, and his thin lips tightened.

"Lass...you're hinting at foul play?" he suggested. "And...and who do you suspect?"

Their eyes met and Browell himself answered the question for both.

"Peter Henneker! That dirty skunk, Peter Henneker!" he exclaimed grimly. It's just the sort of trick he'd get up to!"

"Henneker was here on Friday, as I told you," said Bessie with a nod of her curly head. "And Sally Soper says she is certain she saw him hanging about round the mill on Saturday morning."

"Then you can wager every shilling you have that it was Henneker who spoilt the game," declared Josh Browell, thumping one gnarled fist on his knee. "You've got to be on your guard, Bess, lass. That villain will stop at nothing to get his own back on you."

"I'm not afraid of Peter Henneker," replied Bessie boldly. "The more he tries to interfere with us girls, the more certain I shall be that we're beating him at his own game....and making him feel it too!"

"Well spoken, lass, well spoken!" said the old mill owner, as he rose to his feet. "But all the same, you've got to keep your eyes open for dirty work. Henneker won't try to beat you with fair means, when he can use foul."

Bessie Booth herself assisted the old man across the mill yard and into the old-fashioned carriage that was waiting for him. The she made her way back up the stone stairs.

Here the girl footballers of the Bee-Hive Mill were hard at work - big, gaunt Mary Bonny the centre half; freckle-faced Sally Soper the goalkeeper; slim, fair-haired Connie Tree, the outside right; and Amy Olroyd and Enid Foster, the backs.

But it was Ned Bromley, broad-shouldered, with rugged features and mild sheepish, blue eyes who first approached Bess.

There was a grim look on his plain face as he came up to the mill-girl's side.

"It's right enough, Bess, lass," he said quickly. "The two outside supports of the water tank were half filed through. We found the filings – fresh and bright – on the roof. It must have been done on Saturday. By gum, if Ah knew it were that dirty skunk Henneker, Ah'd go straight along and screw his dirty neck for 'im."

"But we can't be certain...only to our own minds, Ned," said Bessie wisely. "We can't prove anything. Best leave well alone and keep a careful look-out in case Henneker gets up to any more games."

At that moment the midday hooter went and the engines came to a standstill. In a body, the girls flocked down to the canteen that was run in connection with the mill, and Bessie joined her fellow members of the Busy Bees football team.

"You've got some news, Bessie, lass?" said Sally Soper eagerly. "I can see it in your eyes."

"I have received a letter from the secretary of Rigan Rovers," replied Bessie, referring to their opponents the previous Saturday and the flooded, abandoned, game. "They're willing to play the match next Wednesday afternoon, providing our pitch is in a fit condition."

"Ay, that's the question," muttered Mary Bonny. "Will the ground be fit? What has Ned Bromley to say?"

"He's got a dozen men at work and they're doing their best," answered Bessie. "They've drained most of the water away, and if it keeps fine, we should be able to play on Wednesday. I'll write back to Rigan, and say we'll send them a wire on Tuesday evening, or first thing Wednesday morning."

Bessie herself seized the opportunity to visit the ground behind the mill before the looms started working again. The pitch was in a thoroughly sodden condition. Pools of water still lay about, and a dozen workmen were busy draining these away, with the aid of a length of hosepipe and a small suction pump.

At either end of the field nets and goalposts lay in a hopeless tangle, where they had been thrown by the cataract of water that had gushed from the broken tank on the mill roof and swept across the ground.

"Reckon we'll have everything right by Wednesday, lass," said the foreman of the gang of workers, casting a shrewd glance at the sky. "That is, if the rain keeps off. 'An it don't look much like rain at present."

Bessie glanced hopefully at the sodden turf. She had the success of her team very much at heart. It was for the sake of the team that she and her girls had accepted their dismissal from Henneker's Mill and now straining every endeavour to make a success on their own. And it was working, paying its way, despite the low prices they were charging.

Meanwhile, half a mile away across the town, Peter Henneker sat in his office at his mill, glancing at a letter that he had just received. It was a note, roughly scrawled in pencil, on a half-sheet of notepaper, and it was signed with the name, 'Ada Miller'.

Peter Henneker read it through several times, and a little smile of satisfaction curled his thin lips. He pressed a bell and, an instant later, John Smith, his general manager and right hand man entered the room.

"Sit down, Smith," said Henneker curtly. "You remember that girl I sent along to Bessie Booth's mill?"

"Ada Miller, the girl you sent to spy for you!" replied Smith bluntly. "Did they take her on?"

"Take her on? Of course they took her on!" snapped Peter Henneker with a scowl. "Haven't they taken most of my hands away from me? Ada Miller has been keeping her eyes and ears open. She looks like being useful. Listen! This is the note she has sent me."

'I have found out how it is Bessie Booth is able to sell her stuff at such a low price and still make a profit. Old Josh

Browell has an enormous stock of cotton in reserve, which he bought cheap five years ago. He has handed this over to Bessie Booth for the price he paid for it, and allowed her a year's credit. There is sufficient cotton in hand to last over a year'

John Smith uttered a low exclamation of dismay.

"That's bad!" he blurted. "Five years ago. There was a slump in cotton that year, if you remember. It was fifty per cent cheaper than it is today. Why, those confounded girls can undercut you below your cost price and still make a profit!"

"Do you think I don't know that!" snarled Henneker irritably. "And they've got enough stock in hand to last them for over a year. "This spells ruin for us, Smith. We can't last out a year, running the mill at a steady loss. It would take every penny I've got."

John Smith stared gloomily at his boss. He seemed to see the black shadow of certain ruin hanging over Henneker's Mill.

"You've properly put your foot in it, Henneker, he said grimly." You should never have sacked those dashed girls just because they wanted to play football. Is it too late to get them to shut up and come back again?"

"Too late? Of course it's too late!" snapped the mill owner. "Didn't I try last week, and get kicked out of the mill by that lout Ned Bromley?"

"Then we're done. You're going to throw up the sponge.....to a crowd of brainless females."

"Throw up the sponge? By thunder, no!" roared Peter Henneker. "I mean to smash that hussy Bessie Booth before I've finished with her.... and that old fool Josh Browell as well."

"Well, I don't see how you're going to do it," said John Smith candidly.

"There's only one way," said Henneker, lowering his voice. "Those girls are dependent entirely on their stock of cheap cotton. If they hadn't that stock of cotton, and had to pay at the present price, I'd smash them in six months."

"Of course you would!" muttered Smith, with a veiled sneer. "But they have the cotton....."

"Then they must lose it!"

Smith started, and stared at his employer, a glow of understanding kindling in his eyes.

"Lose it?" he echoed. "I....I see what you mean. But how?"

"I'll tell you," jerked Henneker.

He bent down over the desk, speaking in low tones, for several minutes, and Smith drew a deep breath.

"By heavens! But the risk!" he exclaimed.

"Never mind the risk!" declared Henneker recklessly. "It's worth any risk to smash those girls and save ourselves. Send for Ada Miller this evening. I shall want a few details from her before I can put my plan into execution."

Henneker Gets To Work

Bessie Booth sang aloud in sheer happiness and high spirits when she awoke on the Wednesday morning, to find that the sun was shining from a frosty, cloudless sky. The much-feared rain had held off and it was an ideal day for football.

Her first act on leaving the little cottage in Chapel Lane was to send a telegram to Peg Davis, the captain of Rigan Rovers.

'Hurry along. Everything OK for match' was the message she sent, before hurrying along, light-hearted, to the mill, where a roar of delight greeted her announcement that the abandoned match with the Rigan Rovers was to be replayed that afternoon.

Ada Miller, the traitor to the girl footballers and in Peter Henneker's pay, chuckled maliciously as she deftly pierced a thread.

"They're smiling now....they'll be laughing on the other side of their mugs later on," she muttered meaningfully.

Bessie Booth did not look for a big gate that afternoon. There were urgent orders in hand, and the mill was to be kept working by all save those who comprised the footballers.

At midday she went out to examine the ground. The men had done their work well. It was in ideal condition....the turf green and springy.....and new goalposts had been erected and netting rigged to them.

"Dang me, if it don't look better than it did before!" declared Ned Bromley as he followed Bessie around like a faithful dog. "That water seems to have done it more good than harm."

"But it's cost us a bit of money, Ned, and we hadn't really got it to spare," said Bessie with a business-like shake of her head. "It's swallowed up all our last Saturday's gate, and we shan't get many folk up here today."

But here Bessie Booth was mistaken. Quite a goodly few people came tramping up from the town, and many of the Rigan Rover's ardent supporters accompanied their team to Blacktown.

The Rovers, a robust, jolly lot of girls, arrived twenty minutes before the time appointed for the kick off, and by then there were quite a thousand people scattered around the touchlines.

But the greatest surprise of all came when an old-fashioned carriage drove up to the gates, and old Josh Browell stepped out and hobbled across to the rough-and-ready clubhouse.

"See you, lass!" he chuckled, beckoning to Bessie Booth. "Ah've the room to see this 'ere team of lasses play. Good luck to you! You deserve to win after the bad luck last Saturday."

Bessie Booth thanked the kind-hearted old man delightedly as she saw him planted in a comfortable seat close to the centre-line, and left him puffing contentedly on his pipe.

The Busy Bees took the field a few minutes later, and old Josh Browell stared admiringly and wonderingly at the eleven active, pretty girls who came running out in their black-and-yellow jerseys and white knickers.

"Here they come!"

"Book up, the Bees!"

"There's our Bess. Come on, Bess!"

An equally hearty reception was accorded the visitors when they left their dressing room.

The greatest surprise of all came when old Josh Browell hobbled across to the clubhouse. "Good luck to thee, Bessie," he said. "Tha deserves to win"

Straight from the kick off the Rovers attacked strongly, and Amy Olroyd and Enid Foster had all their work cut out to hold their eager forwards at bay. Sally Soper cleared a long, swerving shot, and, for a brief moment, play was transferred to the other end of the field.

Again the visitors attacked. Despite its appearance the pitch was treacherous in places and Mary Bonny slipped and fell on a sticky patch, where one of the pools of water had lately collected.

The Rovers' centre-forward pounced on the ball and the opportunity, and tricked Amy Olroyd with a cunning pass to her inside-left.

But, over-excited, the visiting forward shot straight at the custodian, and Sally leaped up to tip the whirling leather over the bar.

The resulting corner proved of no use to the Rovers. The ball landed on top of the net, and Sally's lusty goal-kick sent the Busy Bees humming to the attack. The game was being played at a pace that sent the spectators into roaring spasms of delight, and that caused old Josh Browell to open his eyes wide with wonder.

Bessie Booth had received the ball from Mary Bonny. She swerved around the opposing half-back and, just as the two backs converged on her, transferred back to Mary Bonny, who was close at her heels.

'Bony Mary' did not hesitate for a fraction of a second. She rammed her right boot against the leather, catching it on the half volley, and it streaked for goal like the bullet from a gun.

A groan of disappointment went up as the ball struck the juncture of post and cross-bar and rebounded into play. The goalie made a dive for it, but a flying figure in black and yellow was even quicker. Bessie Booth seemed to materialise out of the empty air as she breasted the ball over the line and carried it with her clean into the net.

It was a brilliant, spectacular piece of play, and a sudden twinge of rheumatic limb caused old Josh Browell to realise that he was standing up, cheering and waving with the rest of the spectators.

It was first blood to the Busy Bees, and they retained their lead right up to the end of the first half.

The resumption of play brought immediate sensation.....and a well-earned goal to the visitors. By a dazzling, short-passing movement, so different from their lusty tactics in the first half, they weaved a way through the Bees' defences and Sally Soper had no earthly chance with a shot that struck the underside of the crossbar, and hummed over her shoulder into the net!

Level scores, and both teams fighting might and main to snatch the lead. A dangerous five minutes in the homesters' goalmouth brought Ned Bromley's heart into his mouth. But Sally Soper was equal to the occasion, and Mary Bonny was herself a veritable stalwart, both in attack and defence.

Bessie Booth shook the hair out of her eyes. A terse, panting command from 'Bony Mary' told her the ball was at her feet, and she side-stepped as the opposing centre-forward charged into her. Then she was off, running like a hare, with every ounce of speed that remained in her.

She saw the goalposts looming before her, framing the dancing figure of the distracted custodian, and, with a lightening left-footed shot, she rammed the leather into the net, and scored the winning goal for the Bees. Bessie Booth and her chums ran from the field. By their defeat of Rigan they had notched their second victory in the league.

It was a merry little band of girls who gathered in the canteen at the mill after the match. The Busy Bees were entertaining their defeated league rivals to tea, and speeches and compliments were passed from either side.

Bessie Booth and Mary Bonny accompanied the visiting team to the railway station, to see them off on their return journey to Rigan. It was seven o'clock by then, and night had fallen.

As they made their way back through the town the deafening clamour of a gong and the clatter of wheels and hoofs struck on their ear.

"By gum, there's a fire somewhere....there goes the engine!" exclaimed Mary Bonny. "I wonder where it is."

Windows were thrust up and people were running in all directions. A man came clattering past, drawing on his coat as he ran.

"It's up at old Browell's Mill!" he shouted. "The old mill that's just been opened again. I could see the flames from my window."

Bessie Booth uttered a low cry of anguished dismay, and her heart seemed to stand still. It was the Bee-Hive, their mill, which was on fire! Here was a fresh misfortune that seemed likely to end in disaster for her and her girl chums!

If the mill was burnt down, so would all their hopes be destroyed!

Bessie Booth never forgot that night. It was like a terrible dream......her wild dash through the teeming streets, with Mary Bonny by her side, her arrival at the mill, where blood-red flames leaped in the lower windows, black smoke billowed in choking clouds, and Blacktown's fire engines were bravely pumping water into the heart of the fire.

"The fire's in the basement, where all the cotton is stored," someone informed her. "The firemen think that, by flooding, they'll be able to get it under control and save the mill. No one knows how it happened!"

Three hours later Bessie Booth and the haggard-eyed girls around her knew the worst.

The mill had been saved......in fact, it was practically uninjured...but tons and tons of water had been pumped into the concrete-lined basement, and all their store of raw cotton was hopelessly ruined!

"Lass, this is a hard blow, but it might have been worse," said Ned Bromley as he passed a strong, supporting arm around Bessie's shoulders. "Thank heaven the mill has been saved. Ah wonder how the fire started?"

His and the girl's eyes met, and the same thought flashed into each of their minds.

Peter Henneker! This was more of the scoundrel's rascally, revengeful work! He had struck at their weakest point, by destroying the cotton that was essential to their chances of success!

After The Fire

"Well, it's bad enough girls, but it might have been a sight worse."

Bessie Booth infused a cheery tone in her voice, but her heart was heavy with dismay as she gazed around the debris-strewn yard and up at the smoke blackened walls and flame-splintered windows of the Bee-Hive Mill.

Although the mill had been left structurally sound, hundreds and thousands of bales of cotton had been totally ruined, either by the flames or by the tons of water that had been pumped on to extinguish the flames.

Small wonder that there were gloomy faces around Bessie! Sally Soper the goalie was conspicuous by the absence of her usual cheery grin, and the others could not conceal the dismayed, anxious state of their feelings.

"Ay, things might have been a great deal worse, Bess," admitted Mary Bonny, the big centre-half. "But Ah reckon they're quite bad enough. Ah reckon this means that we'll have to shut up shop. Won't Gaffer Henneker just dance for joy when he hears the news?"

Bessie Booth's eyes flashed strangely and she clenched her tiny fists. There was a vague suspicion in her mind that Peter Henneker probably knew more about the fire at the mill than he would have dared to admit.

"Shut up shop? Who's talking about shutting up shop?" she cried almost angrily. "Surely you're not ready to knuckle under at the first bit of ill-luck, Mary?"

"No, that Ah'm not, Bess lass!" declared Mary Bonny stoutly. "What can we do?"

"That remains to be discussed," said Bessie firmly. "There's still a day's cotton on the bobbins and orders to be fulfilled. The best thing you can do is to get on with your work."

There was a moment's silence, and then a cheer of assent went up from the crowd of mill-workers.

"By gum! Our Bess is right!"

"No use crying over spilt milk."

"If there's work to be done, let's do it."

Away they went, clattering across the mill yard and up the stone steps to the spinning rooms. Bessie Booth choked back a big lump in her throat. Her heart held no hope for the future. How was it possible to keep the mill going now that all of their stock of cotton had been destroyed?

She turned listlessly into the little office on the ground floor, but scarcely had she closed the door than there was a rap on the panels and Ned Bromley, the head overlooker, stepped into the room.

Bessie's face lit up as she caught sight of the big, honest fellow who had so often proved himself her tried and trusted friend. She had sent Ned up to Josh Browell's house to acquaint the old mill owner with the news of the disastrous fire at the mill.

"Well, Ned. How did Mr Browell take it?" she asked eagerly.

"That Ah couldn't say. Ah didn't see the gaffer. The maid told me that he was ill in bed. Seems he caught a chill at the football match yesterday, and the doctor had to be called in. But Ah sent a note up to him."

"Oh dear!" cried Bessie anxiously. "I hope he's not very ill. Poor old man! I wonder if *I* could see him?"

Ned Bromley straddled himself across a chair, rested his arms across the back, and his square chin on top of all.

"Well, Bess lass," he said gravely, "what's to be done? Has this darned fire beaten us? Does it mean shutting up the mill?"

"Not while we have an inch of thread left," declared the girl desperately. "We've enough for today, and perhaps tomorrow."

"And after that, lass?"

Bessie's lips quivered and Ned suppressed a wild inclination to take her in his arms and strive to comfort her.

"Surely we can do something!" cried the girl hopefully. "We have plenty of orders in hand, Ned. On the strength of them, surely we can get a fresh stock of cotton on credit?"

"Ay," said the overlooker gravely. "But you forget one thing, lass. All our orders are booked at the old price. We couldn't deliver at that figure with cotton at the present market value."

Bessie's face fell. Ned was right. With cotton at its present price they would have to default with all the undelivered orders they had in hand. The tears sprang to her eyes again, but she dashed them away as a knock sounded on the door, and the gate-keeper poked his grizzled head into the room.

"A young man has just left this note for you," he said, extending a sealed envelope.

Bessie Booth took it mechanically, and her lips tightened as she recognised the writing on the envelope. She tore it open hastily, and a flame of colour crept into her cheeks as she read the enclosure.

Dear Miss Booth....the letter ran.....

Allow me to proffer you my sincere sympathy in the misfortune that has befallen your enterprise. I have quite enjoyed the brief period during which we have crossed swords in business rivalry, and I can assure you that I bear no malice now that bad luck has beaten you before I was able to do so.

I am willing to take back into my employ yourself and all the other misguided enough to folk who were foolish enough to leave my mill.

Sincerely yours

Peter Henneker

Bessie Booth drew a deep breath, and her hands trembled as she passed the letter across to Ned Bromley. The latter's jaw fell as he read it through, and he sprang to his feet with a shout of anger and indignation.

"By gum! The danged smooth-tongued, impertinent dog!" he cried, his normally mild, blue eyes blazing like steel. "He's just rubbing it in, lass. Laughing at us up his sleeve! Take us back! Ah wouldn't go back to him for all the brass in the world! Ah'm as certain as Ah'm standing 'ere that the fire was his doing...more of his dirty, underhand work!"

Bessie Booth nodded.

"I think the same, Ned," she said quietly. "But what's the use of thinking? We can't prove it. Oh, Ned. We must carry on after this sneering letter! We must find a way to carry on! He takes it for granted that we're going to shut the mill up. We must keep it open!"

"Ay, we'll have a mighty good try!" replied the overlooker soberly. "But...."

Ned was interrupted by the shrill whirr of the telephone bell. Bessie drew the instrument towards her and placed the receiver to her ear. Her heart leapt as she recognised the leisurely drawling voice of old Josh Browell.

"Is that the mill? Ah want to speak to young Bess."

"I'm here....I'm here Mr Browell!" cried the girl eagerly. "Oh, I'm so glad! I heard you were ill!"

"Ah'm......Ah'm none too sprightly, lass," replied the old mill owner. "But Ah'm well enough to speak to you. Don't you upset yourself too much over the fire, lass. I hear that the whole stock of cotton has been destroyed. Well, the whole danged lot's insured, so Ah'll see you get a cheque for it almost at once!"

"But.....but it's your money, Mr Browell!" protested the girl shakily. "And besides, the cotton can't be replaced at the same price. Therefore, we can't fulfil our orders."

"Just you sit tight and hold your tongue a minute," jerked Josh Browell with mock severity. "How much cotton at the old price do you want to complete the orders you have in hand?"

In bewilderment, Bessie Booth made a hasty calculation and named a quantity....a supply sufficient for three week's work at full pressure.

Josh Browell gave a scornful click with his tongue.

"When Ah was out to beat that skunk Peter Henneker, years ago, Ah bought all the cotton Ah could lay my hands to," he informed. "Ah hadn't sufficient room to store it all at the mill, so Ah bought Riggs' warehouse down by the railway goods-yard. There's sufficient there now to last you for the next three months. Go and see Riggs, tell him I sent you, and he'll hand over the keys so you can take the cotton away. No, don't thank me, Bess lass. But bear in mind what Ah said the other day. Keep your eyes skinned for Peter Henneker! Ah'm wagering he caused that fire!"

The wires went dumb. In vain, Bessie Booth called imploringly into the transmitter, but Josh Browell had rung off, and the girl turned to Ned Bromley, her face radiant with happiness.

"Ned....Ned, we're saved!" she cried. "It was Josh Browell who rang up! The cotton was all insured, and I don't know how many tons more of it have been stored all these years down at Riggs' warehouse....enough to last us for the next three months! And all we've got to do is send for it. Oh, I feel so excited, I don't know what to do! Run and tell all the others. I can't! I feel I want to cry for sheer happiness.

Ned Bromley sprang to his feet with a great bellow of delight, his honest face glowing with joy. The Bee-Hive Mill was saved! It seemed too good to be true!

A crouching figure, which had been listening outside of the slightly ajar door of the office, straightened up and darted away up the stairs. Ada Miller had overheard every word that had been spoken by Ned Bromley and Bessie Booth, and her pale face and green eyes evidenced her keen satisfaction.

As a spy for Peter Henneker it was her duty to transmit to him all items of interest that she could glean as a worker at the Bee-Hive. The unscrupulous girl did not wait for the twelve o'clock hooter to sound. Wrapping her shawl around her head, she left the big building and hurried away through the town to Henneker's Mill.

John Smith – Henneker's right-hand man – had instructions to admit Ada Miller to his employer's office at all times, and he now did so, entering himself and closing the door behind him.

Peter Henneker's tall lean frame was stretched out as he relaxed in his chair, his sallow complexion and snappy black eyes clouded in smoke as he puffed exultantly on his cigar, evidently highly pleased with himself.

"Hello, Miller!" he exclaimed, as he caught sight of his visitor. "Seems I shan't need you any longer...eh? Never mind, you shall have a good job here, in future. Come to tell me that the other mill's shutting down, I suppose?"

Ada Miller shook her head, a malicious glint in her green eyes.

"No, you've made a mistake there, gaffer," she replied. "You've got hold of the wrong end of the stick. I've come to tell you that the Bee-Hive's going to keep open."

Peter Henneker sprang to his feet in amazement.

"What the deuce are you talking about, girl?" he demanded roughly. "Are you mad? How can the mill keep open? They've no cotton. I know beyond all possible doubt that the whole lot was destroyed."

"Ay, all at the mill," replied the mill-girl. "But there's more of the stuff stored away in Riggs' warehouse, down by the railway goods-yard. T'was Josh Browell himself telephoned Bessie Booth an' told her so, an' Ah heard her tell Ned Bromley with my own ears. There's enough cotton there to last 'em another three months."

Peter Henneker staggered back, a terrible expression of baffled fury convulsing his sallow face. For several minutes he stormed up and down his office, ranting and raving in a manner that caused Ada Miller to shrink back in terror of the vicious evil she had awakened.

Then Peter Henneker suddenly calmed, and resumed his seat.

"Smith, we've failed again!" he said harshly. "I thought that little fire would settle Bessie Booth for good and all.

Who would have dreamed that old fool Josh Browell had another stock of cotton stowed away? Of all the infernal luck!"

"Well, we've achieved one thing," said John Smith tentatively. "We've reduced their stock of cheap cotton from twelve months' to a three months' sufficiency."

"Yes, you're right there," muttered Peter Henneker, thoughtfully. "We can hold out for three months, but it's going to cost us thousands of pounds. But we'll beat them in the end. After three months they'll have to buy their cotton at the present market price."

"They'll still be able to undercut us slightly," said John Smith cautiously. "They're on a profit-sharing basis. They'll reduce their expenses to balance a drop in price."

"They won't!" declared Peter Henneker. "I'll see that they don't get any cotton....not a single ounce. I'll queer their market for them. I can do it, Smith. I'll find a way. But that'll be three months hence. In the meantime I'll find other methods of squaring matters with that cunning cat of a girl. I'll tackle her when she'll least expect it, and least like it."

"How do you mean?" queried his manager curiously.

Peter Henneker was silent for a moment, ignoring the other's question. Then he turned suddenly to the shrinking figure of Ada Miller.

"Do you play football?" he snapped.

"Well...Ah have played," admitted the girl, "but...."

"But you don't play for Bessie Booth's team?"

"No....Ah'm not...."

"Then you must get a place," ordered Henneker grimly. "You understand? You must get a place on her first team. I don't care how you do it.....fair means or foul. But you must do it as soon as possible, and let me know when you have succeeded. You're on a ten -pound note the moment you are selected to play for the Busy Bees. You may go now. I'll post you your usual money tonight."

Ada Miller gathered her shawl around her and shuffled out of the room. John Smith shot a curious glance at his employer.

"What's the game?" he asked. "Why do you want that girl to play for Bessie Booth's team?"

"Because she may be useful," replied Henneker evasively. "Look here, Smith," he continued. "I've got a job for you. Nearly every mill in Lancashire now has its representative team of girl footballers. I want you to travel around the countryside and pick me an eleven that'll hold its own with any team. Big, hefty, capable girls.... and I don't care if some are a bit rough. Tell 'em they can all have a good job here at my mill. Pay them a five- pound bonus to come, if necessary."

John Smith stared at his employer.

"What is the idea?" he exclaimed. "What do you mean to do?"

"Run a team of girl footballers, of course," said Peter Henneker with a cunning smile. "Henneker's Hornets.....the Horrible Hackers.....anything you like. But I want that team as soon as possible. You can start out today to look for 'em. I've got something up my sleeve that'll give Bessie Booth the biggest shock of her life!"

The Return Match

Saturday morning found Bessie Booth with only one disturbing thought to mar her eager anticipation of that afternoon's away match with Rigan Rovers, when the previous week's strenuous battle for league points would be fought over again.

Old Josh Browell was still ill. In fact he was worse than he had been. Having caught a chill watching his first match of girl footballers, the previous Wednesday, pneumonia in a mild form had now developed.

Bessie had paid the kindly old mill owner a visit on the Thursday evening, but when she had called again on the Friday the doctor had informed her that he was too ill to see anybody. 'He'll be all right in a couple of days' the medical man had assured her. 'No need to worry, my dear. Call again on Saturday or Sunday'.

"By gum, we've got a stiff game in front of us this afternoon, girls!" said Mary Bonny as she settled herself into a corner of the carriage on the train which was taking the team to Rigan, and stuffed the bag containing her kit under the seat. "The Rovers gave us a mighty hard tussle on Wednesday and they'll be a different team on their own mud heap."

It was the girls' first visit to Rigan, and they found it very much the same as any other mill town, and very little different from Blacktown. The same narrow streets, rows and rows of little red-brick houses, and towering, smoke-gushing chimney stacks.

Peg Davis, the Rigan Rovers' captain, had given them careful instructions how to find the football ground, and the eleven girls boarded a clattering tram, the destination board of which indicated that it was bound for Thicket End.

Here they dismounted, and had only to follow the straggling lines of people who, evidently, were bound the same way as themselves, only as spectators and not players. A narrow, winding lane brought them to a big, wooden gate, bearing the name *'Rigan Rovers (Girls) Football Club'*.

"We're the team from Blacktown....the Busy Bees," said Bessie Booth to the man taking admittance money at the entrance.

"Eh, what's that?" he exclaimed. "You're the Busy Bees? Are you sure?"

"Reckon we ought to know," said Mary Bonny dryly. "What's wrong with you, lad? Expect to see us drive up in a hive, all buzzing together!"

The gatekeeper shook his head and beckoned to someone inside the ground. The next instant Peg Davis came hurrying up, and she uttered a glad cry as she caught sight of Bessie Booth and her companions.

"Oh, Bess, I'm so glad you've come!" she exclaimed. "I couldn't make it out at all. In fact, I don't understand it now!"

"Understand what?" queried Bessie. "We're not late are we? Kick off's two thirty, isn't it?"

"Yes, but it's not that," said Peg Davis. "But there's another team here, and they say they're the Busy Bees, and that they've come to play us!"

Bessie Booth and her companions stared at one another in amazement, and Mary Bonny uttered a snort of indignation.

"Another team?" she echoed. "Trying to make out they're the Busy Bees! Why, of all the cheek! Where are they?"

"In the dressing room," said the Rovers' captain helplessly. "I.....we didn't know what to do. We thought you might have sent a reserve team."

"Perhaps it's a joke," said Bessie with a frown. "We'll soon find out. It certainly is a cheek."

Peg Davis led the way to the big, wooden shed in which the dressing-rooms were situated, and Bessie Booth passed through the door of one labelled *'Visitors'* to find herself confronted by a dozen strange girls, coolly engaged in removing their hats and coats.

"Excuse me," said Bessie sharply. "What are you doing here? Do I understand you are trying to pass yourselves off as the Busy Bees from Blacktown?"

A thick set girl, with coarse black hair and heavy features stared at her insolently.

"That's right," she said shortly. "We come from Blacktown. We're the Busy Bees."

Bessie Booth halted, speechless with amazement, and Mary Bonny forced her way to the front.

"Why you impudent hussy!" she cried hotly. "Are you crazy? What do you mean? How dare you make out to be the Busy Bees! You're nothing but impostors!"

"Impostors! It's you who're the impostors!" replied the black-haired girl with a scornful laugh. "You've no right to play in the league. You've come here under false pretences."

Mary Bonny nearly exploded and Bessie Booth pushed her gently to one side.

"Look here!" she said quietly. "Perhaps you'll explain."

"Explain? That's easily done," sneered the black-haired girl. "Are you Henneker's Busy Bees?"

"We're the Busy Bees from Blacktown."

"What are you doing here?" said Bessie Booth. "Do I understand you are passing yourselves off as the Busy Bees from Blacktown?"

"Yes, but not Henneker's. You're nothing to do with Henneker's, and Henneker's Busy Bees is the team that was elected to the Lancashire Girls' League."

Bessie drew a deep breath.

"Do you come from Henneker's?" she asked quietly.

"Of course we do!" snapped the girl. "We all work for Henneker's Mill. We're the genuine Henneker's Busy Bees."

"But you're not the same team that qualified for a place in the league!"

"Not the same team...no. But we're the same *club*. And you're not! You've left Henneker's. You've no right to the name, or a place in the league. Now do you understand? You soon will, from the league officials themselves. Mr Henneker has written to them, protesting against your eligibility to compete in the league."

Bessie Booth and her companions stared at one another in silent dismay. Here was more of Peter Henneker's spiteful handiwork! It was true enough that they had applied for membership under the name of Henneker's Busy Bees, and that they no longer had anything to do with Henneker's. But did that rob them of their place in the league?

It was a purely technical point that only the committee of the league itself could decide.

"I'm afraid there'll be no use playing the game, under the circumstances," said Peg Davis, the Rovers' captain, regretfully. "Personally, I think you are in the right, Bess, because we played you last week. But we shall have to wait and see what the league officials have to say. It's an awful shame, but what else can we do?"

It was a miserable, gloomy little crowd of girls who travelled back to Blacktown on the next train. Peter Henneker had dealt them a crushing blow by his cunning move of sending another team to Rigan

For the second Saturday in succession the Busy Bees had been cheated out of their match, and Peter Henneker rubbed his hands together and chuckled gleefully when he learned of the success of his latest plan!

A New Turn of Events

Bessie Booth sat in the general office of the Bee-Hive Mill, running over the pile of letters that the morning post had brought her.

Overhead in the spinning room the busy looms were clattering and whirring. They had been silent for three long years, but now they were working away as though making up for lost time.

Bessie Booth arranged her open correspondence into two little piles.....the one containing orders, the other substantial cheques for goods delivered.

From where she sat, by gazing straight out of the window, Bessie could see the towering, smoke-belching chimney stacks of Henneker's Mill on the other side of town, and the sight accrued a feeling of despair over recent events and the ongoing feud with Peter Henneker, owner of the other mill in Blacktown and malicious business rival who was determined to see Bess and her friends fail, both in business and in their beloved football.

Now, with dispute over their right to play in the league, the situation was one that filled Bessie Booth with dismay and fears for the future of her club. It was evident that Peter Henneker was acting out of spite, else he would have made his protest before the Busy Bees had reached their third league match of the season.

As matters stood, the match with Rigan Rovers was postponed; pending a decision by the officials of the league and it was an anxious time of waiting for Bessie Booth. They had sacrificed everything to keep their team running, and it was quite on the cards that they would be disqualified from any further participation in the league competition.

She glanced up sharply as the door opened and Mary Bonny entered the room.

"Well Bess, lass. Any news?" Mary asked eagerly. "Have you heard anything from the league yet?"

Bessie Booth threw a meaningful glance at the big heap of unopened letters that still lay before her.

"It may be there....I hope to goodness it is," she said wistfully. "It's the suspense of waiting to know what's going to happen that gets on one's nerves. Yes, we ought to have heard from the league by now. Perhaps it's all a bluff.....perhaps Peter Henneker never wrote to them at all?"

Mary Bonny shook her head as she plumped her lean form down into a chair.

"No chance of that, lass," she said grimly. "That skunk Henneker wouldn't miss an opportunity like this. He's been planning this for the last week or more!"

"How do you know that?" queried Bessie eagerly.

"Ah heard it from one of the men up at Henneker's Mill, who's courting my sister. He says he knows for a fact that Henneker sent his manager, John Smith, travelling all over Lancashire in search of a team of girls. He was told to get hold of all of the best players he could find, and bring them back to Blacktown with him. Ay, he was even to offer them a five quid bonus, as well as a good job in his mill."

Bessie's eyes flashed as she heard this news. It was plainly evident that Peter Henneker meant to do them harm in any possible way he could, and that he was quite prepared to spend money freely to achieve his ends.

"And that's the team he sent to Rigan on Saturday, I suppose?" said the Busy Bees captain. "I thought they were all strangers to Blacktown. And are they all supposed to be good players?"

"There's not much supposing about it," grunted Mary Bonny dourly. "That impudent, black-haired hussy who seemed to be the captain......that's Jane Tanner, who played for the Lancashire girls against the Belgian girls last season."

Bessie frowned as she ripped open another letter. She had heard of Jane Tanner. She had seen her photographs in the papers. There was no doubt she was a sound, capable, robust player, but she had an unpleasant reputation for rough play and tricky tactics, that in some quarters would have been called 'foul'.

"An' there's Nell Warren from the Glassbury team," continued Mary Bonny. "They say....."

Bessie Booth interrupted with a little cry of excitement.

"It's come, Mary!" she exclaimed eagerly. "It's the letter we've been waiting for from the league!"

Mary Bonny was at her side in an instant, and together they glanced over the letter that Bessie Booth spread out on her desk.

It bore the printed heading of *'The Lancashire Girls' Football League'* and the address in Ranchester, where the headquarters of the league were situated.

Dear Miss Booth.....the letter ran......*We have received a communication from Mr Peter Henneker, of Henneker's Mill, Blacktown, in which he makes a protest that the club of which you are secretary – Henneker's Busy Bees F.C. – is not the original and genuine club that was nominated to a place in the league.*

He has placed certain facts before us in support of this assertion, and an inquiry into the matter will be held at the above address on Wednesday, the 21st instant.

Will you please present yourself here on the date mentioned, in order to answer Mr Henneker's various charges?

The letter was signed by Mr Hudson, the secretary to the league.

"Humph! Pretty business-like, isn't it?" grunted Mary Bonny, screwing up her somewhat prominent nose. "And the inquiry is to be held tomorrow at Ranchester. Ah wonder if Peter Henneker will be there?"

"He's bound to be," declared Bessie. "He'll have to give his evidence the same as I shall."

"You'd best let me go in your place, Bess," cried Mary Bonny eagerly. "By gum, Ah'd show that skunk up! Ah'd let the league officials know what kind of dirty cad he is!"

"No, I'm afraid you can't go, Mary," replied Bessie with a smile. "Perhaps it's just as well. You might spoil everything with that sharp tongue of yours. Well, I'm glad it's come at last. We shall know our fate by tomorrow evening."

It would have been futile for Bessie Booth to deny that she felt slightly nervous and none too confident as to the probable result of the league inquiry as she took her seat in the train the following morning.

Peter Henneker, with his usual cunning, had evidently made out a fairly strong case. And technically there was no doubt that he was correct in his assertion – that Bessie Booth's present team was not the original Henneker's Busy Bees in name, though in composition and every other detail.

Ranchester was a busy, bustling sort of a place compared to Blacktown, and having almost an hour to spare, Bessie strolled about, gazing into the windows of the big shops.

In the act of crossing the main street she sensed a tall form by her side, and glanced up into the sallow face of Peter Henneker.

Henneker raised his hat with a flourish and there was a glint of admiration in his dark eyes as he confronted the pretty girl who had so far proved herself more than a match for him.

"Just a few words with you, Miss Booth," he said suavely. "Believe me, I have no wish to be too hard on you. This mater can be settled amicably between us if you are willing?"

Bessie stared coldly at the rascally mill owner.

"It will be settled in any case," she said quietly.

"Yes, but not in your favour," jerked Henneker confidently. "You haven't a leg to stand on. Your team will lose its place in the league, and it's only a matter of weeks before you will have to close your mill down. I'm bound to beat you in the end. Come, be sensible. Throw up this mad enterprise. I'm willing to take the whole lot of you back again, and I shan't interfere with your football."

Bessie Booth's eyes flashed scornfully. She knew Peter Henneker too well to be deceived by his hollow promises. The very fact that he was willing to come to a settlement was proof positive that he was beginning to feel the effects of the competition of the Bee-Hive Mill.

"Come back to work for you!" said the girl indignantly. "Not for all the money in the world, Gaffer Henneker! We wouldn't work for you again if we were starving!"

She turned away scornfully, leaving Peter Henneker staring evilly after her, his sallow cheeks flushed with chagrin.

Bessie Booth felt that the brief interview with the mill owner had given her renewed confidence. If Peter Henneker was so certain of his ability to get the Busy Bees thrown out of the football league, and to compel them to close down their mill he would not have suggested a compromise. It was a sign of weakness on his part, and Bessie's previous feeling of nervousness vanished as she made her way towards the offices of the Lancashire Girls' Football League.

A young woman with spectacles – evidently the assistant secretary - admitted her, and, taking her name, ushered her into a cosy little waiting-room, where a cheerful fire was burning. Here also, in a big glass case, was the handsome silver cup and gold-centred medals that at the end of the season would be presented to the champions of the league.

Bessie's eyes glistened as she gazed at the trophies. She had only one wish in the world at that moment, and that was for the Busy Bees to be the successful club! What a day of days it would be if the Blacktown team headed the league! But she also realised that there were many obstacles to be overcome before then, and one of the most serious of all that very afternoon. The next hour would decide the fate of the Busy Bees – whether they were to retain their place in the competition, or be ousted out by Peter Henneker's bogus, hastily-formed eleven

The girl with the spectacles appeared again a few minutes later.

"The committee is just sitting," she said in a friendly tone. "Mr Henneker is giving his evidence. You will be called as soon as he has finished."

Another half-hour passed whilst Bessie sat, a prey to anxious indecision. Would Peter Henneker sway the league officials to his point of view, with his suave tongue and cunning distortion of facts?

There in a glass case was the handsome cup to be awarded at the end of the season. Bessie's eyes glistened as she gazed at it

At last the summons came and a moment later the girl found herself in a big, plainly furnished room, where half a dozen men and women sat around a long mahogany table.

"Take a seat, Miss Booth," said a neatly dressed, elderly woman, with a kindly face and iron-grey hair. This was Mrs. Desmond, the 'chairman' and a well-known lady sportswoman in her younger days. A hockey international, a champion golfer and tennis player, she had been one of the first to espouse the cause of the girl footballers and in the promotion of the Lancashire Girls' Football League.

"The complaint against your club, Miss Booth," said Mrs. Desmond in business-like tones "is that it is not the original Henneker's Busy Bees who were admitted to membership of the league. What have to say to that?"

"It is the original Busy Bees," declared Bessie Booth firmly. "I formed the club myself, and I sent in the application for admittance to the league."

"Yes, the application was certainly sent in your name."

"The team now is exactly the same team that played in the qualifying round and, by winning, became eligible for league itself."

"Yes, that may be so," said Mrs. Desmond. "But Mr Henneker's point is that as you are no longer in his employment you no longer have the right to call yourself Henneker's Busy Bees."

"The team had nothing to do with Mr Henneker," flashed Bessie. "His name was only used to distinguish us from any other club that might call itself the Busy Bees."

"One minute," interposed a man who sat at the other end of the table. "You say your club has no binding connection with Henneker's Mill, yet you used his name, and you played your matches on his ground?"

Bessie Booth bit her lip, and flushed slightly.

"Yes, that is so," she admitted. "We had no ground of our own then, and we played on a piece of waste ground belonging to the mill. But it was without Mr Henneker's permission. When he learned what we were doing he forbade us to use the ground."

"Indeed!" exclaimed Mrs. Desmond. "That does not look as if he was giving your club.....or his club, as he calls it......any support."

"Support?" echoed Bessie. "Why........"

"One moment," interrupted Mrs. Desmond. "I think we had better send for Mr Henneker."

A moment later Peter Henneker came stalking into the room. He sank confidently into a chair, and blinked his eyes maliciously at Bessie Booth.

"Is it true, Mr Henneker," asked the chairman, "that you forbade the Busy Bees the use of a ground belonging to your mill?"

The mill owner's eyes narrowed.

"Yes, that is so," he admitted.

"Why?"

"Because I needed the ground for another purpose."

"Nothing of the kind, ladies and gentlemen," cried Bessie, springing to her feet. "The ground was taken away from us out of sheer spite, and Mr Henneker knows it. He did everything he could to prevent us from playing football. Why.....why do you think we were dismissed from his mill? Simply because we refused to give up the game!"

A ripple of wonderment ran round the long table, and Peter Henneker shot a venomous glance at Bessie Booth.

"Dismissed you because you refused to give up playing football?"

"Extraordinary! And yet Mr Henneker claims......."

"All this is beside the point," rasped Henneker, realising he was losing ground. "What I claim is that Henneker's Busy Bees.....the football club elected by you to the league....is strictly limited to girls in my employ."

Bessie Booth rose to her feet again, her pretty face flushed with excitement.

"If that's the case," she said steadily, "how many league engagements has your club fulfilled?"

Peter Henneker started.

"Not any," he admitted sullenly.

"And why?" continued the mill girl. "Why is it you allowed my team to play two league matches without having made your complaint to the league? I'll tell you now. You never thought anything more about the football club after we had left your mill. And now you are bringing this point up out of sheer spite."

"It seems to me," said Mrs. Desmond, gravely, "that we are getting slightly away from the subject. The point we have got to decide is which of the two teams – yours Miss Booth or Mr Henneker's – is eligible to compete in the league? There is something to be said for each side."

"We will discuss the matter amongst ourselves," suggested the young man who had administered the well-deserved rebuke to Peter Henneker.

Bessie Booth made her way back into the little waiting-room. Ten minutes.....a quarter of an hour's poignant impatience, and then she was summoned back to the committee room to face Peter Henneker's surly visage across the table.

Mrs. Desmond rose to her feet. Her face was no indication to her thoughts.

"It is the opinion of the committee," she said in a clear voice, "that, technically, Mr Henneker has good grounds for the complaint he has lodged. But, considering the various circumstances brought to our notice by Miss Booth, it appears that she is equally deserving of a fair and sympathetic hearing. It is obvious that her team is the original Busy Bees, in all but name. It is our opinion that there is only one way in which to settle this dispute, and that is for the two teams to fight it out between themselves as to which shall remain in the league."

Peter Henneker's dark eyes glittered triumphantly as he stood twirling his hat in his long fingers. The decision was quite satisfactory as far as he was concerned. It gave him the chance to bring still further ignominy upon Bessie and her team.

He hadn't the slightest doubt that his carefully collected team of crack girl footballers would have no difficulty in defeating the Busy Bees. And their defeat would lose them their place in the league. It would be a double victory in every sense of the word.

"I am quite satisfied with your ruling," he said suavely. "And when is the match to be played?"

"The sooner the better," replied Mrs. Desmond. "Otherwise the winning team will find itself with a very congested fixture list, for there is the match with Rigan to be played off as well.....and another league match on Saturday next. I would suggest tomorrow.....Wednesday.....afternoon."

Bessie Booth nodded again. She agreed that the sooner the deciding match was played off the better it would be.

"And what about the choice of ground?" asked Peter Henneker eagerly.

"The choice of ground will be drawn for in the ordinary way," said Mrs. Desmond.

She wrote the names of the two clubs on separate sheets of paper, and, having folded them up, handed them to the league secretary who sat half way down the table. He placed them in a hat and held it above his head, whilst the official opposite inserted his hand.

He drew one of the slips of paper, unfolded it and read out.

"Mr Henneker's team."

Peter Henneker gave a little exclamation of satisfaction.

"Well, I wish you the best of luck, Miss Booth," said Mrs. Desmond, drawing the mill girl to one side before she left. "I wish we could have decided in your favour right away, but in the circumstances it just wasn't possible."

As she sat in the train speeding back to Blacktown, Bessie Booth could not help thinking that the result of the league inquiry that day was more or less in the nature of a victory for Peter Henneker.

The rascally mill owner had proved his point. His objection had been upheld, and, though he had not robbed the Busy Bees of their place in the league, he had laid it open to the possibility that they might be disqualified.

It all depended upon the result of the match that was to be played the following afternoon, and Bessie was none too optimistic as to her team's chances of success.

Henneker had played his cards cunningly and well. He had got together a team of girls that, on paper, seemed strong enough to beat any other girls' eleven in all Lancashire.

"They mustn't beat us........we've simply *got* to win!" muttered Bessie, a little lump of anxiety in her throat. "If we lose this match we lose everything. After all we've done to keep the club together, and keep our place in the league. It would be simply heart-breaking to go under now."

The Traitor

"Peter Henneker's given all his hands a half-day off to see the match this afternoon. Are you going to do the same, Bess?"

Bessie Booth stopped short as Ned Bromley, the head overlooker, addressed her.

"A half-day off? No, we can't afford to do that, Ned," she said grimly. "We're too busy.....too many urgent orders to handle, as you know. If Peter Henneker is giving all his hands a holiday, you may depend that his looms are only working at half pressure. If there was work for them to do, you can be sure they'd get no half-day holiday out of him."

Bessie's thoughts came into sharp focus about the forthcoming match that afternoon.

"We're not going to lose...we mustn't think about losing!" she cried, clenching her little hands. "Oh, I know what it means if we do, Ned. We'll lose our place in the league, we'll be disgraced, and Peter Henneker will have done us more harm than if he'd blown the mill up over our heads!"

"The dirty skunk!" growled Ned Bromley, shaking a brawny fist in the direction of the smoking chimney stacks of Henneker's Mill, half a mile away. "It just isn't fair!"

"It's all fair in one way," said Bessie Booth with a sigh. "They're all employed at his mill, and they're all properly registered. Never mind! When we've beaten them it will be all the more credit to us and.......what was that?"

The sound of a heavy fall and a sharp shrill cry of pain were heard above the noise of the engines and the clatter of the looms. Bessie darted into the mill.

At the bottom of the flight of stone steps leading up to the spinning room a girl was huddled, one foot twisted beneath her and her face white and twitching with pain. Bessie immediately recognised Sally Soper, the Busy Bees goalie.

"Why, Sally, what's happened? What have you done?"

Sally bit her lip to suppress the moan of pain that was rising in her throat.

"Ah slipped," she said faintly. Ah was coming down the stairs when Ah slipped and fell. Ah'm afraid Ah've hurt my ankle, Bess."

Bessie Booth uttered a low cry of dismay as she knelt down by the girl's side. Tenderly she straightened out the twisted limb, and at one glance she knew the worst. Sally's ankle was badly sprained; already it had swollen to twice its normal size. There would be no football for Sally Soper that afternoon, or for many other afternoons. The Busy Bees would have to face Peter Henneker's redoubtable team without their regular goalkeeper.

"It's.....it's badly sprained, Sally," said Bessie huskily. "You mustn't try to walk on it. You must be taken straight home, and see a doctor. Fetch me some cold water, Ned."

Sally's jaw dropped.

"Go....go home," she stammered. "But Ah can't, Bess! You know Ah can't! Ah've got to play this afternoon."

She struggled to rise, and sank back again with a moan of agony. Tears were trickling down her freckled face; but they were tears of disappointment rather than of pain.

"They'll be no football for you this afternoon, Sally," said Bessie consolingly, "or for some weeks, I'm afraid. Never mind, dear! It's bad luck, but it can't be helped."

The clatter of the engines and looms suddenly ceased as the hooter sounded and the operatives came streaming down the stairs from the spinning rooms. The bad news spread swiftly from lip to lip, bringing gloom and dismay wherever it went.

Mary Bonny the centre-half and Amy Olroyd the right-back helped to carry Sally into the general office. Ned Bromley arrived with a tin basinful of water, and Bessie deftly applied a cold compress to the black-and-blue, badly swollen limb.

"To think that Ah can't play this afternoon," sobbed the injured goalkeeper, disgustedly. "Ah must play. Perhaps it will be better by two o'clock."

"It won't be any better by two o'clock tomorrow," said Ned Bromley, gravely. "Dang me, but it's rotten luck!"

The girl footballers stared at one another in dismay.

"What.......what shall we do?" muttered Connie Tree, the outside-right. "Poor Sally! Who is going to take her place?"

The unfortunate accident to their clever, popular goalkeeper seemed to have thrown a cloud of depression over the Busy Bees. They had been none too confident of beating Henneker's before, and now........

Sally Soper was carried away home on a motor-bike and side-car belonging to one of the engineers, and Bessie Booth frowned around at the gloomy faces of her companions.

"What, beaten before the match starts?" she said, with sharp reproach. "Don't you think we're good enough to beat Henneker's without a goalkeeper? Buck up girls! This ought to make you all the more determined to win.

"Hear, hear! Bess is right," cried big Mary Bonny scornfully. "Do you think you're going to a football match or a funeral? We won't need a goalkeeper this afternoon if we play like we ought to do."

"That's rot! We can't do without a goalkeeper," declared Enid Foster the left-back, indignantly.

"We're not going to," said Bessie Booth quietly. "The only thing is.....who shall we play in Sally's place?"

It was a difficult problem to decide. Sally had hitherto never missed a match since the Busy Bees had first been formed, so that no one else had ever had a chance to show what they could do between the sticks.

"Will you give me a chance, Bess? Ah'll do my best. Ah used to play goal for a girls' team before Ah came to Blacktown. Ah don't say Ah'm as good as Sally, but......."

Bessie Booth glanced sharply at the girl who had stepped forward – a thin, pale-faced girl named Ada Miller. There was something about Ada Miller that Bess had never liked – a shifty, furtive look in her grey-green eyes; but it wasn't to say that she couldn't play football.

"Well, somebody's got to take Sally's place," she said resignedly. "Mary, you and the other girls go round to the ground and see how Ada shapes. Get out a couple of practice balls and put her between the sticks."

The girls went clattering away to the football ground at the back of the mill, and Bess sank into a chair with a heavy sigh of despondency.

"Now then, Bess lass, don't you get down in the dumps," said Ned Bromley, laying a gentle hand on the girl's shoulder. "Ah know it's rotten hard luck, but you've got to fight it. If you're beaten this afternoon you won't be disgraced."

"Beaten! We mustn't be beaten, Ned!" cried Bessie desperately, roused by the hint at defeat. "But Sally of all people, and I was depending so much on her. Why, it wouldn't have been so bad if it had been me."

Ned gave a short snort of scorn.

"If it had been you there would have been no sense in playing the match," he declared. "Now just you keep your pecker up, lass, and you'll come through with flying colours! Dang me, Henneker may have a team of cracks, but they're all strange to one another. Doesn't say they can play together."

Bessie nodded hopefully. What Ned Bromley said was sound horse-sense. He had pointed out the one weak spot in Henneker's team. The players had come from all different parts of the country. They had been chosen on their individual merits, and whether they would blend and combine together or not was another matter altogether. A team of cracks does not make a crack team, as many a wealthy football team had discovered.

"Have you heard how Josh Browell is?" asked Ned Bromley, suddenly changing the subject.

"I telephoned up this morning," replied Bessie. "The doctor says he is no better and no worse, but he isn't fit to receive visitors as yet. Poor old man! I hope he'll soon be up and about again. We really owe everything to him, don't we, Ned?"

Ned Bromley nodded his head. He had been more worried over old Josh Browell than he would have cared to admit. Many a time he had wondered what would become of them if the old man were to die, for their tenancy of the mill was a purely verbal one. There was no written agreement on either side.

A few minutes later Mary Bonny came stomping into the room, with Ada Miller close on her heels.

"The lass is none too bad, Bess," announced the Busy Bees' centre-half. "She knows how to kick a ball, and she saved some mighty hot shots. 'Course, she's not in the same street as our Sally, but you might do worse than put her in goal for this afternoon. There's no one else better."

"Then Ada had better play," decided Bess. "Be ready at half past one sharp, Ada, and don't eat a heavy dinner. We're looking for you to help us beat Henneker's and if you do well you can keep Sally's place until she is fit again."

Ada Miller left the office, and there was a peculiar gleam of triumph in her green eyes as she hurried away across the mill yard. A hundred yards down the street she turned into a grocer's shop, where there was a public telephone box, and, closing the door carefully, called a number into the mouthpiece.

"Ah want to speak to Mr Henneker," she said, a few seconds later, and almost at one the harsh voice of Peter Henneker came rasping over the wires.

"Gaffer, this is Ada Miller speaking," said the girl in a low, tense voice. "Ah've got some news for you. You remember what you asked me to do? Well, Ah've done it. Ah've got a place in the Busy Bees team."

"Humph! How did you manage that?" grunted the mill owner sourly.

"Sally Soper's just sprained her ankle and Ah'm taking her place as goalkeeper."

"What!" A note of excitement crept into Peter Henneker's voice. "Do you mean to say you're playing in goal for the Busy Bees this afternoon?"

"That's right, gaffer."

An ugly chuckle of delight came rumbling over the wires.

"Thunder, that's splendid, Miller!" exclaimed Peter Henneker. "You've done better than I expected. This makes it a certainty for my team. Listen! If the Bees lose you're on a ten pound note. Do you understand?"

"Ay, Ah understand," replied the girl eagerly. "The Bees won't win if Ah can help it, gaffer. The money's as good as mine."

And, replacing the receiver, Ada Miller, Peter Henneker's paid spy, left the box, a glint of avarice in her green eyes.

A Fight for Existence

"Is everybody here? Have you all got your bags? Come along, then, girls!"

Bessie Booth picked up the leather satchel containing her own football kit and led the way out of the gates and up the road in the direction of Henneker's Mill. From behind them came a hearty cheer of encouragement, and the girl footballers turned to wave their hands towards the faces clustered at the windows of the Bee-Hive Mill.

There was no half-holiday for Bessie Booth's workers that afternoon. There were many urgent orders that had to be executed, and, after all, business came before pleasure.

"Good luck to you, girls! Good old Bess!"

"See you put it across 'em!"

"Don't forget your shooting boots, Bess!"

Bessie Booth threw a brave, confident smile back over her shoulder.

"We'll do our best," she called sturdily. "We can't do more than that."

It was evident that the importance of the occasion was making itself felt on some of the girls. There was a nervous, strained look on their faces, and few words were spoken as they tramped along.

They all realised they had reached a crisis in the affairs of the Busy Bees Football Club. They would not be fighting for league points that afternoon......they would be fighting for their very existence. Defeat would lose them their place in the league, and if that happened, all the sacrifices they had made to keep the team together would have been in vain.

And they missed the cheery, encouraging personality of whimsical, freckle-faced Sally Soper. Sally had ever a laugh and a joke on her lips, and an unfailing supply of good humour, that no misfortune, however great, could dampen. A smile and a quip from Sally had won more than one game in the past.

Peter Henneker evidently did not intend to lose money over the match. He had had the entire ground fenced in with rough boards and wire, and was actually charging sixpence for admission. Most of the crowd of would-be spectators grumbled indignantly, but they paid up, as Henneker had shrewdly guessed they would.

Already there were quite six or seven hundred people assembled on the ground as Bess and her team passed through the gates and made their way towards the big dressing-tent.

Here they were greeted by a sturdy, black-haired, heavy-featured girl. This was Jane Tanner, the captain of Henneker's new team, who was well known throughout Lancashire as a player.

"You know the way to your dressing-room," she said, with a surly nod of her head to the visitors, and promptly disappeared into her own portion of the tent.

"Nice, pleasant sort of lass, that," said Mary Bonny grimly as she tossed her bag to the ground. "And Ah've heard she plays a dirty, rough game in a clever way. She'd better not try any of her tricks on me."

"Ah heard Peter Henneker picked the roughest players he could find," muttered Enid Foster. "They're a sight bigger 'n older girls than we are."

"Never mind that," smiled Mary Bonny. "We'll see if we can make 'em feel small."

Five minutes later the two teams took the field amid a generous roar of applause from the rapidly swelling crowd.

Henneker's wore plain red jerseys, and the Busy Bees their usual black and yellow hoops.

A few minutes kick-about and the referee – a man specially appointed by the officials of the league – whistled the teams to attention. Bessie extended her hand to Jane Parker, but the girl pretended not to see it, and the unmannerly action brought an angry spot of colour to Bessie's cheeks.

A coin was spun in the air. Bess was wrong in her call and - with a superior sneer - Jane Parker waved a hand towards the goal that was favoured by the breeze.

The two teams lined up, and the next instant the great game, that was to decide the fate of the Busy Bees, had commenced. Bessie Booth's pretty face was pale and set with grim determination. She passed to her right wing, and the winger, grasping the situation, centred rapidly as Bess dashed forward like a flash of lightning. A roar of amazement went up as the girl dribbled straight on down the field.

The opposing halves were temporarily nonplussed. Every second they expected Bessie to get rid of the ball; but they hesitated too long and their tackles were easily encountered. Before they could recover, the girl was passed them and, showing them a clean pair of heels, she raced for goal.

The right-back, a big, red-headed girl, charged at her like a bull at a gate, and Bessie deliberately stopped dead in her stride, stepped to one side to avoid the back's rush, and then ran straight on like a hare and slammed the ball past the amazed goalkeeper into the net.

"GOAL!"

The roar of delight that went up shook the windows of the Bee-Hive Mill, half a mile away! It was the most surprising goal that the Blacktown folk had ever witnessed. In less than sixty seconds from the start of the game Bessie Booth had given her side the lead, and Mary Bonny and Amy Olroyd snatched her up and almost carried her back to the centre of the field.

Peter Henneker, watching from a specially prepared seat on one side of the ground, raved and cursed like a madman as he saw what was happening. He had expected his side to inflict a crushing defeat on the Busy Bees, but already they were a goal to the bad.

A moment later Henneker was smiling again. Jane Tanner & Co. did not mean to be caught napping so easily a second time. Keeping the ball in their midst they swept down the field by sheer force. A heavy charge sent Enid Foster sprawling, but Amy Olroyd filched the ball away from Jane Tanner's toe and slipped it on to Mary Bonny. Mary cleared at the same instant as a lashing boot thudded against her ankle, bringing a yelp of pain to her lips.

"So that's the game, is it?" muttered Mary hotly, as she hopped about for a moment on one leg. "Ah half-guessed as much. Ah hope this ref keeps his eyes open for rough play."

Rough play there was to follow, and plenty of it. Bessie Booth was charged and hustled every time the ball came anywhere near her, and the only occasion when Connie Tree managed to make one of her lightning breakaways, she was bustled into touch with such force as to send her floundering right amongst the spectators.

But the Busy Bees managed to keep their citadel intact until five minutes from half-time, when Jane Tanner sent in a long, drooping shot that Sally Soper would have cleared with ease. But Ada Miller muffled the ball in some extraordinary manner, and it went over her shoulder into the net.

"Good girl!" muttered Peter Henneker. "She's out to win that tenner, and I hope she does."

"Young Ada should have stopped that shot," grumbled Mary Bonny, as she rubbed her bruised ankle in the dressing-tent at half-time. "Twice as easy as picking flowers."

"She was nervous, perhaps," said Bessie Booth, whose right arm was black-and-blue from shoulder to wrist, thanks to the kindly attentions of the opposing centre-half.

As Bessie Booth had foreseen, Henneker's were far from being a well-balanced team; but what they lacked in combination and co-ordination they made up for in dash and unnecessary vigour. Soon, not only Mary Bonny, but Connie Tree as well, was limping from a nasty kick on the ankle, and it was only the dour, resolute play of the Bees' backs – Enid Foster and Amy Olroyd – that prevented the home team from taking the lead.

And then, half way through the second half something happened that brought a groan of dismay to Bessie's lips. Henneker's were granted a free kick for offside and made another sweeping attack. Amy Olroyd slipped and fell in the act of clearing, and with prompt judgement slid her foot along the turf and rolled the ball gently back toward Ada Miller in goal.

All the deputy-goalkeeper had to do was to stoop and pick it up. Instead of that, she aimed a wild kick at the leather, missed it altogether, and clutched at the left upright for support as the ball trickled over the line into the net.

Henneker's had taken the lead, and with only a bare quarter of an hour to go the Bees seemed certain of a defeat that would lose them their place in the league.

"Bess, Ah believe Ada Miller deliberately gave that goal away," said Mary Bonny, as the visiting team prepared to kick-off again.

But the Busy Bees had not yet lost their sting, and the crowd roared its delight a few minutes later when Mary Bonny put the scores level with a rasping shot that gave the goalkeeper no earthly chance.

And it was the very tactics that previously had served them so well that brought about Henneker's downfall.

Three times in succession the referee awarded the Bees a free kick for tripping and rough play, and on the last occasion Bessie booth snapped up a neat pass from Connie Tree and made a rush for goal.

Everything was forgotten, save the ball at her toes. She could see the goalkeeper dancing about anxiously on her goal-line, and then an outstretched leg swept her feet away from beneath her, and sent her crashing to the ground.

It was a deliberate foul, a yard inside the penalty area, and the referee pointed sternly to the fatal spot.

"If the game weren't nearly over, I'd send you off the field!" he said sternly to the guilty right-back.

Bessie herself took the kick, and made no mistake with a rising shot that found the top right-hand corner of the net, and gave the Busy Bees a well-deserved victory.

They had made certain of their place in the league, and once again Peter Henneker found himself defeated and deflated by Bessie Booth and the girl footballers of the Bee-Hive Mill.

Shamed and chagrined, beaten by their own foul tactics, the team that Henneker had been at such pains to get together slunk from the field, whilst the Busy Bees had to positively fight their way through the delighted crowd that swarmed around them.

And up at the Bee-Hive Mill, Ned Bromley sat, white and silent, stunned by the bad news that had just reached him over the telephone. That which he had dreaded had come to pass......old Josh Browell was dead!

It was a deliberate foul, and the referee pointed sternly to the spot. "If the game weren't nearly over, I'd send you off the field." he said sternly to the guilty right-back

A Chance for Henneker

The sudden death of old Josh Browell came as quite a shock to the inhabitants of Blacktown, but the people most vitally affected were Bessie Booth and all the men and lads and girls who assisted her to run and work the Bee-Hive Mill.

And on top of her grief at the old man's sudden death, Bessie Booth was filled with anxiety and fear for the immediate future. The tenancy of the mill was a purely verbal one, with no written agreement between her and Josh Browell; the old man had simply said 'There's the mill so get on and run it', and she had done exactly as he had directed.

It was a disquieting prospect, and small wonder that Bessie Booth's pretty face was pale and wan, and her eyes clouded with anxiety and gloom as she sat in her office at the mill the day after Josh Browell had been laid to his last long sleep at Blacktown Cemetery.

"Ned, I've got a letter here from Mr Chaddon, Josh Browell's lawyer," said Bessie to Ned Bromley, the head overlooker.

Ned sank back into a chair with a stifled groan of dismay.

"Ah, so it's come at last, has it?" he said resignedly. "An' when have we got to clear out, Bess, lass?"

"I don't know at all," replied the girl with a little frown of bewilderment. "Mr Chaddon doesn't say anything at all about clearing out. He simply asks me to come and see him at his office this afternoon. There's another thing that's worrying me, Ned," she went on gravely." What about our match tomorrow with Rigan. Do you think we ought to play football under the circumstances...so soon after Mr Browell's death?"

It was all-important that the league match between her team and Rigan should be played the following afternoon. It should have been played the previous Saturday but Peter Henneker's underhand tactics had put paid to that.

But it was the grim uncertainty of their position that worried Bessie Booth more than anything. Just as they had made a success of the mill it looked likely that they would be turned out into the street and robbed of the fruits of all their toil.

As soon as the midday hooter sounded, Bessie Booth donned her coat and hat and set off briskly into the town, to keep her appointment with Josh Browell's lawyer. With mingled feelings she passed through the door that bore a brass plate with the name 'James Chaddon' inscribed upon it and gave her name to the clerk in the outer office.

Almost at once she was ushered into the presence of Mr Chaddon himself – a tall man with a long, white, clean-shaven face and not unkindly bright brown eyes.

"Ah, Miss Booth," he said briskly. "Take a seat, Miss Booth."

Bessie perched herself on the edge of an old-fashioned high-backed chair, whilst James Chaddon propped his elbow on the edge of his desk, and stared kindly at the pretty girl.

"I fear the untimely death of my client, the late Mr Browell, has left you in a very awkward position, Miss Booth," he said at length.

It was not a very promising start and Bessie's heart sank.

"I....I don't quite know how I stand," she faltered nervously. "That is why I was so anxious to see you, Mr Chaddon."

"I quite understand," jerked the old lawyer with a nod of his head. "At the present moment you are the tenant of my late client's mill, under a verbal agreement very favourable to yourself. You had no written, legally binding agreement with Mr Browell?"

"Nothing whatever," admitted Bess ruefully. "Mr Browell said I could have the use of the mill for what I liked and as long as I liked. I.....myself and my friends.....took advantage of Mr Browell's generous offer. We re-opened the mill and, thanks to his aid, we have made it pay."

"Yes, I quite understand all that," said the lawyer, "and the fact remains that you had no written agreement with my late client. Your tenancy of the mill automatically expired with his death."

Bessie Booth started, and tears of dismay crept into her eyes.

"You....you mean that we will have to leave the mill?" she said anxiously.

"No, I don't exactly mean that," said the lawyer, rubbing his clean-shaven chin. "I am quite willing to carry out, as far as possible, the wishes of the late Mr Browell. I don't mind telling you, Miss Booth, that some time ago Mr Browell asked me to draft him out a new will, in which he left the entire mill property to you."

Bessie Booth gave a great gasp of excitement, but the lawyer raised a warning hand.

"Don't let my words raise any false hopes, Miss Booth," he said gravely. "I regret to inform you that Mr Browell died leaving the new will unsigned."

Chaddon's words dashed Bessie's hopes to the ground again. Fate had played her a cruel trick. Old Josh Browell had wanted to make her a present of the entire mill property, but death had snatched him away before he could carry out his intention in a legally binding manner.

So near and yet so far! It was a bitter disappointment to the mill girl. Things would have been so different had Josh Browell only lived to put his signature to the new will. As it was.....

"How exactly do we stand, Mr Chaddon?" she asked, an eager, anxious look in her brown eyes.

"I will tell you exactly. Miss Booth," replied the old lawyer kindly. "The sole heir to all Mr Browell's property is his son.....his only son"

"His son! Why, I didn't know he had a son!" exclaimed Bessie in surprise.

"That is quite understandable," smiled the lawyer, "but nevertheless Josh Browell had one son....Richard Browell.....who would be about twenty-eight years of age now. He and his father had a slight quarrel some seven years ago, and Dick Browell went abroad to America. I believe he is still there, but I have no knowledge of his address. He did write once to his father, but Josh Browell was a stubborn, stiff-necked old man and he sent the letter back unopened."

"What a shame!" cried Bessie instinctively. "And now he doesn't even know his father is dead?"

"No, he can't know," replied the lawyer. "I shall have to advertise for him in the American papers. In the meantime, Miss Booth, I am going to allow you to carry on with the mill under the same conditions as when Mr Browell was alive. But you must understand that this is only a temporary arrangement," he hastened to add as Bessie Booth gave a little cry of delight. "It will hold good until I have got into communication with Mr Richard Browell, when I shall have to act under his instruction. He will probably want me to sell the mill for him, and realise on all his property over here if he has settled for good in America."

Bessie nodded gloomily. After all, half a loaf was better than no bread. At least they would have a few weeks' respite before Richard Browell could learn of his father's death and claim the property that he was legally entitled to.

The fact that he might wish to sell the mill was a disconcerting one. Bessie Booth instinctively guessed what would happen – the purchaser would be her deadly enemy and business rival, Peter Henneker! There was not the slightest doubt that Peter Henneker would jump at the opportunity to buy the mill over their heads, and turn them out into the streets.

"I.....I hope you will put our case before Mr Browell when you get into communication with him," said Bessie wistfully. "Perhaps if he knew his father intended leaving the mill to me he might...."

"I can assure you, I'll do everything I can for you," promised the old lawyer. "You have my sincere sympathy, Miss Booth. But I shouldn't advise you to build too many hopes on Mr Browell junior. If he has been in America all these years, and is anything like his father was when he was younger, he has probably developed into a shrewd, hard-headed man of business, and there is not much sympathy in business, as you know."

There was a general atmosphere of gloom when Bessie returned to the Bee-Hive Mill and announced the result of her visit.

"So that's how we stand, is it?" muttered Mary Bonny ruefully. "We can stay on here until Mr Richard Browell turns up and sends us packing. It's enough to take all the heart out of you. What's the good of everything carrying on if we're going to be turned out in the end? Might as well chuck it now."

"That's not like you, Mary," said Bess reproachfully. "While there's life there's hope. You don't know what might turn up. Young Mr Browell may allow us to carry on as usual, when he learns that it was his father's wish that we should."

"Ay, but not on the same terms, Ah'll wager," said Amy Olroyd, the right-back. "He'll want all the brass for himself."

"You can't be certain," protested Bessie hopefully. "Supposing he takes over the mill. He's sure to let us work for him."

"No need to borrow trouble," said Sally Soper stoutly. Since spraining her ankle the Busy Bees' goalkeeper still limped, and walked with a stick. "Young Mr Browell knows nothing about his father's death, as yet, and he may not know for weeks...perhaps months. What we've got to do is stick to it, and hope for the best."

A chorus of approval went up.

"All Ah've got to say is that it's danged bad luck," declared Ned Bromley. "Just to think that if poor old Josh Browell had lived just a few days longer, the mill would have belonged to our Bess, lock, stock and barrel."

"Never mind. Buck up the Bees!" cried Bessie. "We're not beaten yet, and we're not going to be. Don't forget we've got Rigan tomorrow in the replay, and on Monday we're to meet Newtown Flyers at home."

Meanwhile, the news of old Josh Browell's came as a pleasant surprise and a distinct pick-me-up to Peter Henneker, the unscrupulous owner of Henneker's Mill. He realised that Browell's death must come as a tremendous blow to Bessie Booth and her companions, and he was shrewd enough to guess that there was a strong likelihood of their being turned out of the Bee-Hive Mill.

"I hope they are turned out into the gutter to starve," he muttered viciously as he strode up and down his office. "I must find out exactly how things stand. I'm certain that girl had no hard-and-fast agreement with old Josh Browell. I wonder who is the old man's next-of-kin?"

He immediately set about finding out, sending for Ada Miller, who worked for Bessie Booth...... but spied for Henneker. Many were the valuable items of information she had brought her rascally employer, and she was now able to give him every detail relating to Bessie Booth's visit to the late Josh Browell's lawyer.

"Ah, so that's the position, is it?" muttered Henneker thoughtfully. "What a stroke of luck for me that old Browell never signed that will! By heavens, guess I've got Bessie Booth where I want her now! You say that Richard Browell is the old man's sole heir, and that he is now in America?"

Ada Miller nodded her shawl-swathed head.

"Ay, he went there seven years ago," she informed. "No one's heard anything of him since."

"Doesn't the lawyer know his address? How's he going to get into communication with him?"

"Advertise in the papers, so Ah understand."

Peter Henneker sent for his manager, John Smith.

"Smith," said Henneker tersely. "I want you to send a cable to Carl Lehmann, our agent in New York. Tell him to get in touch with a young Britisher named Richard Browell, who arrived in the States some seven years ago, and to offer Browell any sum he likes for the mill property here in Blacktown, that belonged to his father, Josh Browell."

A flicker of interest crept into John Smith's dull eyes.

"So you mean to buy up the Bee-Hive Mill?" he asked.

"Of course I do. Do you think I'm asleep?" snapped his employer. "Do you think I'm likely to miss such a chance as this? Lehmann is a smart man. He'll soon trace this fellow Browell, and persuade him to sell the mill, and once it becomes my property I'll sling Bessie Booth and her confounded gang into the gutter."

John Smith nodded, showing little emotion.

"It's a good plan," he said quietly. "Your luck has turned again, Mr Henneker. Nothing could have been more Providential than old Josh Browell's death. He is better out of the way!"

On the following afternoon the Busy Bees entertained Rigan Rovers on their trim ground at the back of the Bee-Hive Mill. It was not until the last minute that Bessie decided to give Ada Miller another chance in goal, in place of the injured Sally Soper. In the previous match she had put on a deplorable display, almost losing the match for them; but Bessie was not to know that the girl – on instructions from Peter Henneker – was deliberately trying to let the Busy Bees down. But Mary Bonny half-suspected the truth and said so to her chum.

"No, I can't believe it, Mary," said Bess, the last person on earth to think ill of anyone else. "What object would Ada have in trying to lose us the game? Think how anxious she was to take Sally's place. It was nervousness that caused her to play so badly. She's sure to play better this afternoon."

As a matter of fact, Ada Miller put up quite a respectable performance. She tried to, this time, in order to keep her place in the team as Peter Henneker had advised her to do.

It was a fast and gruelling game that ended in a draw of two goals each, but the Busy Bees were disappointed that they did not win outright and secure both points. With Sally Soper in goal there was not the slightest doubt that they would have done.

BEES
TBALL
LUB

"Still, not so bad," said Bessie cheerfully. "We've only played three league games and we've got five points out of a possible six. And we ought to beat Newtown Flyers on Monday."

On the following Monday morning, James Chaddon, lawyer and sole executor to the will of the late Joshua Browell, sat in his gloomy office opening his correspondence. He had cabled an advertisement calculated to catch the eye of Richard Browell, to the foremost American press agencies, but he did not expect to hear anything from, or of, the missing heir for several days, perhaps weeks.

Chaddon glanced up sharply as his clerk rapped on the door and entered the room with the announcement that there was a gentleman waiting to see him.

"What is his name?" jerked the old lawyer irritably.

"He didn't give a name, sir. Says you'll know him all right when you meet him.

A moment later the visitor was ushered into the office, and Chaddon stared half-angrily at the man who refused to give his name. He found himself confronted by a tall, broad-shouldered young fellow, with lean, bronzed features, and a firm, square jaw. He was neatly dressed in a blue suit and a grey velour hat.

"I am afraid you have the advantage of me, sir," said the old lawyer at length. "May I ask the reason for this...er.....intrusion?"

The newcomer smiled a trifle sadly.

"You don't remember me, Mr Chaddon? Have I changed so much?"

The lawyer stared, clutched at the arms of his chair, and sprang to his feet with a cry of amazement.

"Good heavens, you're young Dick Browell!" he almost shouted. "How in the name of all that's wonderful did you get here so soon? I only cabled last Friday!"

"I don't know anything about your cables, " said Dick Browell as he shook hands warmly with the old lawyer, whom he had not seen for eight long years. "I only landed at Fishguard yesterday morning.....came over from the States on business, and also to have a look at the old dad. But it appears I've come just too late. I happened to notice a paragraph in one of the Sunday papers announcing his death some days ago, and I came along here at once. I should like to have seen him before he died."

"And he would like to have seen you," said James Chaddon consolingly. "His last words were of you, Richard. He bitterly regretted the stupid quarrel that had separated you for all these years."

Dick Browell was not ashamed of the tears that crept into his steady, blue eyes. Death had played him a cruel trick in claiming his father only a bare few days prior to his long-delayed return to his home country.

James Chaddon stared curiously and admiringly at the stalwart young man who was heir to considerable fortune and properties. Strangely enough his first feeling was one of sympathy for the plucky girl footballers down at the Bee-Hive Mill.

For over an hour the two men – lawyer and client – were closeted together. Chaddon did much of the talking, whilst Dick Browell listened in grave silence.

"So, you see," concluded Chaddon, "you are a rich man, Richard. All the money that you will require is at your disposal."

"I don't need money," replied Dick Browell simply. "I have made a good bit for myself in the States. But I don't mind telling you that the old mill interests me. It fits in with a scheme I have had in my head for some years. But I don't quite understand. Do you mean to say that father handed the mill over to a crowd of men and women operatives and let them open it on their own?"

"Yes, on a profit-sharing basis," replied Chaddon slowly. "And they're doing very well. You see....."

"I should dashed well think so," interrupted Dick Browell a trifle indignantly. "Paying no rent or anything like that. It's ridiculous....more like a charity scheme than a business proposition."

"I hope you will continue to allow them the same privilege as your father did?" said the old lawyer hastily.

Dick Browell shook his head.

"That's impossible," he said bluntly. I tell you I want the mill for myself."

"But, good heavens, it will throw all these unfortunate people out of work......"

"Not necessarily," declared young Browell."If I decide to keep the mill open they can continue to work only for me, instead of themselves."

Chaddon clutched eagerly at this straw of hope.

"You will keep the mill running?"

"I don't know for certain," said Dick Browell, rising to his feet. "I must think the matter over. In the meantime I'll just run along to the mill and introduce myself to the present boss. He must be expecting something like this. See you later."

Chaddon opened his mouth, but Dick Browell had vanished from the office before he could find words. He had meant to inform him that the present 'boss' of the mill was not a man, but a young girl......and a particularly pretty girl at that.

"Never mind. Let him find out himself," decided the old lawyer. "Perhaps when he learns the truth and sets eyes on

Bessie Booth he'll think twice about taking the mill away from her."

This was the soundest supposition that James Chaddon had made that day. Many peculiar things were to come of the approaching meeting between Bessie Booth and Dick Browell.

But for the moment the fate of the Busy Bees hung in the balance!

A New Employee

For the first time in eight long years, Dick Browell strode through the narrow grimy streets of Blacktown and up the hill towards the towering, smoke-belching chimney stacks that marked the position of the mill that had once belonged to his father but that now, following his parent's sudden death, belonged to him.

"Eight years!" muttered Dick under his breath, his young handsome face and determined chin turned upwards as his clear grey eyes surveyed the building in front of him. "Eight years!" he said again. "What a lot had happened in that time! And...I'm back just too late to see the old dad before he died. What cruel luck!"

Dick now regretted the sudden quarrel between father and son – equally as pig-headed and stubborn as one another – that had caused him to shake the dust of Blacktown from his feet and seek an independent career abroad.

Many changes had taken place over the years as he had learned from James Chaddon, his father's solicitor. He now knew the whole story...the unscrupulous Peter Henneker, the closing of the mill, and the reopening of it by, of all things, a group of mill workers!

Dick Browell already admired their guts and determination, but he wanted the mill for himself and saw no way that the workers could continue with their profit sharing scheme they had created. That is why he was now on his way to the mill, to introduce himself to the present 'boss' and inform him that his tenancy would have to be terminated.

Dick paused half way up the hill to thumb a wad of tobacco into his pipe. To his left and a short distance away was the towering bulk of Henneker's Mill and Dick's gaze was one of reflection as to what had happened, and what may be yet to come. His eyes returned to the mass of dark red brick and glass in front of him.

"I can't understand father handing over the place to a crowd of operatives," he muttered. "He used to be such a crusty old fellow and dashed tight where money was concerned."

The young man was soon to find out the reason for old Josh Browell's amazing act of generosity.

After a few moments he was at the gates of the mill, and here he stopped short again, staring with bewildered interest. The name 'Browell' no longer graced the front of the building. Instead, the words 'The Bee-Hive Mill' were painted in its place.

And the place was throbbing and buzzing like a veritable hive of industry. The engines were roaring, the looms clacking and whirring. And men were bustling about, loading big lorries in the stone-paved yard.

"The Bee-Hive...of all the dashed extraordinary names!" exclaimed Dick Browell. "And they seem to be working like real game 'uns! I shall be sorry to take the mill away from them but, hang it all, I want it for myself! I must see if I can keep them all employed."

He crossed the yard and ran up the steps into the mill. He passed through a door on the right and into the general office. To his surprise the place was utterly deserted. The desks were empty; there was not a living soul to be seen.

"Well, this is a rum sort of a general office!" muttered the young man. "Hallo, there! Anyone at home?"

He awakened echoes in the long, silent room by banging his clenched fist noisily on one of the wooden desks.

"Have you any business here, or are you just amusing yourself?"

Dick Browell spun around sharply on his heel. He was no longer alone. Someone had entered the room close behind him. He found himself confronted by a slim girl in neat overalls, and instinctively he realised that she was the prettiest girl he had ever seen; curly brown hair, big brown eyes, a perfectly curved mouth, and a dimpled, softly rounded chin.

She stared at him steadily, a faint smile lurking in the depths of her eyes.

"Are you here on business?"

"I....I beg your pardon!" Dick Browell whipped off his hat, stammering and blushing like a schoolboy. "I didn't mean to kick up such a confounded row...but there doesn't seem to be anyone about!"

"Is there anyone you particularly wished to see?" queried the girl.

"Well, yes, there is. I want to see the boss...the...err... person who is running this show."

"Take a seat, will you? What is there I can do for you?"

Dick Browell sank meekly into a chair and fiddled bashfully with his hat.

"Why...err...just tell the...err...boss that I would like to see him," he suggested. "If you would be so kind....."

"*I* am the boss," said the girl with a smile that revealed tiny pearl-white teeth. "*I* am in charge here."

Dick made a futile clutch at his hat, and almost fell off his chair.

"You...you're the boss?" he gasped. "Do you mean to say that you're running this mill? Hang it...you're pulling my leg!"

"I assure you I'm not!" declared the pretty girl. "My name is Booth...Bessie Booth...and this mill belongs to me, for the present."

Dick noted the sudden glint of sadness that crept into her brown eyes, and his head swam as he knew what it meant, and realised the truth.

The mill was being run by this girl - the prettiest girl he had ever set his eyes on - and he had come along to claim his property and tell her that she would have to terminate her tenancy of the premises. His heart almost failed him. How was he to broach the subject? He had never dreamed that it was a girl he would have to deal with...especially a girl like Bessie Booth.

"Confound old Chaddon!" he muttered under his breath. "Why didn't he tell me? That accounts for the twinkle in his eyes! Then he stammered aloud. "Really, this is quite a surprise to me. I didn't imagine...."

"Why shouldn't a girl run a mill as well as a man?" asked Bessie Booth quietly. "It has been a sort of experiment, but quite a success. Of course, the mill isn't really mine. It has been loaned to me....."

She broke off with a sigh, and Dick Browell felt like kicking himself. He wanted to get away...... to think and readjust his plans. It was all wrong! What was he to do?

"I'm rather busy," hinted Bessie Booth. "If there is anything I can do for you? What did you wish to see me about?"

Dick Browell gulped and floundered. He couldn't do it. He could imagine the tears of dismay springing to those pretty eyes were he to announce his business.

"Why...it's like this Miss...Miss Booth," he faltered. "As a matter of fact...why...I came to ask you for a job. That's it...I want a job!"

Dick sighed triumphantly. He had found one way out at any rate.

Bessie Booth smiled in surprise at the handsome, well-dressed young man.

"You want a job!" she echoed. "What sort of a job? What can you do? You don't know anything about the trade, do you?"

"Yes, but I do!" declared Dick, which was perfectly true. As a boy he had spent many hours wandering through his father's mill, soaking up knowledge of every branch of the great industry. "You don't seem to be over-staffed here!" he said, glancing around the desolate office. "Plenty of room for one here. I'm a first-rate bookkeeper and clerk. You just try me!"

Bessie Booth looked interestedly at the young man. If there was one thing the mill lacked it was the service of a competent general business manager. Then her face suddenly fell and she shook her head.

"I'm sorry...I'm afraid it can't be done," she said wistfully. "You see, I couldn't offer you a definite salary. This is not like an ordinary mill. We work on a profit-sharing basis and..."

"Hang the salary!" blurted Dick recklessly. "That is...I don't care what I get. I'll take what comes to me..."

"But it's not only that," added Bessie Booth. "You see, we may have to leave the mill at any moment. The dear old man who loaned me the use of it is dead, and he has a son somewhere who is likely to turn up and throw us out..."

"Not he!" declared Dick without thinking. "That is to say...he may not. He may never turn up. At any rate, let me work for you as long as the old mill stays open? I'll risk it.....I can work all right."

Bessie Booth smiled kindly at the eager, impetuous young man.

"You're a stranger to Blacktown?" she suggested.

"No....not exactly. I've been here before...some years ago."

"You haven't told me your name."

"Richard.....Richard Trueman," he replied after a moment's hesitation. It was true up to a point. His full name happened to be Richard Trueman Browell.

"Can you supply references?"

The young man nodded. He was dead serious. He meant to go through with this business now. He had met the prettiest girl in all the world and he didn't mean to lose sight of her, or frighten her away by revealing his true identity. That could wait for another time. It would be easy enough to supply references. He had friends in London – old school chums – he could write to and arrange matters with.

"You haven't told me, Miss Booth," he said eagerly, "how you come to be here, running this mill?"

"It's all through football," replied Bessie Booth gravely.

"Football! Why, how on earth..."

"It is evident that you are practically a stranger to Blacktown," smiled the girl. "It was when I was working for Peter Henneker's mill. I started a team of girl footballers."

"Girl footballers!" Dick Browell nearly exploded. Having been out of England for eight years the girl footballer was a new species to him.

"Yes, girl footballers," repeated Bessie severely. "There are hundreds of teams all over England." She then proceeded to tell Dick everything that had happened; being dismissed from Henneker's for wanting to play football, saving Josh Browell's life, and restarting the mill.

Dick Browell stared admiringly at Bessie Booth. She had saved his father's life, and he had actually been contemplating throwing her out of the mill!

"And your team...The Busy Bees.....how are they doing?"

"We're doing splendid!" Bessie's eyes flashed with pride. "We haven't lost a league match yet!"

"This Henneker fellow must be pretty sick, eh?"

"He does everything he can to harm us," said the girl, and she informed Dick of all the devious schemes that Henneker had hatched to try and ruin Bess, her team, and their business, ending with their defeat of Henneker's bogus team of girl footballers.

"Bravo! That's splendid!" exclaimed Dick Browell enthusiastically. "I must certainly see your team play, now that I'm a member of your staff. I am, aren't I?"

"Well, I suppose you are, by the way you talk," laughed the girl. "You seem to have engaged yourself, as if the mill belonged to you."

The young man gave a start. Bessie's random remark had hit the truth. The mill did belong to him, but he did not mean to admit ownership just yet awhile. He was embarking upon an adventure that thrilled and interested him more than anything he had come across during the past eight years.

A raucous screech on the mill hooter suddenly announced that it was twelve o'clock. The throb of the engines and the click and whir of the looms ceased, and was succeeded by a deafening clatter of feet as the operatives – minders, piercers, and weavers – came pouring down from the spinning rooms.

"You'll be able to see my team play this afternoon, Mr Trueman," said Bessie a trifle shyly. "We're meeting Newton Flyers in a league match on our ground at the back of the mill, at two fifteen."

"Then you can depend I shall be there," declared the young man, with great emphasis. "Soccer is my favourite game, and the next best thing to playing is to watch it."

At that instant the door opened and the big, broad-shouldered, roughly dressed figure of Ned Bromley tramped into the office. He stopped short and ran his fingers through his fair hair as his mild blue eyes caught sight of the handsome, well-dressed young man with the clear grey eyes and the eager, happy smile.

"Is there anything Ah can do for you, Bess lass?"

"Come in, Ned," said Bessie, blushing for some reason that she could not then understand. "This is Mr Trueman. You know how badly we have needed someone to look after things here in the office? Mr Trueman is going to take charge here."

Ned Bromley blinked at the girl in surprise, and extended a hand like a leg of mutton.

"Pleased to meet you, Mr Trueman," he said bluntly. "Ah doubt you'll have long to do anything. The old mill is likely......"

"Yes, Miss Booth has told me all about it," said Dick cheerfully. "I'm willing to take things as they come. Who knows? This young Browell may never turn up to claim the mill. Or else he may write and say you can hang on to it.....make you a present of it, as his father meant to do. At any rate, until something does happen, I mean to help you keep the old flag flying."

Ned Bromley stared approvingly at the young man. He liked the look of him; but his heart sank as he realised instinctively that here was a dangerous rival for the affections of pretty Bessie Booth.

At that moment a crowd of eager, excited, noisily chattering girls came pouring into the room, and Dick Browell scarcely knew if he was standing on his head or his heels as he was introduced to the various members of the Busy Bees football team.

Finally, Sally Soper, the freckle-faced, snub-nosed goalkeeper came hobbling forward with the aid of a stick. Having sprained her ankle the previous week she was still a crock and would not be able to turn out for the team for some weeks to come.

It was a disconcerting experience for Dick Browell, and he made his escape as soon as possible, after promising not to fail to attend the match that afternoon. His first action upon leaving the mill was to enter a little general shop, where there was a public telephone box, and apply for the number that would put him in communication with James Chaddon.

Almost at once the clear voice of the old lawyer answered him.

"Is that you, Chaddon?" called Dick Browell eagerly. "This is Browell speaking. Have you told anyone else that I'm back in Blacktown? You haven't...splendid! Well don't.....don't breathe a word to a soul. I don't want anyone to know that I'm here.....that I'm even in England. You understand?"

"Well, I do...and I don't!" replied the puzzled Chaddon. "What sort of game are you up to now? Have you been to the mill? Have you given them notice?"

"What?" exploded Dick Browell indignantly. "Give that stunning, pretty girl notice? Not on your life! Why didn't you tell me it was a girl in the first place, you old villain? No, I haven't given her notice, and I haven't told her who I am. I don't want her to know at present. That's why I'm asking you to keep mum. So remember, you don't know me....anywhere or at any time."

Dick rang off and the lawyer replaced the receiver at his end of the line before leaning back in his chair with a chuckle of satisfaction.

"I thought as much," he muttered under his breath. "I knew that he'd alter his mind as soon as he set eyes on Bessie

Booth's pretty face. But I wonder what sort of a game he is playing, and who he told her he was? I dare say I shall learn all in good time."

Meanwhile, Bessie Booth was being assailed by a volley of questions as she and her companions sat down to their dinner in the mill canteen.

"Say Bess, where did that young fella come from?"

"By gum, he's a good looker, ain't he?"

"Ever met him before, Bessie?"

Bessie Booth blushed in spite of herself as she bent over her plate.

"I've never met him before in my life, and I know no more about him than he has told me himself," she replied bluntly. "His name's Dick Trueman and I believe he used to live in Blacktown some years ago."

"It's a rum thing him coming here to the mill for a job," said Mary Bonny. "Smart fella like him with them posh clothes 'an all."

"Doesn't say he isn't in need of a job because he's got smart clothes," championed Sally Soper. "And it's just what we needed...a manager for the office. And he looks the goods and no mistake. And Ah reckon he's mighty struck on you, Bess. Didn't you notice the way he kept eyeing you and....."

"Don't talk so foolish, Sally!" cried Bessie Booth, blushing more furiously than ever. "Mr Trueman is an absolute stranger to me. I've never seen him before, and he's never seen me. He wanted work and that's the end of it."

Big Ned Bromley, sitting silently at the other end of the room, thought otherwise. He had a vague, instinctive idea that the coming of Dick Trueman to the Bee-Hive Mill was only the beginning of it.

"Ay, he's stuck on Bess, and Ah'm reckoning she's stuck on him," he muttered shrewdly. "Well, Ah've had my turn and Ah've failed, and Ah wish no harm to the man who's lucky enough to win the lass."

Bessie found herself analysing her feelings as she made her way round to the football ground that afternoon. Her heart gave a guilty throb as she caught sight of the tall figure of Dick Trueman standing by the entrance to the ground, and she knew the colour was flooding up into her cheeks.

Dick whipped off his cap with a smile of greeting.

"By Jove, what a topping little ground, Miss Booth!" he cried enthusiastically. "I never dreamed you were running your club on such thorough lines. It's splendid! And the people! Do you mean to say you get as many spectators as this every time you play?"

"Why, there's hardly any here as yet!" laughed Bessie happily.

She hurried off to the dressing room, shyly aware of the honest light of admiration in Dick Trueman's grey eyes.

The visiting team had already arrived and were changing in the adjoining compartment. A couple of minutes later the home team took the field and Dick Browell drew a deep breath as the eleven trim, active girls in yellow and black jerseys came running out.

"Dick, my boy, you've copped it!" muttered the young man under his breath. "You're in love....there's no getting away from it!"

The Newton Flyers came streaming out in their green and white hooped shirts and the referee whistled the rival captains to the centre of the field.

Bessie Booth lost the toss, and started the game with a neat dribble and a nice pass to Connie Tree on the right wing.

“What dost tha think of our Bess?” asked Ned. “Why, she’s splendid, wonderful!” cried Dick Browell

Half-way through the first half she opened the scoring with a neat header and beat the goalkeeper all ends up, and no one cheered more loudly or excitedly than Dick Browell.

"Goal! Well played, Bessie Booth!" he shouted, throwing his cap recklessly in the air. It was Ned Bromley who picked it up and brought it back it back to him.

"What d'yer think of our Bess, Mr Trueman?" he asked gruffly.

"Why, she's splendid...wonderful!" cried Dick eagerly.

Half time came with the Busy Bees still leading by one goal to nil; but no sooner had play resumed than Bessie Booth ran clean through the Flyers' defence and put her team still further ahead.

There was only one team in it now, and when the final whistle blew, the home side were victors by the sweeping score of five goals to nil.

Bessie Booth found Dick 'Trueman' waiting by the exit gates when she left the football ground half an hour later.

"It may sound a bit of a cheek, considering that you're really my employer," said the young man firmly, "but I'm going to take you out to tea, Miss Booth. Now mind, I'm determined......I won't take a refusal."

But Bessie Booth did not refuse; nor did she notice Peter Henneker as she and Dick strolled down the street. Henneker scowled blackly as the handsome young man and the pretty girl passed him by without seeing him.

"Now who the dickens can that fellow be?" he muttered curiously. "I've never seen him before. I must find out who he is. Probably Ada Miller can tell me."

Not for one moment did Peter Henneker realise that the young man who had attracted his interest was none other than old Josh Browell's son!

Memories

"Good Morning, Miss Booth."

Bess gave a start as she came through the office door and glanced up into the handsome face of Dick Trueman. He stared admiringly at the pretty, curly-haired girl in the neat overalls and serviceable boots.

"Good morning, Mr Trueman," replied Bessie with a blush. Why she should blush she did not know, unless it was because she could read the honest admiration in her new manager's eyes.

The admiration for his pretty employer grew in leaps and bounds as Bessie Booth dealt briskly with her correspondence. The girl's memory and business acumen were remarkable. She was never at a loss for a detail or an instant decision.

"Miss Booth, you amaze me," said the young man at length. "Anyone would think you had been running a mill all your life.....and that wouldn't be very long after all."

And not only was the mill doing well, but Bessie's football team – the Busy Bees – was going ahead like wildfire, and Dick Trueman admired the pretty mill girl's bravery in how she had overcome all the obstacles placed in her way by her rival, Peter Henneker.

"Hallo, here's a letter addressed to you, Miss Booth," said Dick changing the subject.

Bessie's attention was immediately drawn to the imprint of the Lancashire Girls' Football League on the envelope as it was handed to her. A low gasp of amazement passed her lips as she read the letter within that bore the signature of the League

Secretary. It gave the shocking news of Henneker's success in gaining admission to the league.

'*Dear Miss Booth* – the letter ran – *I beg to notify you that, owing to unforeseen circumstances, the Ecclesfield United F.C. have been compelled to resign from the League. Under the circumstances, Henneker's Ramblers have been elected in their place, and have taken over the United's fixture list. They will be credited with what league points the latter have won up to date. Please revise your fixture list according to the substitution of clubs.*

Bessie Booth scarcely believed the evidence of her own eyes when she had read the letter. Peter Henneker's luck was phenomenal! He had failed to get the Busy Bees dismissed from the League, but sheer chance had given his team an opening to participate in the competition!

Not only were she and Henneker rivals in business, but they were now rivals on the football field as well. There was no doubt that Peter Henneker would leave no stone unturned to stimulate his team to vanquish the Busy Bees in the stern struggle for championship honours, and win the coveted cup and medals.

Dick Trueman, staring at Bessie's flushed, dismayed countenance, was unable to repress his curiosity.

"I say...what's the matter, Miss Booth?" he queried anxiously. "Anything wrong? Is it bad news?"

"I'm not certain. It's.....it's unexpected news," the girl replied slowly. She handed the letter to her manager and he gave a long low whistle of surprise as he read it through.

"Well, I'll be hanged!" he exclaimed. "Of all the infernal.....I beg your pardon.....confounded luck! So this fellow Henneker's got his team into the League after all. They say that the Devil looks after his own. But, by Jove, I shouldn't consider this bad news, Miss Booth."

"Why, how do make that out?" cried Bess.

"Because it'll give you the opportunity to wallop Henneker on the football field the same as you are doing in business," declared the young man enthusiastically. "Go in and win the League Championship and you'll be rubbing it in with a vengeance."

Bessie's eyes brightened.

"If only we could," she said eagerly.

"Could? You can....and must!" pronounced Dick encouragingly, thinking of the defeat of Rigan Rovers. "If Henneker's can play half as well as you did last Saturday, my name's not Brow...er...what it is."

"He's got a very strong team," remarked Bessie gravely. All good players, from all over Lancashire, taken into his mill."

"You beat them before."

"Yes. But it was a close game, and his team hadn't had time to get acquainted with one another's play."

"When is your first league match with them?" asked Dick.

Bessie looked at a sheet of paper on her desk and gave a start, her brown eyes widening.

"Well I never!" she breathed. "According to the fixture list we're at home to Ecclesfield United this Saturday. The means we'll have to play Henneker's!"

"Good egg!" Dick Trueman cried boyishly. "Aren't I glad I shall be here to see it? And Henneker's have taken over Ecclesfield United's points. How do they stand in the league?"

Bessie opened the local paper and studied the up-to-date Lancashire Girls' League table.,

"Darkpool Albion is on top with ten points," she announced. "We come second with nine, and Ecclesfield tie for third with Lanchester. They are a point behind, but they have played one more match than we have."

"Hum, close thing," muttered Dick. "If you beat them on Saturday it will strengthen your position and send them sliding down a few pegs."

Bessie jumped to her feet as the midday hooter suddenly blared out, and the roar of the engines and the busy chatter of the looms faded away into silence.

"I must go and tell the girls," she said eagerly. "This'll come as a big surprise to them, and I'll put it to them from your point of view, Mr Trueman. I...I think you're right. Perhaps it's not bad news after all. Thank you...for your encouragement."

She made a hasty retreat out of the office, blushing, leaving Dick Trueman staring after her slim, graceful form with the light of admiration in his eyes.

"Dick, my boy, you've got it mighty bad," muttered the young man, running his fingers through his crisp, curly hair. "That's a girl in a million...the sweetest pluckiest girl that ever breathed. Thank my lucky stars I came back to Blacktown when I did. Dear old dad. He obviously thought a heap of her, but he didn't think one hundredth part as much of her as I do. He meant to give her the mill. I mean to give her my name and myself...if she'll have me!"

Meanwhile, Bessie Booth had hurried straight along to the recreation room and canteen, where the mill girls had gathered for their midday meal. Her pulses were throbbing with the excitement of the news she had to announce, but perhaps it was not all due to the letter from the secretary of the league! Something seemed to have changed in her since she had appointed Dick Trueman as her new office manager.

A welcoming chorus greeted her as she entered the big room.

"Has Dick Browell come back to turn us out?" asked the girls

"Come on, Bess, where've you been all morning?"

"First sight we've had of you!"

"I thought you'd engaged a manager fella to do all the office work?"

Bessie blushed again. It was most annoying and inexplicable that she should blush at the bare mention of Dick Trueman. They could all see from her expression that she had news of some sort and an instant silence fell over the canteen, with every member of the Busy Bess football team present.

"My word, Bess, lass. Don't say it's bad news," said Mary Bonny anxiously. "Don't say as old Browell's son has turned up and we've got to clear out of the mill!"

A general sigh of relief went up as Bessie shook her head.

"No. It's nothing so bad as that," she smiled, reassuringly, and with further preamble she proceeded to read out the letter from the secretary of the league.

A gasp of consternation had echoed through the room, and the girl footballers stared blankly and incredulously at one another.

"What! Henneker's team in the league?"

"You're joking, Bess!"

"It can't be true!"

"Here it is in black and white...signed, sealed and official," Bessie declared, waving the letter above her head. "Ecclesfield United have resigned from the League, and Henneker's have taken their place!"

"Well of all the blessed luck!" exclaimed Mary Bonny with disgust. "We had to fight mighty hard to get our place in the League, and Henneker's simply waltz in and collar eight points without having played a match."

"An...an we've got to play them this Saturday, on our ground!" gasped Sally Soper, suddenly grasping the awful truth for her. "An I shan't be able to play!"

Poor Sally nearly burst into tears. It was a bitter disappointment to her that her ankle injury would, for the second time, leave her unable to turn out for the Bees against Peter Henneker's team.

"What are you looking so gloomy about, girls/" Bessie Booth chided reproachfully. "You ought to be delighted at the prospect of lowering Henneker's colours again. We must beat his team on Saturday. We must play as we have never played before. And we must carry off the championship of the League, and show him which is the best club in Blacktown....... in all Lancashire for that matter."

A rousing burst of cheers greeted Bessie's spirited words, and she smiled strangely as she realised she had she had stirred the girls with the sentiments expressed by her new manager, Dick Trueman.

"Beat Henneker's? We'll wipe the field with 'em!" shouted Mary Bonny.

"They'll get no points out of us!" declared Amy Olroyd determinedly.

Even though they knew they would have to take the field without their regular goalkeeper, Sally, they were determined to win. Sally Soper had clenched her fists and blinked her eyes bravely. She would have willingly given all she possessed to take her accustomed place between the sticks on the following Saturday. But nothing less than a miracle would mend her ankle in time! Or so she thought.

The girl footballers had something to talk about as they went chattering back to the spinning rooms, and Bessie had found herself with Ned Bromley, the head overlooker.

"Ah reckon Henneker must be feeling pleased with himself, Bess," he said gruffly. "He seems to have all the luck!"

"He'll want more than luck to beat us on Saturday," replied the girl grimly. "You're just the fellow I wanted to see, Ned. I've received a repeat order of two thousand pounds from Manders of Leedfield. They want delivery by November 21st. We can do it?"

Ned Bromley rubbed his chin and nodded his head.

"Ay, we can do it," he said slowly, "but do you know we're turning out twice as much work as we looked for, Bess?"

"All the better," replied Bess with sparkling eyes. "We can't refuse orders. Every one we accept is a loss to Henneker's."

"Ay, but it's the cotton Ah'm thinking about," said Ned. "The supplies of the cheap stuff old Browell let us have won't last three months at this rate. We've only a couple days of supply left in the mill at present."

"Then you must send and fetch the remainder from the warehouse down by the railway good yard," Bessie said.

"And what are we going to do when that's gone, lass?"

"We'll have a bit of capital behind us by that time," said Bessie hopefully. "And though we won't be able to quote the same low prices, we'll still be able to undercut Henneker's....unless he's willing to sell at a loss."

But she did not realise how Henneker would fight and what foul methods he would employ.

A Foul Plot

That same day Peter Henneker chuckled triumphantly as he glanced over the letter he had received from the Lancashire Girls' Football League, notifying of his team's inclusion in the league.

"What a stroke of luck!" he muttered gleefully, with an excited flourish of a bony hand. "This is the best news I have had for a long time. I'd like to see Bessie Booth's face when she hears how things have turned out. So, I've not gone to the trouble and expense of getting a team together for nothing."

John Smith, Henneker's manager and general confidant, gave an impatient shrug of his broad shoulders.

"I can't understand you, Henneker," he said in a deep guttural tone. "You mean to say we are going to carry on with this foolish football business. I do not see the object."

"Then you must be confoundly dense," snapped Henneker irritably. "You know very well I'm out to crush and humiliate that girl. I want to strike her at her weakest point. What would you say that was?"

"The mill, of course....."

"Nonsense! Her football team!" Henneker declared. "She thinks more of that football team than anything else. Didn't she accept her dismissal from here rather than throw up the game? She has set her mind on winning the championship of the league, and if I can prevent her, I'll have dealt her a blow that will almost break her heart. And I can do it, now that my team has been admitted to the League."

John Smith shrugged his shoulders again.

"But that won't save you and your mill," he said sullenly. "We are losing money every day. We can't go on like this forever."

"Do you forget that old fool Josh Browell is dead!" exclaimed Peter Henneker. "Soon...any day...his son may turn up and turn that pack of girls out of his mill. Perhaps he may not come back to England at all. My agent is still searching for him in America, and when he finds him he will buy the mill...for me."

"Well, let's hope he soon finds him and completes the purchase," said John Smith pointedly. "It will take us all out time to get back our trade again. We are not paying our way, we....."

"What a confounded creaker you are, Smith," scowled the mill owner. "Go away...you annoy me. Send that Miller girl in to me."

A moment later the thin girl, with pale face and sly green eyes entered the office, a shawl wrapped around her head.

"Well, Miller, what have you to tell me today?" Henneker asked his spy brusquely.

"Their stock of cotton won't last three months. Ah heard Ned Bromley say so this morning."

"That's worth knowing at any rate," the mill owner muttered. "The sooner it goes the better. I'll see that they don't get any more."

"All they've got left," continued Ada Miller, "is stored in the old warehouse down by the railway goods yard, and they're sending for that this week."

Peter Henneker's eyes glittered with sudden interest and a thoughtful scowl furrowed his sallow forehead.

"So all the cotton they have left is down in Riggs' warehouse," he muttered under his breath. "By heavens, if only I could get hold of it. It would mean *'Finish'* ...they wouldn't have a bale left to work on. It might be done...it *must* be done! I must think it over. It's a chance not to be missed!"

Henneker gloated in silence for a moment before a thought struck him.

"What did this Booth girl say when she heard my team had been admitted to the League?"

"They all cheered," replied the girl maliciously. "Bessie said she'd beat you in football as she was doing in business."

The mill owner ground his teeth in silent fury.

"By thunder, we'll see about that!" he snarled. "We're playing them on Saturday on their own ground. Is the Soper girl still crocked?"

"Ay, she won't be able to play."

"And you'll be playing in goal in her place. Splendid! You'll have to let them down this time. There's a sovereign for you for every goal you let through."

Ada Miller hurried from the office and Peter Henneker sprang from his chair and waved his arms above his head with evil exultation.

"By heavens, I guess I've got you beat this time, Bessie Booth," he cried gleefully. "I don't mean you to have that cotton, and if only I can get hold of it it'll put paid to the Bee-Hive Mill!"

Another Calamity

Bessie Booth scribbled a list of names on a sheet of notepaper, and then came to a sudden stop, tapping the end of her pen against her white, even teeth, a dubious frown on her pretty face.

"Forwards....Peggy Lang, Rose Taylor, myself, Violet Gibbs and Connie Tree," she read out in a low deliberate voice. "Half-backs.....Joan Brown, Mary Bonny, and Minnie Wells. Backs....Enid Foster and Amy Olroyd. Goal......"

Here Bessie came to a full stop again and heaved a puzzled sigh that attracted the attention of the other occupant of the office...the handsome young man who was busily pounding a typewriter.

There was something more than respect in his eyes as he gazed across at the slim, curly-haired girl in the neat overall.

"You look a trifle....err....perturbed, Miss Booth," he said politely. "Anything I can do?"

Bess turned to face her business manager, shaking her head.

"No, I'm afraid there's nothing anyone can do," she said ruefully. I'm making out our team for our match against Henneker's Ramblers on Saturday. There's nothing particularly difficult in that but.....oh, I do wish Sally Soper were able to play!"

Dick Trueman leaned back in his chair and raised his eyebrows in polite interrogation. Bessie looked away with a sudden flush. It was a funny and most annoying thing that she always flushed when she met the full gaze of Dick Trueman's steady gaze.

"Sally.....Sally Soper, our regular goalkeeper," she explained hastily. "You know, she injured her ankle.....I told you.

She hasn't been able to play in our last two matches, and she won't be fit to turn out against Henneker's."

"You have a reserve goalkeeper," said Dick.

"Yes, Ada Miller, but she's not a patch on Sally. And....and somehow the girls don't trust her. They've got an idea that she's likely to let us down, and you know how important it is......how keen we are to beat Henneker's?"

Dick Trueman nodded. He knew exactly how important it was that the Busy Bees kept their unbeaten record in the new Lancashire Girls' League. The greatest ambition of Bessie Booth was to lead her side to victory. But the injury to Sally could not have come at a worse time.

Bessie sighed again, and Dick Trueman suppressed a frenzied desire to take her in his arms and comfort her; for he had fallen head over heels in love with the pretty mill girl the first moment he has set eyes on her.

"But.....haven't you another goalkeeper," he asked lamely, "besides this Ada Miller?"

"No. We've always depended upon Sally Soper," said Bess ruefully. "There's no one else even as good as Ada."

"Hang it! I wish I could help you," cried the young man vehemently. "No good me buying a wig and powdering my nose and playing in goal for you, I suppose?"

"Not the slightest!" said Bessie severely, though there was a twinkle in her brown eyes. "Besides, our regular goalkeeper doesn't wear a wig or powder her face."

"Oh, I say, I didn't mean that," protested Dick Trueman.

"I hope you didn't. Sally Soper would be awfully annoyed," smiled the pretty mill girl. "Well, there's nothing else for it, Ada Miller will have to go in goal."

Bessie Booth scribbled the name down with an air of resignation, and then suddenly changed the subject.

"I had a letter from Mr Chaddon this morning," she announced.

Dick Trueman gave a start and his lips tightened at the mention of the name – his late father's solicitor and executor of his will.

"I wrote and asked if there was any news of young Mr Browell," continued the girl.

"And what does he say?" queried the new manager eagerly.

"A very un-business-like letter," replied Bess. "Not like a lawyer's at all. He simply says 'When Mr Richard Browell wants his mill he will come and claim it. Meanwhile, sit tight, and don't worry'."

"Bravo! Good old Chaddon!" cried Dick Trueman enthusiastically. "That is to say," he continued confusedly, "quite a sensible letter to write. You sit tight, and don't worry, as he says, Miss Booth."

Bessie Booth could not hide the puzzled look she gave the young man as she rose.

"You seem very flippant and optimistic this morning, Mr Trueman," she said severely. 'Good old Chaddon' is scarcely the way to speak of a stranger...and a lawyer at that. I must go and pin up this list in the recreation room."

Dick Trueman heaved an explosive sigh of relief as the door closed.

"By Jingo, I nearly gave myself away that time," muttered the young man to the empty office. "I shall have to be more careful. I mean to stick to this job. It's quite an adventure. And Bessie Booth! If I don't make her Mrs Browell one of these days, I'll....I'll go back to the States and breed chewing gum!"

Dick Trueman was quite sincere in what he said, and for his love for Bess. He knew she was the only girl he would ever love. He didn't like the subterfuge he had entered upon, but he could see that Bessie's one aim in life – besides her football team – was to make a success of the Bee-Hive Mill, and he meant to let her achieve her objective before he made his true identity known.

And if he could help her, well, he could help her in a more pleasing and acceptable way as Dick Trueman than as Richard Trueman Browell, the wealthy mill owner.

A few minutes later the midday hooter uttered its hoarse, noisy bellow and the young man donned his hat and coat and left the office. As he passed down the corridor an unusual sound came to his ears....the sound of someone in trouble....a choking, pathetic sob.

Instinctively he opened a door to his right. It led into a bare, dusty room where old Josh Browell's callers had once had to wait. It was occupied now by a girl who stood by the window, leaning on a crutch. The startled face she turned towards Dick Trueman was pale and freckled, with a turned-up nose and big, grey eyes that were full of tears. Immediately the young man realised who she was.

"You're Sally Soper," he said with a friendly smile. "I hope I'm not intruding. Can I do anything for you? Does your ankle pain you?"

Sally Soper shook her head and mopped fiercely at her eyes.

"No, my ankle doesn't hurt...much," she said huskily. "It's not that Ah'm crying about. Ah'm just crying with disappointment. Ah came here to have a good howl all on my own."

Dick's heart quickened with sympathy as he moved across to the Busy Bees' injured goalkeeper."

"I'm so sorry," he said gravely. "What a beastly shame. You're disappointed, because...."

"Because Ah shan't be able to play against Henneker's Saturday," admitted Sally. "Ah....Ah would try and play, but Bess won't let me."

"And quite right too," said Dick stoutly. "You don't want to run the risk of crippling yourself for life. Is your ankle very bad?"

"No, it's much better. The pain's gone, but it's weak and Ah can't stand on it. But Ah do so want to play."

"You're plucky at any rate," said Dick warmly. "I know a bit about sprains. Would you mind letting me examine your ankle?"

Sally Soper whipped off her stocking and Dick Trueman took the slender foot gently in his strong hands. At the same instant a sudden sound caused him to turn quickly towards the open door.

On the threshold stood Bessie Booth, big Mary Bonny the centre-half, and several other members of the football team.

"I didn't know you were a doctor, Mr Trueman," said Bessie with a smile.

"I'm not," replied the young man promptly, "but I've played football myself and I know how bad a sprain can be. I don't think this is so much a sprain as a displacement of one of the small bones in the foot. See....there is no swelling or discolouration....."

"D'yer mean Ah might be able to play by Saturday!" cried Sally eagerly.

Dick Trueman sat back on his heels. A sudden idea had flashed into his mind. He was anxious to do all he could for the Busy Bees' plucky goalkeeper.

"Look here, I know a doctor chap in London," he said brightly. "He is what is known as a professional bone-setter, and he's an old pal of mine. There was a professional footballer who went to him who'd been hobbling around on crutches for weeks with a bad knee. Harker treated him and he was playing football again two days later."

Sally Soper gave a gasp of excitement and a flush of colour crept into her pale cheeks.

"Oh, do you think he could get me right for Saturday?" she cried eagerly, and then her face dropped. "But of course he wouldn't come right up from London," she finished wistfully, "and I dare say he'd want an awful lot of money."

"He's an old pal of mine," said Dick Trueman. "He'd do anything for me. I'll send him a wire. If anyone can put you right, he will, Sally."

He hurried away, leaving Sally Soper bright-eyed with fresh hope and excitement.

"By gum, there's a real gentleman for you," she exclaimed emphatically. "Ah...Ah like him, Bess. He's a real good 'un, isn't he?"

"Yes, he is," said Bessie, and blushed again.

"Bessie thinks more of him than that," whispered Mary Bonny with a sly wink."

Meanwhile, Dick Trueman had hurried straight away to the post office to write a telegram to one Horatio Harker, at Park Crescent, London.

'Catch first train in morning. Urgent. Expense no object. Will meet you station.....Dick Browell.'

"That'll fetch him," he chuckled. "It'll cost me fifty guineas, but I wouldn't mind paying five hundred under the circumstances."

The circumstances, of course, were that he was in love with Bessie Booth!

At ten o'clock the following morning a tall, strong-featured man, clad in a heavy travelling coat, alighted from a train at Blacktown station where he was greeted by 'Dick Trueman' with a grin of welcome on his face.

"Good man Harker!" said the latter eagerly. "I knew you'd come. Good job I wrote you I was back in England."

"Dick Browell!" exclaimed the Londoner. "Why, I haven't set eyes on you for..."

"Sssh! Not that name here!" cautioned the other. "Call me Dick if you like, but cut out the Browell. I'm known as Trueman in Blacktown, for the present."

He briefly explained the circumstances to his companion as they strode briskly through the narrow streets to the Bee-Hive, and Horatio Harker listened calmly throughout.

"I'm not surprised at anything you do Browell....I beg your pardon, *Trueman*," he said with a smile. "You always were a mad-headed beggar....up to all sorts of funny dodges. But this is the limit...working for some other fellow in your own mill....."

"It's not a fellow....it's a girl. The sweetest...."

"Ah, that explains everything," said the other dryly. "No need to say any more, Dick. And it's a girl you want me to treat....a girl footballer. I can't mend broken hearts man..."

"Don't be a silly ass! It's a bad ankle, and you ought to be able to put it right in ten seconds."

A wave of excitement swept through the Bee-Hive Mill when it was known that the famous surgeon had arrived from London to examine Sally Soper's sprained ankle. Eager faces were pressed to all the windows as Dick Trueman and his companion crossed the mill yard, and Sally trembled like a leaf when she was summoned to the general office.

Harker's kindly manner assured her at once as he bid her be seated.

"If you'll just leave me alone with my patient," he smiled, rolling up his sleeves, and Bessie Booth and Dick Trueman retired to an adjoining room.

"Oh, Mr Trueman, do you think he'll be able to make it possible for Sally to play on Saturday?" whispered Bessie, her cheeks flaming with excitement.

"If it can be done, Harker will do it, Miss Booth," replied Dick. "We...we must hope for the best."

Two minutes later Harker flung the door open and stood smiling on the threshold, calmly fastening his shirt cuffs. Sally Soper lay back in the big armchair, pale-faced, but with her eyes glittering like stars.

"You, you haven't finished.....you haven't done anything, have you?" cried the goalkeeper. "Why, you didn't even hurt me."

"It wasn't necessary," laughed Harker. "Get up, and walk!"

Reluctantly, nervously, Sally Soper stretched out her injured limb and placed her foot on the floor. Then she stood up and threw all her weight on it and took a couple of steps.

"Why, there's nothing wrong.....I can't feel anything," she almost screamed.

Bessie Booth clapped her hands together wildly, and Dick Trueman beamed.

"Good man, Harker," he enthused. "I knew you could fix it."

"And will Ah be able to play football on Saturday?" gasped Sally timidly.

"Where do you play?" queried the surgeon.

"Ah play in goal."

"You'd be able to play in goal tomorrow, but I should advise you to rest your foot if you want to be at your best for Saturday and now, Dick, what's my next train back to London? I've got an appointment at seven o'clock this evening."

Tears of joy were trickling down Sally Soper's cheeks. Bessie Booth was glowing with excitement, and as the glad news filtered upstairs to the spinning rooms, a tremendous burst of cheering seemed to shake the mill.

"The London gaffer has done the trick!"

"Sally is walking about again!"

"She'll be able to play against Henneker's this Saturday!"

Horatio Harker fled towards the station with his coat tails flapping in the wind and a cheery wave of his hand towards the myriad faces at the big windows.

"And that's that!" said Dick Trueman cheerfully. "Isn't Harker a trump, Miss Booth?"

Bessie nodded her curly head.

"Yes, but it's you we have to thank, Mr Trueman," she said in a low voice. "You sent for Mr Harker......otherwise this never would have happened."

"That's just what Ah was going to say," cried Sally Soper. "Mr Trueman's a real gradely sport." And she suddenly flung her arms around the young man and kissed him soundly on the cheek.

Ten minutes later the looms were humming away again, and Dick Trueman was pounding strenuously on the typewriter in the general office. He was highly pleased with himself. He had banished the worried look from Bessie Booth's brown eyes and, unknowingly, put in a big spoke in Peter

Henneker's wheel by ousting his paid spy – Ada Miller – from her place in the Busy Bees team.

But it was only the sunshine before the storm. Black clouds were even then gathering over the Bee-Hive Mill.

"By the way, Miss Booth, where's Ned Bromley?" asked Dick Trueman, swinging around in his chair. "I want to see him about that order for Messrs. Maunders of Leedfield."

"He's gone down with the lorries to Riggs' warehouse to collect our reserve supply of cotton," replied the girl. "I don't expect they'll be back yet awhile. It'll take them a couple of hours to load it."

Scarcely had Bessie spoken than there came the sound of hurried footsteps across the cobbled mill yard. Then someone came leaping up the steps and along the corridor; the office door was flung open and the tall figure of Ned Bromley stumbled into the room.

His rugged face was as white as a sheet. Beads of perspiration were dripping down his forehead, and there was a strange look of dismay in his normally mild blue eyes.

"Ned, what's the matter?" cried Bessie, springing to her feet. "Are you ill? What's happened?"

"Bess, lass..... it's gone!" gasped Ned wildly. "Every bit of it! Gone....stolen!"

"Gone?" echoed the girl. "What's gone? What do you mean, Ned?"

"The cotton, lass. All the cotton! It's been stolen. The warehouse is empty. There's not a bale left, and no one knows anything about it. It must have been taken last night!"

Bess dropped back in her chair with a sharp cry of dismay and despair, and Dick Trueman sprang to her side.

"Good heavens, Bessie.....Miss Booth, what's the matter?" he demanded anxiously. "What does all this mean?"

The girl looked up in a daze.

"If it's true, it means that we are ruined.....that the mill will have to close down," she said shakily. "Our whole stock of cotton was stored in a warehouse down by the railway goods yard. It was cotton bought at a low price five years ago that the late Mr Browell handed over to us."

And the tears started afresh in Bessie's eyes; tears that sent a stab of pain through Dick Trueman's heart.

"Bromley, what are the facts?" he demanded almost fiercely, turning to the panting figure of Ned.

"The cotton's gone," repeated the man huskily. "The locks must have been picked and the bales taken away some time last night. No one seems to have seen it go. Ah've told the police. It's just gone."

"Hmm," said Dick Trueman softly. "This is more of Peter Henneker's dirty work I suppose."

"What's the use of supposing," breathed the girl despairingly. "We...we can't prove anything against him. This.....this is the end!"

"Nothing of the sort!" snapped the new business manager briskly. "This is only the beginning. No use crying over spilt milk. We must order some more cotton at once and get on with the good work."

Bessie Booth's eyes brightened, her little hands clenched, and the colour came back to her pale cheeks.

"You're right, Mr Trueman," she said with a grateful glance that set Dick's pulses racing. "I ought to be ashamed of myself for....for being so weak. How long can we keep the looms working on what supplies we have in hand, Ned?"

"'Till Saturday.....and not a day more," replied the overlooker, after a hasty mental calculation.

"Then we must order some more cotton for immediate delivery......Monday at the very latest," said Bess bravely. "We shall have to fulfil what orders we have in hand at a heavy loss, and after that quote new prices. We shall be able to undercut Henneker's slightly. It'll be a tight thing.....but I think we'll win through."

"Of course we shall win through!" declared Dick Trueman confidently.

In his office at the mill on the other side of the town, Peter Henneker was chuckling maliciously.

The Match with Henneker's

All Blacktown was agog with excitement. Everyone seemed to know that Bessie Booth's Busy Bees and Peter Henneker's Ramblers were to meet on the Bees' ground that Saturday afternoon.

All roads seemed to lead to the trim little enclosure behind the Bee-Hive Mill. A constant stream of people clattered up from the town, and Dick Trueman opened his eyes wide in amazement as he saw the great crowd that was assembling around the touchlines.

"By Jove, this is the way to fetch 'em," he said brightly. "There won't be much room left for the players by the time they all get in. And how's the ankle Sally?"

"It's just as though Ah'd never sprained it at all," she declared, and to prove her words, she went tearing away like a hare to the dressing room.

Peter Henneker himself arrived on the ground with a sullen scowl of disappointment wrinkling his sallow countenance. He had learned that Sally Soper in some miraculous manner had recovered sufficiently to take her accustomed place between the sticks, which meant that Ada Miller – his paid spy, and the Busy Bees reserve goalkeeper - would be unable to sell her team down the river as he had bribed her to do.

Punctually to the minute the two teams took the field, amid roars of welcome from their respective supporters – the Bees in their black-and-yellow jerseys and the Ramblers in red-and-white. A special cheer was accorded Sally Soper as she made her appearance.

Jane Tanner, the Ramblers' black-haired, sullen-faced captain, won the toss, and Bessie Booth kicked off to set the game in motion.

It was the most strenuous, thrilling game that any Blacktownite had ever witnessed, and one continuous roar of excitement rippled around the touchlines.

From end to end of the field the ball was swung. The Ramblers were combining far better than they had done on the previous occasion the Busy Bees had met them, and Bessie Booth knew that her team would have to play as they had never played before if they meant to carry off the spoils.

"Go on...into 'em!" growled Peter Henneker as he sat chewing the end of an unlighted cigar. "Hack 'em! Barge 'em! Knock the stuffing out of 'em! Bravo! That's the style."

The Ramblers needed no encouragement to rough play. They used their weight freely, and Connie Tree, the Bees' speedy right winger, was limping badly long before half time.

But the interval came with a blank score sheet, and five minutes after the resumption of play the Ramblers' forwards broke away with a sudden, sweeping rush, and swarmed down upon the home goal. An over-vigorous challenge that the referee did not see sent Amy Olroyd crashing to the ground and, snapping up a short pass, Jane Parker sent in a rasping, curving shot from ten yards range.

Dick Trueman uttered a groan of dismay, and the word 'Goal!' boomed across the field.

But it was no goal! In some miraculous way Sally Soper flung herself headlong and just managed to get her straining finger tips to the ball and turn it round the post.

The corner kick proved of no use to the Ramblers, and a fierce bout of mid field play ensued.

It seemed almost certain that the game was to end in a draw, and it was only a couple of minutes from time when brawny Mary Bonny – the Bees' centre half – pounced fiercely on the ball, drew the defence, and passed squarely to Bessie Booth.

It was now or never! Bessie set her teeth and made a lightning spurt that carried her clean passed the opposing backs. Now she had only the opposing goalkeeper to beat, and just as she was steadying herself to shoot, her legs were swept from under her, and she crashed to the ground.

It was a distinct foul, well within the penalty area. In vain the Ramblers clamoured and protested. The referee pointed sternly to the fatal spot and, bruised and dizzy as she was, Bessie took the kick and slammed the ball into the net.

An instant later the final whistle shrilled amid frenzied roars of delight. The Busy Bees had triumphed again, and it was the Ramblers' own foul tactics that had brought about the defeat.

"Never mind.....winning a paltry game of football won't save you!" snarled Peter Henneker, shaking a fist towards the slim figure of Bessie Booth. "I've got you beat in any case. You can't run your mill without cotton, and of that you haven't got a scrap, I do know. And you won't get any....I'll take jolly good care of that!"

The following week certainly held many troubles in store for plucky Bessie Booth and her faithful supporters.

“ I have you beaten in any case ! ” snarled Henneker as Bessie and the Busy Bees left the field

Bad News

It was scarcely more than daylight when Bessie Booth left her aunt's little cottage in Chapel Lane and hurried through the narrow streets of Blacktown with a shawl wrapped tightly around her head and shoulders.

Half way up the steep hill that led to the Bee-Hive Mill she stopped and glanced grimly towards another cluster of buildings and towering chimney stacks that lay to the south of the town....Henneker's Mill. Bessie's thoughts wandered to the previous Saturday and the league match between the Busy Bees and Henneker's Ramblers. The result of the clash – a clever and well-deserved victory for the Bees – was still fresh in her mind.

"Those two points put us at the top of the league table" she muttered proudly to herself and starting off up the hill once again. "If only we can manage to remain there until the end of the season....to be champions in our first year and carry off the cup and medals!"

With a nod and a smile the girl hurried past the timekeeper at the mill gates and almost ran across the cobbled yard. Standing waiting for her at the top of the stones steps was the broad-shouldered and roughly dressed figure of Ned Bromley, the head overlooker. His mild blue eyes looked troubled, and his hands were thrust despondently into his pockets.

"Why, Ned," cried Bessie in surprise at the sight of her friend. "What are doing here? I thought you would be down at the station. Where's the cotton?"

"It hasn't come, lass," replied Bromley gravely. "Ah've been down to the station goods yard, but there's no cotton for us."

Bessie Booth uttered a low cry of dismay. It was the worst possible kind of news Ned had brought her, for it meant that there would be no work done at the Bee-Hive that day, or perhaps for several days, and there were several urgent contract orders on hand! In spite of having had their reserve supply of cotton obviously stolen, the local police could find neither trace of it, nor any clue to the thieves.

This had left Bessie and her co workers at the Bee-Hive with barely enough cotton to the end of the week, and she had sent out urgent letters to suppliers requesting delivery no later than the following Monday morning. And now Ned Bromley had met her with the staggering news that the supplies had not arrived!

"Ned, what can it mean? What are we going to do?" cried the girl anxiously. "We must have cotton! There's Manders order...it must be completed this week or we face a heavy penalty!"

Ned laid an encouraging hand on the girl's arm.

"Don't upset yerself, Bess," he said gruffly. "There's plenty of time yet for the cotton to arrive. There's another train due in almost at once. They'll 'phone us from the station if the stuff's on it. If so, we can get the looms running by ten o'clock."

Bessie Booth nodded and turned away into the general office. All over the weekend she had been painfully aware of a strange, unexplainable, sense of uneasiness. Something seemed to tell her that everything was not as it should be, and it was this vague instinct that had got her out of bed and brought her up to the mill an hour before the ordinary operatives were due to arrive.

"Why should I worry? The cotton is sure to arrive," she muttered hopefully as she sank back into a chair and stared at the pile of unopened letters on her desk. "There is no reason why it shouldn't arrive. It's been delayed, that is all. It will come by the next train."

Mechanically, she ripped open the first letter she picked up. Her eyes brightened as she caught sight of the printed heading – *Cardross & Blane, cotton importers* – one of the firms with whom she had placed an order.

'Dear Madam' – the letter ran – *We regret we are unable to meet your order of the 16th of this month, now, or at any other time in the next six months. We are fully booked up and unable to open any new accounts.'*

Bessie Booth bit her lip in keen disappointment. She had never dreamed that such a vast firm as Cardross & Blane would be unable to supply her small requirements.

"Never mind. They're not the only ones," she muttered under her breath. "I'm glad I split the order up to make certain of getting one delivery."

Half way through the pile of correspondence the mill girl came across another letter that brought another gasp of amazement and dismay to her lips. It was from Fairfax and Player, another firm with whom she had placed an urgent order for immediate delivery. Their reply was even more curt.

'Dear Madam, We regret that we are accepting no new accounts...and your name is not on our books.'

Bessie's face was pale now, and her heart was throbbing as if it would burst. With trembling fingers she turned over the remainder of the letters, until she came across an envelope bearing the imprint of Messrs. Cole & Scriven. They were the only other firm she had written to!

Now her pulse quickened, and her fingers trembled as she slowly tore open the envelope. She knew the worst almost before she had read the typewritten words of the letter.

Dear Madam: We regret we are unable to fulfil your esteemed order....'

The sheet of paper fluttered from Bessie's hand as she fell back in her chair with a little sob of dismay. Her last hope had failed her! Every single request for cotton she had sent out had been refused. There would be no fresh supply arriving that day; the looms would have to remain silent and the workers idle.

Bess felt stunned by this fresh calamity which threatened to bring ruin and disaster upon the Bee-Hive Mill, and undo all the brave work that she and her companions had performed during the past few weeks. She had not anticipated the slightest difficulty in obtaining a fresh supply of cotton, and she was prepared to pay cash on delivery. Yet every firm she had written to had politely, but firmly, declined her order.

It almost seemed as though there was a conspiracy afoot to place every obstacle in her way to success. Surely there was no shortage of cotton in the country? Why should her order be turned down? The excuse that no new orders were being opened was scarcely a reasonable one.

Large tears gathered in Bessie's brown eyes as she sat staring miserably at the abrupt, business-like letters that had come as such a staggering, unexpected surprise.

At that moment the door of the office was flung open and Richard Trueman, business manager to the Bee-Hive Mill, swung into the office. He stopped short, a look of surprise in his eyes as he caught sight of the trim figure of Bessie Booth seated at her desk.

"Why, Miss Booth. I didn't expect to see you here so early," he exclaimed, tossing his hat dexterously on to a peg. Then he suddenly noticed the girl's pale, agitated face and her hasty action to wipe the tears from her cheeks, and in an instant he was at her side.

"I say, what's the matter?" he queried anxiously. "Bess...Miss Booth, what's happened? Tell me, why...why are you crying?"

Bessie dashed the tears fiercely from her eyes.

"It's...it's bad news, Mr Trueman," she said shakily. "The cotton hasn't arrived. They...they won't accept my order."

"What?" Dick Trueman's handsome face flushed with anger. "Why? Who won't accept your order?"

"None of them .The three firms we wrote to. And the looms are at a standstill. We haven't a scrap of cotton in the place. And our contracts...we are under a heavy penalty if we don't deliver this week."

"But why won't they accept your orders? It's preposterous. You offered cash. Hang it all..."

Bessie Booth silently passed across the three letters, and Dick Trueman read them through with growing indignation and bewilderment.

"Not opening any fresh accounts," he repeated slowly. "Of all the confounded rot! Your money's as good as anyone else's. There's more in this than meets the eye, Miss Booth. It sounds almost like a dashed conspiracy to prevent you getting any supplies. By Jove...."

The young man's eyes flashed, and he brought his fist crashing down on the top of the desk.

"I bet that scoundrel Peter Henneker's at the bottom of this," he said grimly.

Bess gave a start. The same idea had occurred to her, but she had dismissed it as preposterous...impossible.

"How could that be, Mr Trueman?" she exclaimed. "How could Peter Henneker prevent us from getting cotton? He has no control over the market."

"I don't know...we'll have to try and find out," said Dick pointedly. "The beggar's capable of any villainy. Just you sit tight while I use the telephone, Miss Booth."

The young man put through a trunk call to Ranchester, and gave the number of Cole & Scriven, one of the firms that had refused Bessie's order.

Bess cast a side glance at the handsome profile of her new business manager, and knew she had no cause to regret employing him. Her heart beat faster with renewed hope as she noted the glint of battle in his eyes. He was not deterred or dismayed by the blow that the morning's post had brought.

"Is that Cole & Scriven?" rapped Dick Sharply. "This is the Bee-Hive Mill. Blacktown, speaking. What about that order we sent you last week?"

"We have already acquainted you by post that we are unable to fulfil it," replied a calm voice.

"And why?"

"Because we are unable to accept any fresh accounts."

"Rubbish! That can't be the reason at all!" declared the young manager boldly. "You are always opening fresh accounts. With the present state of trade you can't afford to do otherwise. Why not be candid and admit the truth?"

There was a momentary pause before the reply came.

"We please ourselves as to whether we accept orders or not," said the voice coldly. "As a matter of fact, I see no reason why I should not inform you that we have received certain complaints as to the manner in which your mill conducts business. You are undercutting other firms' prices and ruining their market. You are selling your goods at a ridiculous figure. It is sheer...sheer Bolshevism."

"Bolshevism be blowed!" snorted Dick Trueman. "We pay you the same price as anyone else for your goods, and it's nothing to do with you how little profit we care to make."

"No, but it has a lot to do with our other customers. We do not care to upset them by selling to you to enable you to take their trade away by undercutting their prices. We cannot....will not....accept any orders from you."

There was a click as Messrs. Cole & Scriven rang off, and Dick replaced the receiver, saying something under his breath that was far from polite.

"Miss Booth, it's just as I thought," he declared grimly, turning to the girl footballer. "Peter Henneker is at the bottom of this. He has evidently written to all the wholesale firms, prejudicing them against your mill, and threatening to withdraw his custom if they supply you with raw cotton. The low-down scoundrel. I'd like to wring his beastly neck for him."

Bess clenched her tiny hands as she made a brave attempt to repress her tears of dismay.

"What...what can we do, Mr Trueman?" she asked shakily. "If we can't get any cotton we...we will have to close the mill down."

"Not if I have anything to do with it!" declared the manager firmly. "There are plenty of other firms besides the three you wrote to. Let us see what they have to say. It will give us some idea of the extent of Peter Henneker's powers."

Dick Trueman drew the telephone towards him again, whilst Bess supplied him with a list of wholesale merchants and importers and their telephone numbers. Three quarters of an hour later he replaced the receiver for the last time, leaning back and biting his lip savagely. Peter Henneker had done his foul, underhand work only too well. He had rung up half a dozen different firms, and each one had promptly and decisively refused to consider any order from the Bee-Hive Mill.

Bessie Booth rose to her feet, sick at heart with dismay. This was the end of all her hopes, plans and ambitions. The mill would have to be closed down, and the little capital she and her chums and fellow workers had accumulated would have to be paid out in penalties for broken contracts!

In another few minutes Mary Bonny, Sally Soper and the others would be arriving to start their day's work, and she would have to break the news to them. It was a task that she dreaded. The mere prospect appalled her, knowing as she did the dismay and despair it would bring to all concerned.

"Well, Mr Trueman," she said bravely, "this...this is the end. Thank you for all you have done. But we have failed. Peter Henneker has proved too strong for us."

Her voice broke, and it was all Dick Trueman could do to prevent himself from snatching the pretty girl in his arms and kissing her tears and troubles away. He loved her. He had loved her since the first time he had set eyes on her.

"Miss Booth, you mustn't give in...we're not beaten yet!" he cried vehemently. "We *must* get some cotton and keep the mill running night and day to deliver the goods. It can be done...we've got five days before us!"

"But it's hopeless...impossible. You know it's impossible," said Bess sadly. "Where are we to get the cotton from? No one will supply us"

Someone will supply us!" declared Dick with peculiar confidence. "I'm not going to lie down and allow that scoundrel Henneker to walk all over us with both feet. I can get some cotton..."

"You can get it!" gasped Bess. "Are you a magician, Mr Trueman? Is there anything you can't do? First, you fetch a famous London surgeon to mend Sally Soper's sprained ankle, and now you say you can get us the cotton we need. Where? How?"

"Never mind about that now, Miss Booth," said Dick evasively. "You just leave this to me. I'll have the cotton here by tomorrow morning. You can bank on me, and I'll get it for you at ten per cent below the market price."

With these amazing words the young man snatched up his hat and almost ran out of the mill.

Dick Gets Busy

There was a peculiar smile on Dick Trueman Browell's clean-cut face as he left the mill and hurried into the town. He entered the post office where there was a closed-in, soundproof telephone box and put a call through to a Liverpool number. A voice answered at the other end of the line.

"That you, Saxby?" asked Dick curtly. "This is Browell speaking."

An exclamation of surprise came from the other end of the wire.

"Great Scott, sir! I was wondering what had become of you, and I didn't know where to write."

"Saxby, is the Seaspray in yet?"

"Yes, sir. She docked two days ago."

"Good. Is she unloaded?"

"No. I've been waiting to hear from you..."

"Unship the cargo at once and despatch every ounce of cotton to the Bee-Hive Mill, Blacktown. It must reach here by tomorrow morning..."

"Great Scott, Mr Browell! I don't think it can be done!"

"It *must* be done!" ordered Dick grimly. "Invoice it at ten per cent below the market price...quote six months' credit, and no mention of my name. Is that clear?"

"Yes, but..."

"That's all, Saxby. See that my instructions are carried out to the letter. Goodbye."

Dick Trueman rang off and left the box with a smile of satisfaction. Few people knew that he was the sole owner of some of the biggest cotton areas in America. When he had gone to America seven years previously - following a hot-headed quarrel with his father – he had started in a small way, and gradually built up a vast and prosperous business.

It had always been his idea to work hand-in-glove with his father, and supply his mill with cotton direct. It was his agent in Liverpool, Saxby, whom he had just telephoned.

All day long the looms at the Bee-Hive Mill remained silent, and the news spread through Blacktown like wildfire, until all sorts of disturbing rumours were added to it.

"The Bee-Hive Mill's closed down!"

"They're not working...can't get any cotton!"

Seated in his office up at his own mill, Peter Henneker rubbed his lean hands together and chuckled aloud in malicious triumph.

"Didn't I say I would get her, Smith," he gloated to his manager.

Smith nodded his big, square head.

"Yes, I don't think we have anything more to fear from the Bee-Hive Mill," he said stolidly. "You were bound to win in the end. But supposing someone else buys the mill and opens it up again?"

"I mean to buy it myself, just as soon as I can get in touch with young Browell," declared Henneker.

Peter Henneker could not settle down to work, so elated was he with his success in holding up Bessie Booth's supplies of cotton. Finally he put on his hat and coat and strolled along to the Bee-Hive Mill to see for himself the result of his cunning scheme.

The mill was silent and desolate. The fires were banked down, and the only person in evidence was the watchman at the gate. But from the rear of the mill came certain sounds that attracted Peter Henneker's attention and caused him to wind his way in that direction.

The men, boys and girls who should have been working in the spinning and carding rooms were congregated around the touch lines of the Busy Bees football ground.....and Bessie and her chums were playing a practice match.

He turned away with a curse. Somehow, his triumph was not so complete as he thought it to be. As he strode away from the mill someone suddenly barred his way; a sturdily built young man, with clear grey eyes and clean-cut, determined features.

"Are you Mr Henneker?" he asked quietly.

"And what if I am?" snapped the mill owner. "What do you want?"

"My name is Trueman. I am the business manager of the Bee-Hive Mill," said the young man.

Henneker stared with fresh interest.

"Indeed!" he sneered. "One of the rats from the sinking ship, eh? Want me to give you a job?"

Dick Trueman's cheeks flushed and his eyes hardened.

"I wouldn't work for you for all the money in the world," he said sharply. "And to give you a word of warning. If ever you molest Miss Booth again, either by word or deed, openly or in your own particular foul, underhand way, I'll give you such a hiding as you'll remember all the days of your life. Just bear that in mind you low down hound."

Henneker aimed a murderous blow at Dick's head

In an excess of passion Henneker raised the stick he was carrying and aimed a murderous blow at Dick Trueman's head.

But the blow never fell. The next instant the stick was wrenched from his grasp and sent spinning yards away, and a particularly hard and bony bunch of knuckles caught him fairly on the bridge of his somewhat prominent nose.

With a squeal of pain Henneker fell to the ground. That one blow was sufficient to disperse any courage he might have had.

"All right, you low-bred beast. I'll pay you out for that blow!" rasped Henneker, mopping his bruised and bleeding nose as Dick walked away. "This is more of Bessie Booth's work....she put you up to assaulting me. Never mind, I can afford to wait! In another few weeks you'll be crawling in the gutter, begging for work. Then you'll see who's top dog!"

Dick Trueman glanced happily at his grazed knuckles "That's just a little bit off the account, Mr Peter Henneker," he muttered darkly. "I'll settle the rest in full on some future occasion!"

Saved!

Motor lorry after motor lorry, laden high with great bales of cotton, came thundering up the hill from Blacktown and turned through the gateway into the spacious yard of the Bee-Hive Mill. As each vehicle made its appearance a hearty cheer of delight burst from the big crowd of operatives who packed the windows and doorways of the big square building. Above them all the towering, smoke-belching chimney stack reared its slender brickwork body a hundred and fifty feet in the air.

"Hurrah! Here comes another!"

"Now we shan't be long."

"Who said we were beat? Three groans for Peter Henneker!"

The three groans were given with much gusto and eager eyes followed the rapid unloading of the half dozen or so lorries.

At the eleventh hour someone had come to their aid. Bessie's eyes were swimming with mingled gratitude and bewilderment as she turned to the handsome young man who stood by her side as they watched the unloading of the motor lorries.

"Mr Trueman, I don't know how to thank you," she said in a low voice. "Not only for myself, but for all my good friends here, whom you have saved from unemployment. You....you must be a magician. How did you do it? Where did you get the cotton from, and how did you manage to get it delivered so quickly....within twenty four hours?"

Dick Trueman blushed slightly as he met the instant gaze of the pretty girl by his side.

"What's the use of being a business manager if you can't....err....do business?" he replied lightly. "You wanted some cotton, and it was up to me to get it for you, Miss Booth. By a stroke of luck I was able to do so."

"Yes, but where from?"

"Well, you see, I have a pal who's just launched out in business as agent for a big cotton exporter in the States," explained Dick slowly. "Naturally, he was only too willing to accept my order and make delivery at once."

"Who is he? What firm is it?"

"Here is the invoice. It came this morning," replied the young man, handing over a slip of paper.

"Charles Saxby, sole British agent for the Top Notch Cotton Alliance, U.S.A." Bessie Booth read out keenly. "Why...why this is extraordinary, Mr Trueman! They have allowed us six months credit, and quoted us ten per cent below the present market price!"

"I told you Charles Saxby is a pal of mine," blurted Dick Trueman. "And he's just starting over here, so naturally he quotes a lower price than other firms. You can have all the cotton you want at that figure."

Bessie Booth's brown eyes positively danced with delight, and then a thoughtful expression crept into them as she gazed at her new business manager.

"You seem to have a lot of influential friends, Mr Trueman, and a happy knack of getting me out of trouble," she said. "First there was the help for the goalkeeper, Sally...... now conjuring all this cotton out of thin air from another 'old pal'. I wonder they can't assist you to find something better to do than a situation in my poor little mill."

I don't want anything better to do," declared Dick Trueman hastily. "I wouldn't leave here for an offer of a hundred pounds a week."

Bessie Booth turned quickly away. There was a note in Dick Trueman's voice, and a light in his grey eyes that set her heart racing and brought a rich flush of colour surging up into her cheeks.

The last of the motor lorries discharged its load and Ned Bromley came striding across the yard.

"Bess, lass. Ah don't know if Ah'm standing on my head or my heels," he cried gleefully. "Ah'm fair amazed. How did you manage it? Where did you get the cotton from?"

"Ask Mr Trueman here," smiled Bess. "It's nothing to do with me. He did it all."

Ned shot out a large, strong hand and Dick grasped it willingly.

"By gum, you're a real trump, Mr Trueman," said Ned bluntly. "You've saved our Bess, you've saved the mill...in fact you've saved the whole bunch of us! An you've put one over on that dirty skunk Peter Henneker. He thought he'd fixed us good and proper this time. Say, lads and lasses," went on Ned, turning towards the waiting operatives who thronged the mill yard and packed the windows overhead. "Do you know who we've got to thank for getting the cotton for us? Young Mr Trueman here. Three cheers for Mr Trueman!"

The roar of applause that went up seemed to split the very skies and, blushing crimson to the roots of his hair, the young business manager turned tail and dived headlong into his office.

A few minutes later the powerful mill engines commenced to roar and rumble, and the busy looms swung into their chattering song in the spinning rooms overhead..

All was well with the Bee-Hive Mill and Bessie Booth's eyes were misty with tears of relief as she stared across to where Peter Henneker's mill reared itself up on the skyline, listening to the hum of the looms that was music to her ears. With a spring in her step she danced up the stone steps to the spinning room and attended two looms herself until the midday hooter sounded, and the girls flocked down to the canteen where they had their meals.

"It'll be overtime all this week girls," said Bessie gravely, as she took her seat one of the long tables. "We're a day behind as it is and there's another contract for Burtons to be completed by Saturday."

"Don't you worry about Burtons, or any other contract," said big red-haired Mary Bonny. "We'll get them finished, if we have to work all night, every night. Ah'm thankful we've got the work to do, and the cotton to work on."

"Ay, that's a fact," cried Sally Soper the goalkeeper, and a murmur of agreement arose from the other girls.

The events of the past couple of days had filled them with dismay and uncertainty, and now that the crisis was past, and it was certain the mill was safe, their relief knew no bounds.

"Dick Trueman's a champion....a real top-notcher!" cried Sally, enthusiastically waving her knife and fork. "Ah only wish he thought as much of me as he does of Bess there."

Bessie Booth sat bolt upright, her cheeks crimson with confusion.

"Why, Sally, what do you mean?" she exclaimed indignantly. But the Busy Bees' goalkeeper only winked slyly at no one in particular and busied herself with her meal. Sally Soper was no dunce. She did not need any telling that the new business manager was head over heels in love with his new employer.

And at that moment, Dick Trueman was striding up and down his office, his hands jammed deep into his trouser pockets, and a heavy frown on his handsome face. The game he was playing and the deceit it brought with it – his real identity as the son of Josh Browell and the true owner of the Bee-Hive Mill – was playing heavily on his mind.

"What the dickens is the right thing for me to do?" he muttered for the hundredth time as he stamped up and down the room. "Keep up this idiotic deceit, or admit the truth…tell Bess I love her, ask her to marry me, get turned down, and then clear off back to the States."

Dick Trueman Browell groaned aloud at the very idea of the latter prospect. Life without Bessie Booth would not be worth living. He dared not put his luck to the test.

Suddenly, he took a coin from his pocket and spun it in the air.

"Heads I own up…tails I sit tight, and then see how things turn out," he muttered grimly.

The coin chinked to the floor, rolled around in a circle, and flattened out with a last rattle.

"Tails it is!" cried Dick thankfully. "Dick Trueman I remain…..for the time being at any rate."

Henneker's Revenge

Peter Henneker stepped down from the big motor car that deposited him outside the gates of his mill and a sullen, puzzled frown wrinkled his narrow forehead as he stared across the vista of huddled, grimy houses and narrow streets to where the Bee-Hive Mill loomed grey, square and solid.

He felt his plot to ruin both Bessie Booth's football and business ambitions had been a success. So why was it that smoke was rising from the towering chimney stack at the rear of the Bee-Hive Mill? What was the use of keeping the furnaces alight when there was no work for the engines to do?

Henneker scowled again as he stomped into his private office, removing his hat and coat before ringing for Smith, his manager.

"Smith, what does all this mean?" he snapped, pointing through the window towards the smoking chimney stack of the Bee-Hive Mill.

"I don't know.....although I overheard," he said with obvious reluctance, "one of the men telling how there are people in the Bee-Hive Mill today. That the engines and the looms are running just as usual."

Peter Henneker puffed out his sallow cheeks and his eyes positively blazed.

"Thunder and lightning! How can that be?" he snarled. "How can they run the looms without the cotton? Where did you get that lying tale from? Who told you? Give the fool a week's notice and tell him to clear out!"

John Smith nodded matter-of-factly. He was used to Peter Henneker's sudden burst of rabid, ungovernable fury.

"That girl....the one who gives you information...she is waiting to see you," he announced calmly.

"What, Ada Miller?" rasped Henneker. "Why the dickens didn't you say so in the first place? She is just the person I want to see. Send her in."

The pale, sly-faced spy came sidling into the office, a shawl wrapped around her head.

"Well, Miller, what do you want? Come for a job here, now that the Bee-Hive has closed down?"

Ada Miller shook her head and shuffled her clogged feet.

"The Bee-Hive ain't closed down," she said hoarsely. "It's bad news for you, gaffer. They're working same as usual, all the looms going an'......"

Peter Henneker's face was livid as he stared across the desk at the trembling girl.

"By heavens! If you're lying to me I'll ring your neck for you!" he gasped acidly. "What do you mean? How can the looms be running? They've got no cotton."

"Ay, but they have, gaffer. They've all the cotton they need. It arrived early this morning."

Peter Henneker fell back in his chair, his hands and face twitching, his teeth grinding and clamping so that a line of foam formed on his thin lips. John Smith coolly handed him a glass of water and Henneker drank deeply, recovering some of his composure.

"Cotton....cotton! Cotton!" he croaked. "Where did they get it? Where did it come from?"

"It came by road from Liverpool," volunteered Ada Miller. "In motor lorries...twenty or more of 'em."

There was a moment's silence as Henneker stared across at the flabby, immobile face of John Smith.

"Who can have let us down, Smith?" he mused with an evil edge to his tone. "Who can have supplied Bessie Booth with that cotton?"

The manager shook his head and Ada handed across a soiled, crumpled square of pasteboard.

"Here's a label off one of the bales," she said quietly. "You can see where it comes from."

"Charles Saxby, agent for the Top-Notch Cotton Alliance, USA," read out Peter Henneker hoarsely. "And the label is addressed to Bessie Booth, Bee-Hive Mill. Smith, who the devil is this fellow Saxby?"

"Apparently he is only an agent...but I have heard of the Top-Notch Cotton Company," said Smith slowly. "I did not know they exported to England. Evidently, they have just started, and Miss Booth has been clever enough to get in touch with them."£

Almost choking with rage, Peter Henneker twisted and turned in his chair. Once again his cunning scheme had miss fired. Despite all his efforts to the contrary, Bessie Booth had succeeded in gaining a fresh supply of cotton.

"It weren't Bessie Booth as got the cotton," said Ada Miller. "It were Mr Trueman, the new business manager."

Henneker's lips parted in a snarl, and his eyes gleamed red. The two men had only met the once, and the young manager had warned Peter Henneker to leave Bessie Booth alone. And Henneker had not forgotten Trueman's fist, or the crunching blow he had received, and he did not intend to forget it until he had squared accounts with Bessie Booth's new business manager.

"Smith, you must write to this fellow Saxby. Warn him not to accept any more orders from the Bee-Hive Mill, if he wants to do trade with any other mills. Rub it in pretty thick, the same as we did with all the rest who gave Bessie Booth the cold shoulder."

"Yes, I'll write to this Mr Saxby," said Smith, "but it's rather like locking the stable door after the horse has been stolen. The cotton has been delivered....the Bee-Hive Mill is in full swing again."

"Ay, they'll be working late nights to catch up with their contracts," chimed in Ada Miller.

"You clear off.... and let me know if anything else turns up!" ordered Peter Henneker. "And now, Smith," he went on after the sly girl had left, "where's my little black book? I want to send a wire to Hamburg."

"To Hamburg!" echoed John Smith, displaying surprise for the first time. "And why are you wiring to Hamburg?"

"To send for Carl Hinck and Otto Wohl."

"Hinck and Wohl!" Smith's heavy jaw dropped. "Why do you send for those cut-throat villains?"

"Because I have work for them to do," snarled Peter Henneker menacingly. "I don't mean to waste any more time and money, Smith. This business has got to be settled this week, and there's only one way to do it. Bessie Booth must be got out of the way for good and all, and while I'm dealing with her, I'll also deal with that whelp of a manager of hers. No man has ever yet struck me and lived very long to brag about it! Hinck and Wohl will know how to deal with the dog. Wire them to come at once, Smith."

John Smith wrote out the telegram with ill-concealed reluctance. Scoundrel as he was, he drew the line at seeking the assistance of two such cold-blooded, murderous scoundrels as Carl Hinck and Otto Wohl.

Never had the workers of the Bee-Hive Mill known such a busy week. From early dawn 'till eight or nine o'clock at night the looms clicked and whirred and the dispatch office had all it could do to keep pace with the output.

No one slackened; no one grumbled or complained beneath the constant strain. They all knew they were working in a good cause, and none worked harder than Bessie Booth herself. There was nothing she could not or did not turn her hand to. Part of the day would be spent in the spinning room, attending to as many as four looms; then she would pass on from department to department, and finally finish up in the general office to assist Dick Trueman with his books and correspondence.

But even then she and the rest of the Busy Bees did not neglect their training. They managed to snatch an hour every evening on the football ground in exercise and ball practice, and there was no question about their fitness.

It was a stiff match that they ahead of them on the coming Saturday. Darrington Crusaders had proved a tough nut to crack on their own ground. They had yet to suffer their first home defeat, and with Henneker's team running them so close in the league, it was essential for the Bees to get one point, if not the two.

There was a look of relief and satisfaction on Bessie Booth's pretty face as she burst into the general office on the Friday afternoon and placed some papers on her desk.

"Burton's order will be completed tonight, Mr Trueman," she beamed, "and we'll have the whole lot on rail by tomorrow morning. I never thought we'd get it done in time. One day's work lost takes a lot of catching up. Do you mind working late again tonight? I want to get everything cleared up so that I can go to the Darrington game with an easy conscience tomorrow."

"Mind? I'll work all night if it's necessary!" declared Dick Trueman willingly. "And then I shan't have done half as much as you, Miss Booth. You've been splendid! If only Henneker realised the sort of spirit he was up against, he'd pack up and clear out of Blacktown before he jolly well had to!"

"If you'll wait until after the engines have stopped and all the other workers have gone this evening I'll come and give you a hand with the books," promised Bessie. "We'll have a quiet hour between eight and nine to get everything up to date."

Ada Miller had been listening outside the office door and now drew her shawl around her head and hurried away to a telephone call box, in a little general shop opposite the mill.

Five minutes later Peter Henneker replaced the receiver of the telephone in his private office and turned towards John Smith, his dark eyes blazing with excitement and triumph.

"At last! A message from Ada Miller," he said in a low, tense voice. "Bessie Booth and that manager of hers will be working late tonight. They will be all alone at the mill between eight and nine. It's the chance I've been waiting for, Smith. Send Hinck and Wohl in to me. They'll not get such an opportunity again!"

Peter Henneker threw back his head with a harsh chuckle of delight. It seemed that Fate had delivered Bessie Booth and Richard Trueman into his hands!

Trapped!

All day long the engines and looms of the Bee-Hive Mill in Blacktown had been roaring and clattering; but now the big, square-faced many-windowed building was silent and deserted, and wrapped in darkness save for a glow of light that shone steadily in the general office.

Two persons were seated in the long, sparsely furnished room with the distempered walls and swinging electric lights. The girl –young and distinctly pretty with curly brown hair and big brown eyes – wore a frown, clattering the end of a pencil thoughtfully against her white even teeth as she bent over the big pile of letters, receipts and invoices on the desk before her.

At an adjacent desk a few yards away sat the broad shouldered young man, with strong clean-cut features and steady grey eyes. He had a fat ledger set out in front of him into which he was making many neat entries and rows of figures. There was no sound save the scratch of his busy pen and the occasional rustle of paper.

Bessie Booth stifled a yawn behind a dainty hand and glanced at the clock that hung on the wall. The hands pointed to a quarter to nine.

"Nearly finished Mr Trueman?" she enquired.

Dick Trueman answered without looking up from his work.

"I shan't be another ten minutes, Miss Booth" he assured. "But there's no need for you to wait any longer. You've had a hard day of it, and you've got another hard day before you tomorrow."

"Oh, football's not hard work, it's a pleasure" said Bessie lightly, knowing he was referring to the league match against Darrington Crusaders that the Busy Bees were to play the following day. It was an away match and the long journey to Darrington was the most tiresome part of it all.

Bessie picked up the bundle of letters and invoices and crammed them away in her desk. All that week she had been working late at the Mill, for the Bee-Hive was under contract to deliver certain goods for certain firms by a certain date, and failure to do so meant being given a heavy financial penalty.

Bessie reflected on how the seemingly insurmountable problems of the last few days and weeks had been overcome by Dick Trueman her business manager.

She was conscious of an overwhelming sense of relief as she closed her desk and glanced again at the clock on the wall. It was the end of the most strenuous working week she had ever known, and it was with an easy mind that she could look forward to the morrow's league match against Darrington Crusaders.

"If you're only going to be ten minutes I think I'll wait for you, Mr Trueman," she said a trifle shyly. "Then I can see the mill safely locked up. And besides, we both go the same way into town."

Dick Trueman's pulses leapt as he bent over the big ledger before him. He knew beyond any possible doubt that he had lost his heart to the pretty brown-eyed girl by whom he was employed. As a matter of fact, he had fallen head over heels in love with Bessie Booth the first moment he had caught sight of her, and the past week had only made it more clear to him that she was the only girl in the world so far as he was concerned.

"I'm coming to Darrington to see you play tomorrow," he said as he made a neat entry on the ruled page.

"You've got to see to it that the Bees keep their unbeaten record, Miss Booth."

Bessie's pretty lips tightened and she nodded her head. So far her team had not lost a single match, and they stood firmly planted at the head of the league table. "We ought to beat Darrington all right," said the girl thoughtfully. "They've only won two matches this season, and Henneker's defeated them easily last week."

"And you've beaten Henneker's once, so it ought to be a walk-over for you" smiled Dick Trueman as he flung down his pen and closed the ledger with a bang. "I'll just get some of this ink off my fingers and then we can toddle along."

Bessie Booth commenced to put on her coat and hat as the young man grabbed up his towel and slipped out of the office. The stone-paved corridor was in darkness, save for a solitary flickering gas-jet; but Dick could have found his way blindfold to the cloakroom.

As he flung the door open and stepped over the threshold, he fancied he heard a slight gasp and a light footfall close behind him. Even as he swung round on his heel something descended upon his head with crushing force, and he knew no more

Meanwhile Bessie Booth was waiting back in the office, perched on the edge of a desk and swinging her neatly shod feet. Ten minutes passed; but Dick Trueman still did not appear and she glanced at the clock with a little frown of impatience. She had been hard at it since eight o'clock that morning and she was anxious to get a good night's sleep in view of the morrow's match against Darrington Crusaders.

She did not turn her head as she caught the faint creak of the door being pushed open.

"I'm still waiting, Mr Trueman," she said severely. "I thought you had forgotten all about me and gone home."

Dick Trueman made no reply, which was unlike him, and Bessie wheeled round towards him. But the young manager was not there, and what she did see brought a sharp gasp of amazement and dismay to her lips.

Within a couple of yards of her stood two men, who had evidently crept stealthily into the room. Their menacing appearance was sufficient to alarm anyone, let alone a young girl. Each was muffled up to the eyes in a heavy jacket and a scarf that entirely concealed the lower part of the face.

"Who are you? What do you want here?" demanded Bessie Booth.

Strangely enough she was not so much alarmed as indignant at the impudence of these two strangers, who had forced their way unannounced into her private office.

But the men made no reply. Simultaneously they leaped forward and flung themselves on the unprotected girl. Iron hands pinned Bessie's arms to her sides, and a grimy paw was clapped roughly over her mouth.

But not before she had time to fling back her head and utter a ringing cry for help.

"Mr Trueman – come quick! Oh, help! Dick...Dick!"

Even in that moment of terror she realised that, for the first time, she had called her new manager by his Christian name. Then a wad of cloth soaked in some sickly, suffocating drug was pressed over her mouth and nostrils, and the first long gasp for breath sent her senses spinning away from her.

Bess looked round and saw two menacing-looking men. "What are you doing here?" she asked

Brusquely the two men lowered the girl's limp figure into a chair.

"Well that was easy enough," grunted the one, flashing a quick glance around the room. "Who d'you think she was calling for? That fellow we cracked on the head a moment ago?"

"Must have been," jerked the second man. "There's no one else in the building. Give the boss the tip that it's all right."

His companion went to the door and gave a low whistle. Almost at once a third person stepped silently into the room – a tall, lean man in a long dark overcoat. He flashed a nervous glance around the office, and then raised his head so that the light shone full on his face and revealed the sallow features and snapping black eyes of Peter Henneker.

The unscrupulous mill owner gave a little grunt of satisfaction as he caught sight of the unconscious figure of Bessie Booth huddled limply in a chair.

He crossed over and stood staring grimly down into the pale face of the girl whose plucky enterprise in starting a rival mill had brought him almost to the edge of ruin.

"Well done," he said harshly, turning to his two hirelings. "And what about the other – the cub of a manager?"

"We settled him first," replied the taller of the men. "Laid him out with a crack on the head. They were both easy game, though the girl did manage to let out a couple of yells.

Peter Henneker gave a curt order and the two men vanished, to reappear bearing the senseless form of Dick Trueman between them. They dropped him callously to the floor, and Henneker's eyes blazed with evil hatred as he dealt the man a brutal kick in the ribs.

"That's for the blow you struck me the other day, you arrogant dog," he hissed venomously. "I'll pay you back a hundredfold before I've finished with you. You've brought it on yourself. You shouldn't have meddled in my affairs. Get busy you two...tie them up."

One of the men opened his overcoat and drew out a length of thin but strong rope that had been wound around his waist. Quickly and dexterously they went to work, whilst Peter Henneker sat himself in a chair and coolly watched them.

In less than five minutes Bessie Booth and Dick Trueman had been securely pinioned hand and foot. Wrists and ankles were lashed together and finally a padded cloth was swathed around the lower part of their faces so that even had they been conscious it would have been impossible for them to utter a sound.

At another order from Henneker the one man swung Trueman's limp figure over his shoulder, whilst his companion did the same with Bessie Booth. They left the office together and after a brief survey of the room Henneker switched off the light and followed suit. He saw to it that the front entrance of the mill was closed, and then by the light of an electric torch made his way to the rear of the premises.

Another door gave on to a stone-paved yard adjoining the engine-house, which was enclosed by a high brick wall. Here the other two men were waiting with their helpless human burdens dumped at their feet.

The taller of the two made a nervous little gesture as he glanced at the towering chimney-stack that reared itself a hundred and fifty feet up into space towards the star-spangled sky above.

"This is the part of the job I don't like," he said bluntly. "I think you'd better change your mind, guvn'or. I don't fancy......"

"Never mind what you fancy," snapped Henneker fiercely. "You'll do as I say. You're being well paid for it, aren't you? And it's work you've been accustomed to all your life. The sooner you get the job finished the better. It shouldn't take you long with a block and tackle."

With a resigned shrug of his shoulders the man jerked off his overcoat and rubbed his hands briskly together.

"One thing, there's no wind," he muttered meaningfully. "If there had been I wouldn't do what I'm going to do for all the money in the world."

A moment later he had vanished, and Peter Henneker and the other man stood with their heads thrown back staring up into the night-darkened sky.

Missing!

Ned Bromley stepped out of the general office, closing the door behind him, and stood for a moment rubbing puzzledly at his square chin.

It was ten o'clock on the Saturday morning – the day on which the Busy Bees were to journey to Darrington to play their league match with the Crusaders. For two hours or more the looms had been clacking and whirring, and for the third time Ned Bromley had made his way to the general office, only to find it deserted.

Neither Bessie Booth nor Dick Trueman seemed to have put in an appearance. It was an unusual occurrence, for Bessie was generally one of the first to arrive of a morning.

"Never knew the lass to be so late," muttered Bromley as he left the empty office. "An' on a Saturday, too! Happen she's got some other business to attend to. But that's no reason why young Dick Trueman shouldn't be here."

With a vaguely uneasy shake of his head the overlooker tramped up the stone stairs and passed into the vast spinning-room where the looms were roaring and clattering, under the keen observance of the girl operatives.

Here worked most of the Busy bees football team – Mary Bonny, the gaunt, raw-boned centre half; Connie Tree, the diminutive light-footed outside right; Amy Ackroyd and Enid Foster the backs; and Sally Soper, the freckle-faced, snub-nosed goalkeeper.

"Hast seen owt o' Bess, lass?" asked Ned Bromley, approaching Mary Bonny and placing his lips close to her ear in order to make his voice heard above the din.

Mary Bonny – more usually known as Bony Mary – shook her red head and flashed a surprised glance at the overlooker.

"Isn't she in the office?" she jerked, one vigilant eye on her looms.

"Nay, she hasn't been there all morning. An' Trueman's missing as well."

"They were working late last night," said the tall centre-half. "Ah heard Bess say as she didn't expect to leave the mill until nine or ten. Reckon she's entitled to a couple of hours extra sleep this morning."

"Ay. Ah never thought o' that," grunted Ned Bromley with a little sigh of relief. "She's sure to turn up in time to catch the train to Darrington."

For the next couple of hours Ned busied himself with his duties, and when twelve o'clock came and the buzzer sounded its harsh order to cease work he made his way again to the general office.

Mary Bonny and Sally Soper met him on the threshold, both looking considerably perplexed and uneasy.

"Ned, what can have become of Bess?" exclaimed the Busy Bees' goalkeeper. "She hasn't arrived yet. She hasn't been her all morning. And no more has young Mr Trueman."

"Perhaps she's ill. But even then she would surely have sent us word by now?" hazarded Mary Bonny. "An we've got to catch our train in just over an hour's time. Ned, tell young Tom Gandy to jump on his bike and go round to Bess's house an' see what's wrong."

The news sped swiftly from one end of the mill to the other. Bessie Booth was missing! She had not put in an appearance that morning! It was such an unusual happening that it created quite a mild sensation, and there was a big crowd of puzzled operatives congregated in the mill-yard when Tom Gandy came flashing back on his bicycle.

"Bess's not at home," he panted as he ran up the steps to where Ned Bromley and the anxious members of the football team were waiting. "Her aunt tells me that she hasn't been home all night. She reckoned she'd stayed with Amy Olroyd as she did last time she worked late."

"She never came to me last night," declared Amy Olroyd bewilderingly, "though she did sleep at my place last Wednesday."

Consternation fell over the little group. Some of the colour left Ned Bromley's florid cheeks, and his heart gave a great leap of anxiety.

"An' there's Dick Trueman hasn't arrived either," he exclaimed hoarsely. "He an' Bess were working together late last night! Tom Gandy, hurry round to his digs. He rooms with Mother Andrews in Carson Lane. Ask him where he left Bess......and bring him back here with you."

But Tom Gandy came racing back alone, crimson-faced with excitement. From lip to lip spread the amazing news he brought. Dick Trueman's landlady had seen nothing of him since he had left the house the previous morning to go to work at the mill.

He had not been in all night! What had become of him, and what had become of Bessie Booth?

"Ah reckon she's run away wi' that fellow Trueman, the new manager," muttered Ada Miller, the green-eyed spiteful-natured girl. "Many's a time I've seen 'em wi' their heads together....."

"Hold your tongue, dang thee, girl," blurted Ned Bromley sternly. "Our Bess is not one to run away and leave us in the lurch......especially on a day like this. She'll turn up in time to catch the train to Darrington. If she don't then Ah'm reckoning there's summat badly wrong....that she's met wi' foul play."

A gasp of alarm ran through the group of operatives. There was not one there – except perhaps Ada Miller – who would not have gone through fire and water for Bessie Booth, and the possibility that some misfortune might have befallen her filled them all with dismay.

One o'clock.........half past one came, and still no sign of the Busy Bees' missing captain. And their train for Darrington left at two o'clock.

"Girls, we'd best get down to the station," said Mary Bonny huskily. "We may find Bess waiting for us there. In any case we must go to Darrington to keep our date with the Crusaders."

It was a dejected, white-faced, anxious-eyed little bunch of girl footballers who stood on the departure platform of the railway station, gazing hopefully towards the entrance.

Reluctantly they filed into the waiting train as the guard prepared to give the 'right-away', and Ned Bromley gave them a brave, determined glance of encouragement.

"Don't worry lasses," he cried stoutly. "Ah'll find out what's happened to our Bess if I have to search every inch o' Blacktown. 'Appen, she may be at Darrington all the time waiting for you. In any case she'd wish you to play up with a stout heart and give the Crusaders a sound trouncing."

The Busy Bees glanced gloomily at one another as the train rolled out of the station. What with the anxiety of Bessie Booth's mysterious disappearance, and the fact that they would have to play one short – and that one the captain and crack centre-forward – they had but faint hopes of defeating the crusaders that afternoon.

A cool, refreshing breeze blowing across her face brought Bessie Booth's senses drifting back to her. She opened her eyes and blinked puzzledly up at a purple, star-scattered vault of sky that was just streaked with the first grey fingers of dawn.

In the next moment she realised that she was trussed up like a chicken, bound hand and foot, unable to stir an inch, and a thick cloth was wrapped over her mouth so that she could not utter a sound.

Bessie closed her eyes again. Surely it must be a dream? Then everything came back to her with a rush. She remembered waiting for Dick Trueman in the general office, and the sudden appearance of two strange, evil-looking men, who had leaped upon her and clapped a sickly smelling cloth over her mouth.

Blackness had swooped down upon her, and now she found herself flat on her back, bound and gagged and staring up at the open sky.

And as she lay helpless, bewildered, and not a little alarmed, night gradually gave way to day. The stars paled and faded – the rising sun shot a shaft of gold across the sky, and she was better able to take stock of her surroundings.

So far as Bessie could make out, she appeared to be lying at the base of a low brick wall, not less than three or four feet in height. This was on her right. To her left she could see nothing save open sky. She was also cognisant that the ground on which she lay, and the brick wall, seemed to sway gently but perceptibly backwards and forwards.

It was a nasty, sickening sensation, and Bessie put it down to the after-effects of the vile drug that had robbed her of her senses.

Struck with a sudden idea, she drew up her knees and rolled over so that she now lay face downwards. Once, twice again she rolled, and then Bessie Booth's blood seemed to turn to ice in her veins and a fear and horror such as she had never known before sent a rasping shock through her slender figure.

She lay with her head and shoulders jutting out into space, and a hundred and fifty feet beneath her was the roof of the Bee-Hive Mill, lying at the other end of a slender, swaying brick column. And beyond the whole of Blacktown was spread out like a map.

She lay on the edge of eternity...... bound and helpless, peering over the lip of the big chimney stack that towered up above the Bee-Hive Mill!

Bessie Booth closed her eyes again. Her throat was dry, her pulse leaping widely with horror. Surely it was all a dream, a terrible nightmare! It was impossible, how did she get up onto the narrow ledge that ran around the top of the factory chimney?

But it was no dream. She had only to open her eyes to realise that, to feel the breeze in her face, and the steady sway of the well-balanced stack. She also realised that if she had rolled over once more she would have launched herself into empty air and dropped like a plummet to be dashed to fragments on the stones below.

Even now she was in a none too secure position. The narrow rim on which she lay sloped slightly, and it was as much as she could do to roll back the way she had come. She made one half-turn that left her on her side a foot from the edge over which she had hung, and her eyes suddenly revealed to her that she was not alone in her misfortune.

A yard away, close to the circular brickwork that formed the neck of the shaft, lay a man, bound hand and foot in the same manner as she was bound. But though his face was half-concealed by the thick cloth that effectually gagged his mouth, Bess at once recognised the crisp, fair hair and clear grey eyes of Dick Trueman.

Dick Trueman's eyes were wide open, and something of relief and something of dismay clouded them as he caught sight of Bessie Booth. He did not know where he was, but the fact that he was bound and helpless, and Bessie Booth was in the same unpleasant state was quite sufficient to dismay him.

He knew nothing of what had happened. All he could remember was that just as he was entering the cloak-room at the mill to wash his hands someone had come up behind him, and struck him senseless with a smashing blow to the head.

Bessie Booth clenched her dainty, pinioned hands in chagrin at her helplessness to communicate in any way with her companion. Some time later – how long she had not the vaguest idea – the harsh screams of a siren came echoing up to her ears, and she knew that it was eight o'clock, and that her chums would be flocking into the Bee-Hive Mill to commence their half-day's work.

And she would be missing – she and Dick Trueman, the new business manager! What would they think? How would they act when they failed to put in an appearance? Even if they searched Blacktown from end to end, no-one would dream of climbing to the top of the big chimney stack that towered above the Bee-Hive Mill.

Not until that moment had Bessie Booth fully realised the horror of her position. A terrible, lingering death by starvation and exposure lay before her. Far better to roll off into space and end it right away!

She heard the mill hooter sound again at twelve o'clock, and knew that in two hours' time the Busy Bees were due to catch the two o'clock train to Darrington to play their match against the Crusaders.

And she would not be there. She had probably played her last match for the Bees!

Half a mile away across the town Peter Henneker stood on the roof of his mill and, placing a pair of powerful binoculars to his eyes, carefully focused them.

By reason of the height at which he stood he could just distinguish two dark objects stretched on the narrow rim of the lip of the chimney stack that reared up above the Bee-Hive Mill.

"You're there, and there you'll remain," muttered Henneker evilly. "No-one would dream of searching in a place like that. You've brought it on yourself, Bessie Booth. One of us had to go under, and I didn't mean to be that one. I don't suppose you'll be up there very long. They're sure to find you in the end, but it'll be at the foot of the shaft, not at the top, and you'll be beyond doing me any further harm!"

Fifteen miles away to the westward, people were flocking into the cosy little ground of the Darrington Crusaders, and punctually at two-thirty ten figures in the yellow and black jerseys of the Busy Bees filed out onto the field.

And when it became known that the visiting team were one girl short – and that they were without their redoubtable captain and centre-forward, Bessie Booth – a murmur of disappointment ran round the field.

"It's a walk-over for the Crusaders," murmured one Darringtonite. "I wanted to see them win, of course....but I wanted to see Bessie Booth play as well. Never mind. Now then, Crusaders. Show 'em what you can do!"

Five minutes later the Crusaders were one goal up, and Sally Soper, the Bees' goalkeeper, realised that her side were in for certain defeat....... unless the missing Bessie Booth turned up in time to take her place as centre-forward, and save the situation!

In Dire Peril

There was a stiff breeze blowing, and the tall, well-balanced chimney stack swayed gently from side to side, a good four inches out of the perpendicular. It was an unpleasant, sickening sensation and Bessie Booth closed her pretty brown eyes and clenched her white, even teeth.

From far away beneath her came the faint rattle and clatter of Blacktown's tramway service and the occasional toot of a railway engine. The Bee-Hive Mill itself was silent, for it was a Saturday and the engines and looms had ceased running at twelve o'clock.

Tears of disappointment welled in Bessie Booth's eyes. The peril of her position – her utter helplessness and the hopelessness of it all – was blunted in the dismay that came to her in the knowledge that the Busy Bees had their league match against Darrington that very afternoon.

And she would not be with them. By now they had probably gone.

Bessie screwed her head round and shot a puzzled glance at her companion in misfortune. At first she feared that Dick Trueman was writhing in the throes of suffocation, for what part of his face that was visible was crimson and his jaws were grinding steadily beneath the thick cloth that swathed his mouth.

A moment later she realised that for the past hour he had been steadily chewing through his gag. He suddenly spat out a sodden mouthful of wool through the hole he had made and heaved a great sigh of relief.

"Bessie....Miss Booth.....are you all right?" he said huskily, and somewhat irrelevantly considering the circumstances. "Good Heavens! What does this mean? How did we get up here? What a fool I am asking such stupid questions when I know you can't answer. Keep a stout heart. I think I can see a way out of this mess. No sense shouting. No-one will hear us up here."

Inch by inch the young man wriggled his way snakewise along the rough brickwork. It was dangerous work – a slip, a roll and he would have gone plunging down to certain death a hundred and fifty feet below. Now he was close by Bessie's side, gazing anxiously into her brown eyes.

"I've one object in life now," he said with a grim laugh, "and that's to lay my hands on the person or persons responsible for this villainy. I have one other object, but it purely concerns you and I, and this is no time to discuss it."

Dick Trueman bent down, and Bessie booth's heart gave a leap of fresh hope as she felt his strong white teeth tearing at the cords that bound her wrists. Ten minutes later the last one fell apart, and Bessie eagerly raised her cramped hands and tore the gag from her mouth.

"Knife in my coat pocket, "instructed her companion crisply.

Trembling with excitement, Bessie felt for the knife, and in less than a minute she had freed Dick Trueman, and severed the remaining cords that bound her ankles. Then side by side they sat, propped against the circular rim of the chimney, staring blankly into each other's eyes.

"Well, this takes the biscuit," said Dick Trueman at length, suppressing a little shudder as he gazed down at the town of Blacktown spread out far below like a toy model. "I can't realise it....I thought it was a ghastly nightmare. How...how did we get here?"

Bessie shook her curly head vaguely.

"Years ago.....at least it seems years," went on the young manager, "I left you in the office whilst I went to fetch my hat and coat. The corridor was in darkness, and something or someone hit me on the back of the head with a steam-roller. That's all I knew until I woke up in this delightful, airy spot."

"It must have been the man...two men in fact....the same men who attacked me," cried Bessie Booth eagerly, and she quickly proceeded to relate the incident of the two strange individuals who had forced their way into the office and overcome her with a drugged cloth.

Dick Trueman's lips tightened as he listened, and a hard light crept into his grey eyes.

"The dirty scoundrels.....the villains.....they dared to lay their hands on you!" he exploded. "Did you recognise them? Would you know them again?"

"No, I'm sure I wouldn't," replied the girl ruefully. "They were all muffled up, and had their caps pulled down over their eyes. And they didn't speak a word. They...seemed strangers to me."

"They'd seem stranger still if I laid my hands on them," growled Dick Trueman. "Why, it's sheer murder. We might have lain up here for weeks. Who can be at the bottom of it? Who......."

The young man broke off short. He glanced at Bessie Booth, and then his gaze wandered to a cluster of buildings and chimney stacks that lay across town.

"Peter Henneker!" said Dick Trueman in a low, tense voice. "I bet every penny I possess that this is more of Peter Henneker's foul work!"

Bessie nodded, and her tiny hands clenched. Down in the town a clock chimed the half-hour and Dick glanced at his watch.

"Two-thirty!" he exclaimed, "and....."

"And the Busy Bees are on their way to Darrington to play the Crusaders," said Bessie wistfully, and two big tears of disappointment clouded her brown eyes.

"By Jove, I'd forgotten all about your match today," he cried ruefully. "The Bees won't win without you, Bess......Miss Booth. If we could only get you down this confounded chimney there might still be time to get you to Darrington."

The Escape

Bessie drew in a sharp breath, and her face paled. There was only one way to reach the ground, and that was by means of the slender steel ladder that was bolted to the tapering side of the stack, and the upper end of which curved up over the edge of the rim on which they sat.

It was a journey to strike fear into the heart of the bravest man, or girl. But Bessie Booth set her teeth and squared her slim shoulders. No danger was too great when the possible defeat of the Busy Bees hung in the balance.

"It's the only way," she said quietly. "I'm ready when you are."

Dick Trueman gazed at her with admiration.

"It's the thought of it that's worse than the actual thing," he said. "As a matter of fact, I remember climbing up this very chimney as a boy."

Bessie stared amazedly at the young man.

"Why, I thought you were a stranger to Blacktown?" she exclaimed.

The young manager flushed up confusedly.

"Well, yes, for a good many years, "he replied. "But I was born in Blacktown."

"Who owned the mill then?"

"My.....why, old Josh Browell. And now we'd better make a start, Miss Booth."

Bessie Booth shot a puzzled glance at Dick Trueman. She was beginning to think that her new business manager was a bit of a mystery.......that he was something more than he made himself out to be.

"We'll tackle this job without further waste of time," said Dick, eager to change the subject. He was not anxious to stand any cross-examination from pretty Bessie Booth, particularly at that giddy height. Besides, time was getting on.

"I'll go first," he said confidently. "Just forget where we are, Miss Booth, and try to imagine that we're climbing down from an apple tree and that even if you fell you couldn't hurt yourself. Here goes!"

It was the first part of the decent that presented the greatest difficulty. The lip of the chimney stack jutted out a good three feet beyond the main body itself, and the flimsy-looking ladder inclined inwards at an angle of about fifty degrees.

Bessie Booth closed her eyes instinctively as her companion lowered himself over the edge. For a moment Dick found himself suspended by his hands only, his feet groping for a hold on the slippery rungs. It made him sick to think of the dizzy gulf of space beneath him, but he set his teeth and actually hummed a little tune under his breath as, like a fly on a ceiling, he safely negotiated the almost horizontal length of ladder and was once again upright.

But there were beads of perspiration on his forehead as he gave the signal to his companion.

"Right away....don't look down, Miss Booth!" he called. "There are only four rungs, and then you'll be as safe as if you had one foot on the ground. And don't forget not to look down. It's not exactly safe."

Bessie did not give herself time to think of the terrible fate that awaited her if she were to lose her head and slip. She was in fine trim, thanks to her football training, and with memories of horizontal-bar exercises in the school gymnasium not so many years ago, she stood erect on the rim of the stack, grasped the top rung of the ladder and, turning her back on the

Hand over hand Bessie worked her way along, and soon she found herself standing serenely on the ladder

yawning gulf of space, commenced the descent. Almost at once the whole weight of her body was flung onto her arms as the ladder canted sharply inwards, and she lost her foothold.

"Steady," came Dick Trueman's cool voice. "Three more rungs and you'll be all right. That's the style."

Hand over hand Bessie worked her way along, and in a couple of seconds, though it seemed like as many hours, she found herself standing securely on the ladder, with Dick Trueman below her, his head on a level with her feet.

Never so long as she lives will Bessie Booth forget that terrible descent, clinging like a fly to the rugged face of the chimney stack. There was barely room for her toes on the narrow steel rungs, and the strain on her ankles was tremendous.

Several times she had to halt to rest, and Dick Trueman shouted cheery words of encouragement up to her.

"Stick it out, Miss Booth. Not much further now. Take your time. We're over half way!"

Soon Bessie's hands were stiff and aching with the cold. Every minute she feared she would have to release her hold and topple backwards into space.

Her head was spinning dizzily and her throat was parched with thirst. Down, down, down! Step by step...step by step, no sound, save the scrape of her shoes on the steel rungs, and the fierce throbbing of her heart.

Then, all of a sudden, just as she thought her strength could not endure a moment longer, strong arms clasped her around the waist and lifted her down onto the cobbles of the mill yard.

"Splendid!" exclaimed Dick Trueman enthusiastically, now that the strain of that perilous descent was over. "No other girl in the world save you could have done that, Miss Booth. How are you feeling? I think you'd better let me take you straight home. You're in no fit state to play football."

The words acted upon Bessie like a spur. Her eyes flashed and she straightened up and threw back her slender shoulders.

"I'm quite all right," she said stoutly. "And I mean to get to Darrington if I only have time to play for ten minutes. The Bees need me!"

"Well spoken!" exclaimed the young manager heartily. "And I'm coming with you. How do we go?"

"There's a train at three-five. We might catch it. We must try."

Apparently no-one had noticed the thrilling descent from the chimney stack. The watchman on duty at the gate of the mill uttered yell of amazement as two dishevelled figures, in whom he recognised the missing girl and man, dashed past him and went speeding down the street.

Many other people stopped to stare after Bessie Booth and Dick Trueman, and many an eager question was flung at them, but they had not time to spare to satisfy idle curiosity.

Side by side they dashed through the main street, up the station approach, and out on to the departure platform.

A shrill whistle, the clang of a gate, and the three-five to Darrington glided under their very noses. Tears of disappointment and dismay crept into Bessie Booth's eyes.

"There......there's no other train till four o'clock," she said brokenly. "And the match would be over by the time we got there. It's no use, Mr Trueman. It's hopeless!"

Dick's jaw hardened and he turned swiftly to the station-master, who stood nearby.

"I want a special train to Darrington," he said curtly. "At once!"

The man's eyes widened, and he stared aghast.

"A special!" he gasped. "Ah couldn't get you a special under an hour. Ah've no engine here."

Dick Trueman turned away with a gesture of disgust, and his gaze fell upon a big, open-bodied motor-car that stood outside a block of offices opposite the station.

He grabbed Bessie Booth by the arm and hurried her across the street.

"We'll get to Darrington somehow," he said grimly. "Who does this car belong to?"

The uniformed chauffeur, seated at the wheel of the big Vauxhall, stared coldly at the young man with the dusty clothes and soot-encrusted face and hands.

"This here car happens to belong to Mr Henneker" he said brusquely, "and take you filthy paws off my brass-work!"

Dick Trueman uttered a shout of mingled surprise and excitement. Peter Henneker's car! Without hesitation, he whipped the door open and hustled the bewildered Bessie Booth inside.

"Here, what are you doing!" yelled the chauffeur indignantly. "What's your game? I'll have the police on you!"

"I want you to drive me to Darrington!"

"Drive you?" the chauffeur choked with fury. "I'll see you in....Help!"

Dick Trueman shot out a muscular arm, grabbed the spluttering chauffeur by the nape of the neck, and dumped him down in the gutter. With one bound he gained the driver's seat, and touched the electric starter.

"Tell Mr Peter Henneker that Miss Bessie Booth has borrowed his car!" he shouted, and sent the powerful Vauxhall streaking down the road in a thunderous roar.

Bessie leaned back, her cheeks flushed with excitement and her curly hair rippling in the breeze.

"Mr Trueman, you're just wonderful," she whispered admiringly, and Dick grinned happily as he spun round an amazed policeman and took the road to Darrington.

"Poetic justice," he chuckled. "I'd like to see Henneker's face when he learns who's borrowed his car. He'll be as mad as a sackful of hornets. Get out of the way, you idiot!"

A bewildered and indignant chicken soared high in the air amid a cloud of feathers, and a farm labourer who was about to cross the road fell backwards into a muddy ditch with a howl of alarm.

It was thirty miles to Darrington by road and the powerful car ate up the distance like a voracious monster. Through village and hamlet they whisked, exhaust roaring, and it was twenty minutes to four when the Vauxhall gained the outskirts of Darrington.

And then the motor suddenly coughed, spluttered and lapsed into silence, and the car came to a stand-still.

"Of all the luck," groaned Dick Trueman, "every drop of petrol gone! Hi, you old sport, halt!"

A young man on a motor-bike pulled up with a jerk and a blank stare.

"Can you help us?" asked Dick.

"Dunno you!" he grunted suspiciously.

"Never mind about that," replied Dick cheerfully. "Where's the Crusaders' ground?"

"Other end of the town."

"Well, take this young lady on your pillion and get her there as quickly as you can. Go on Bessie....I'll wait with the car."

The young man was too surprised to make any demur. Besides, Bessie Booth was a particularly pretty girl. She sprang out of the car, perched herself on the seat at the rear of the motor-bike, and with a wave of her hand was wafted away down the street.

Dick Trueman straightened his aching back and glanced at his watch.

"They'll be just about starting the second half," he muttered."She'll be in time, and I'll wager ten to one the Bees win....even if they are six down!"

His Secret Out

"If only Ah was sure......if only Ah was certain that 'twas Peter Henneker's doing, by gum, Ah'd go straight along now and wring his danged neck for him."

Ned Bromley clenched his big, brawny fists, and his normally mild blue eyes flashed like chilled steel. It would have gone hard for anyone who fell foul of him in his present mood. Ned Bromley was as quiet as a lamb in the usual way, but once he was roused he was a nasty customer to deal with.

Dick Trueman laughed softly and flexed his arms above his head.

"I should have performed that operation long ago had I been able to verify my suspicions, Ned," he said grimly."I'd like to get the beggar in a ten foot ring and hammer the life out of him."

"There's no use talking about what you would do, or could do, and would like to do," said Bess, glancing up at the two men. "You've only got your suspicions against Peter Henneker. You can't prove anything.....he's too cunning to commit himself in any way."

They all knew, and Peter Henneker knew, that unless he could break the Bee-Hive Mill he was bound to be broken himself. And the supposed accidents that had befallen the Bee-Hive, the underhand business dealing, and even the abduction and possible murder of Bess and Dick, proved that he was prepared to stop at nothing to win.

When Bess had arrived at the Darrington game it was half-time, and the home team was leading by three goals to one. Bess had taken her place on the field, and played as she had never played before. She scored four goals off her own boot, and in the end the Busy Bees snatched a dramatic victory by five goals to three, and so consolidated their position at the head of the league table – two points ahead of the team Henneker was running out of sheer spite.

"Never mind, we'll get the better of the brute," said Dick. "And then it will be 'goodbye Mr Peter Henneker'. He deserves a ten foot drop with a rope round his neck."

"Ay, and that'd be a sight too good for the skunk," declared Ned Bromley savagely. "It was an attempt at sheer cold-blooded murder, hoisting you up to the top of the chimney stack and leaving you there."

Bessie Booth shuddered at the bare recollection of the terrible experience she had undergone.

"We've got some accounts to clear up, Mr Trueman," she said, hurriedly changing the subject as Bromley left the office. "What about paying your Mr Saxby, the agent for the Top-Notch Cotton Company, for the goods he sent us? Shall I send him a cheque? Besides, we want some more cotton almost at once."

"Saxby will supply you with all the cotton you can use," declared Dick Trueman confidently, "and his terms are three month's credit. If you've no objection, I'll run into Liverpool this afternoon and see him."

Bessie Booth nodded her curly head.

"I wish I could see him to thank him," she said gravely. "He saved the mill by sending the cotton along so promptly. And that reminds me, I.......I haven't thanked you for what you did for me on Saturday, Mr Trueman. You saved my life........."

"Nonsense," jerked the young manager clumsily. "I wish I thought so. I....I'd claim it. It isn't one millionth part of what I would like to do for you, Bessie."

Bessie Booth flushed up to the roots of her curly hair and dropped her eyes nervously.

"Why....I don't understand, Mr Trueman," she said in a low voice. "What do you mean?"

Dick Trueman drew a deep breath and squared his shoulders like a man about to plunge into ice-cold water.

"Bessie......Miss Booth, I must tell you...I can't keep silent any longer," he blurted out vehemently. "I've tried.....I've done my best, but it simply must come out. I love you.....I've loved you ever since I first saw you. I shall always love you, even if you send me away for my cheek. Bessie, tell me.....look at me darling. Do you think anything of me......could you ever learn to care enough.....just enough to......."

Bessie Booth lowered her head, and all Dick Trueman could see were the soft tendrils of brown hair curling on the nape of her slender white neck.

"Bessie....do you hear?" he said huskily. "Dear.....I have made a fool of myself. Do you want me to go...."

Then Bessie Booth suddenly raised her head and Dick Trueman read his answer in her gentle brown eyes. With a cry of joy he gathered her slender, unresisting form in his strong arms.

"Bessie, you do care?" he cried wildly. "Is it possible.....am I so lucky? The luckiest man in the world? I can't believe it!"

The girl looked at him shyly beneath her long lashes, and her slender arms crept up around his neck.

"You'll have to believe it...Dick." she said gently. "Because it's true. Yes I do care....I love you...I think I've always loved you, yes even before I knew you, and I've just been waiting for you, the right man to come into my life."

Their lips met in a first long kiss that set Dick's head swimming dizzily with rapture and his heart throbbing as though it would burst the confines of his chest.

Unseen and unheard, Ned Bromley opened the office door and stopped dead on the threshold as though turned to stone at what he saw. Then gently and reverently he whipped off his cap and retired as silently as he had come.

Poor Ned, he had worshipped Bessie Booth in vain ever since she had been a little girl in pigtails and pinafore, and now the long-expected blow had fallen.

"Ah knew it......Ah knew t'was coming!" he muttered huskily. "Ah could see it...t'was just bound to happen. Them two was made for one another. Dick Trueman's a gradely lad.....one f the very best, and Bessie....Heaven Bless Her!.......she's the sweetest lass in the whole world. Bless 'em both!"

"And you'll be my wife, Bessie darling?" Dick Trueman said eagerly two minutes later. "You'll marry me as soon as possible...at once. I can't wait long...I seem to have waited too long as it is!"

A serious expression suddenly crept into Bessie Booth's eyes.

"Yes, Dick, I'll marry you...but not now," she said gently but firmly. "You must wait....until I'm ready. I haven't completed what I set out to do yet and I don't mean to get married until I have. I made a vow that I'll make a success of the Bee-Hive Mill, all on my own, by my own efforts, and I'd drive Peter Henneker out of business the same as he did poor old Mr Browell who lent me this mill. He's dead now, but I promised him I'd pay Peter Henneker back in his own coin and I mean to keep my promise."

"You darling. I love you all the more for that," cried Dick Trueman.

Unseen and unheard, Ned Bromley opened the office door and then stood as if turned to stone at what he saw

A strange thrill ran through him as he spoke – a passing sense of dismay for the other secret regarding his real identity he had locked away in his heart that he longed to reveal to his sweetheart, yet did not dare until the time was right.

"Very well, darling," said Dick with a sigh of resignation. "I suppose I'll have to wait. But I hope it won't be long, because I have something very important to tell you."

"I don't think it will be long now," said Bess gravely. "I believe we shall have Peter Henneker beaten in less than a couple of months. My only fear is that young Mr Browell may turn up and give us notice to vacate the mill before I am quite ready."

"Hang young Mr Browell!" exclaimed the very man himself, drawing the girl to him and kissing her fondly. "Don't you worry about him. I'll find a way to settle things with him. He won't trouble to claim the old mill...I feel certain of that."

Henneker is Worried

"Something must be done, and done at once, Smith. I tell you that we are faced with certain ruin. That confounded spitfire of a girl has cost me twelve thousand pounds in the last month. Another month at the same rate and we shall have come to the end of our tether. We can't stand the constant drain on capital."

Peter Henneker paced heavily up and down his private office, swinging his long arms savagely at his sides.

"Well, you have brought it all on yourself, Henneker," said John Smith with a phlegmatic shrug of his fat shoulders. "You should never have forbidden the girls to play football in the first place, and then dismissed them because they would not obey you."

"How was I to know she would go to that doddering old fool, Joshua Browell, and wheedle around him to allow her to open up his mill? As it is, I can only see one thing left, Smith."

"And that is?"

"Is to get hold of young Browell....the old man's son.... and persuade him to sell me the Bee-Hive Mill. Once it is mine I can turn those girls out into the street."

"But young Browell is not to be found," said Smith stolidly. "He is somewhere in America, and you already have your agents searching for him."

"And even they have failed me," declared Peter Henneker thickly. "Have I no-one on whom I can rely? Send a cable to Hart in New York, Smith. Tell him that if he doesn't unearth young Browell in the next seven days he is no longer in my employ. And tell him that I'll pay him five hundred pounds if he finds the chap, and persuades him to sell the Bee-Hive Mill to me."

"That is good," grunted Smith approvingly. "And in the meantime what about this agent fellow in Liverpool who is supplying Bessie Booth with the cotton?"

"His name is Saxby and he is English agent for the Top- Notch Cotton Company," replied Henneker. "It is a new agency....just opened I believe."

"And why not interview Mr Saxby," suggested Smith menacingly. "Perhaps you can persuade him to knock off the supply of cotton. A couple of hundred pounds might do the trick and it would be well worth the money."

"Great Scott, Smith!" exclaimed Henneker, "I never thought of that! Why didn't you suggest it before instead of wasting all this time? This man, being a new agent, is probably keen for business. That is why he immediately accepted Bessie Booth's order. I'll soon bring him round to my way of thinking."

Henneker made a dash across the room and dived into his overcoat.

"I'll go to Liverpool right away...at once!" he said grimly. There is a train in ten minutes time. Don't forget to send that telegram to Hart."

A moment later he left the mill and stepped into the motor car that was waiting for him. He ground his yellow teeth in savage chagrin as he glanced across at the Bee-Hive Mill with its smoke-belching chimney stack.

"Go on....use your cotton up as fast as you can!" he snarled, shaking an impotent fist. "You'll get no more when that's gone. I'll make certain of that before I am many hours older!"

Peter Henneker caught the two o'clock into Liverpool, and at just about that time Richard Trueman Browell walked into the office of Saxby, British Agent for the Top Notch Cotton Company of U.S.A.

The young man walked in with an unassuming air of proprietorship, which was distinctly justified, for Dick Browell was the sole owner of the prosperous business concern, thereby accounting for the prompt manner in which Bessie Booth's order was accepted, and delivery made. And the low price quoted.....*and* the three month's credit!

"Mr Browell.....you at last?" I am glad to see you" cried Saxby, springing up from his desk and extending his hand. "I was beginning to wonder if you were ever coming back to Liverpool."

"I came as quickly as I could," replied Dick Browell cheerfully, lighting a cigarette and flinging himself into a chair. "Everything all right? I want you to send another load of cotton to Miss Bessie Booth at the Bee-Hive Mill, Blacktown."

Saxby made a note of the order on his blotting pad and glanced puzzledly across at his employer.

"Mr Browell, excuse me, but you've got me guessing," he said hesitantly. "Exactly what sort of game are you playing in Blacktown.....if it isn't an impertinent question? I thought you were going there to settle up your late father's affairs and arrange to open the mill he left you. The next thing I know is you ring me up and tell me that you've got a job as a business manager under somebody else in your own mill, and in the name of Richard Trueman!"

"Well, it's like this," said Dick Browell. "As you know, I came back to England with the intention of reopening my father's mill and keeping it going with my own cotton. The first thing I learned when I landed at Liverpool was that my father was dead."

Dick Browell's voice grew a trifle husky, and he was silent for a brief moment, saddened by the memory of his father's sudden death.

"I hurried straight away to Blacktown and saw the old man's lawyer," he continued, "and found that before his death he had let the mill to a crowd of operatives who were now running it on a profit-sharing basis....and making it pay, though they were up against a regular tartar in the shape of a man named Peter Henneker, who owns the only other mill in the town."

"However, I wanted the mill for myself," went on Dick Browell. "You can imagine my surprise when I discovered it was being run by a girl....a dashed slip of a girl and a dashed pretty one at that. I don't mind telling you, that I fell head over heels in love with her the moment I saw her."

"All right, I understand everything now, Mr Browell," said Saxby with a knowing smile. "Excepting how you come to be business manager of your own mill."

"I hadn't the heart to tell her who I was," admitted Dick candidly. "I blurted out that I was looking for a job, and to my surprise Miss Booth engaged me as business manager on the spot. So there you are....I've got to carry on now, until Bessie has knocked out this fellow Henneker. He's been doing his best to smash her...stopped her from getting any fresh supplies of cotton by prejudicing all the wholesale firms against her."

"Not knowing you were the proprietor of the Top Notch Cotton Company," chuckled the other.

"Not even knowing that I am the real owner of the Bee-Hive Mill. Even Bessie doesn't know that yet. We are engaged of course......"

"Congratulations, Mr Browell," said Saxby sincerely. "I hope I shall soon have the pleasure of meeting...."

A knock at the door interrupted the conversation, and a clerk came in from the outer office.

"Gentleman to see you, Mr Saxby," he said.

Saxby threw one glance at the card, and almost leaped out of his chair. He handed it mutely to Dick Browell, and the latter gave a gasp of amazement.

"Peter Henneker, by all that's wonderful!" he exclaimed. "Bessie Booth's rival, the fellow I was telling you about. Ask him in, Saxby.....you know how to deal with him. And not a word about me!"

With a warning gesture, Dick Browell slipped behind a large screen in the corner of the room, and a moment later Peter Henneker was admitted.

"Mr Saxby?" he said with an oily laugh that gave Dick Browell a hearty desire to kick him soundly. "You are agent of the Top Notch Cotton Company? I am proprietor of one of the biggest mills in Lancashire."

"Indeed?" said Saxby politely. "And what can I do for you, Mr Henneker?"

"I have come to give you some good advice, Mr Saxby," continued Peter Henneker. "You have just started in business....you want to get on, I imagine? And you have accepted and fulfilled an order from the Bee-Hive Mill in Blacktown?"

Saxby nodded, and Dick Browell clenched his fists behind the screen.

"By so doing you stand a chance of being boycotted by the whole cotton industry," said Henneker with a grave shake of his head. "I suppose you are aware that no other firm will accept an order from the Bee-Hive Mill?"

"You surprise me," murmured the other, with assumed alarm.

"Ah, I thought you were acting in ignorance," continued Henneker. "You realise now that you must supply the Bee-Hive with no more cotton. I can find you plenty of other business."

Saxby rested his elbows on his desk and stared straight at his visitor.

"Supposing I have a contract with the Bee-Hive Mill?"

"You must break it."

"And if I don't?"

"That would be foolish, Mr Saxby. You would ruin your business. No other mill owners would deal with you."

Saxby straightened up with a jerk.

"You are wasting your time, and mine, Mr Henneker," he said coldly. "I shall be quite satisfied to do business only with the Bee-Hive Mill."

"Why, you must be mad!" gasped Peter Henneker, his face crimson with chagrin. "Listen, Mr Saxby. I want to buy all your supplies of cotton for the next six months...every scrap of it!"

"Impossible. The Bee-Hive Mill has a price claim."

"Ignore it. I shall make it worth your while. Perhaps a couple of hundred pounds..."

It was all Dick Browell could do to control himself from springing out and laying heavy hands on the unscrupulous mill owner. He itched to grab him by the scruff of the neck and kick him through the door.

Saxby rose to his feet, his eyes flashing with indignation.

"I am not open to bribery, Mr Henneker," he said grimly. "Not two hundred pounds or two thousand pounds. I wish you good day."

Peter Henneker spluttered and turned with impotent rage.

"You will regret this," he snarled, reaching for his hat. "I'll turn the whole trade against you.....I'll smash you......I'll write to your firm....."

Saxby made a menacing step forward, and Peter Henneker dived ungracefully through the door, gnashing his teeth with baffled fury. His trip to Liverpool had been in vain. He had not dreamed that the agent from the Top Notch Cotton Company would ignore his warnings, and turn down his generous offer.

As he passed through the outer office one of the clerks handed another a letter that had just come.

"Take this to Mr Browell," he said, and Peter Henneker frowned puzzledly as he whirled out into the street.

"Browell...Browell," he muttered under his breath. "Someone else in the building, I suppose. Confound it! I wish I could get in touch with young Richard Browell, the owner of the Bee-Hive Mill!"

Little did he realise how close he had been to Dick Browell in the last half hour, or just how narrowly he had escaped a sound thrashing at his hands.

"The dirty hound!" Dick Browell was saying as he perched on the edge of Saxby's desk. "Another minute and I should have to come out, or burst. Never mind...he'll get what's coming to him before very much longer."

But a great deal was to happen before Peter Henneker received his just deserts, and paid the penalty for all his villainy!

Good News

PHEEP!

The referee's whistle sounded sharp and insistent, a command not to be ignored, and a murmur of disapproval went echoing around the packed touch lines of the trim little home ground where Bessie Booth's Busy Bees – by now one of the best known girls' football teams in the whole of Lancashire – were playing a league match with one of their closest rivals, Hitchdale Villa.

There was only ten minutes to go to full time, and there was dismay written on the faces of the Bees' supporters, for the Villa were leading by two goals to one. Bessie Booth and her companions were attacking with might and main, and a dozen times they had come within an ace of scoring. But the Villa's defence held firm.

They were a big, sturdy set of girls, and keen as mustard to lower the colours of the redoubtable Bees, who held a clear lead of two points over all the other clubs in the Lancashire Girls' Football League.

Content with their lead, the Villa were concentrating all their efforts in defence – and their right-back, a tricky, black-haired girl, time and again caught the Bees' forwards off-side whenever they threatened danger.

"Play the game Villa! Not so much o' the one back business," shouted the excited crowd. "Go it, the Bees!"

Bessie Booth pushed a waving tendril of curly, brown hair out of her eyes as she pulled up at the first note of the referee's whistle. Another minute and she would have been clean through with the ball at her toes, but the official had – rightly or wrongly - ruled her off-side.

A pretty slender figure in the yellow-and-black jersey and black knickers of the Bees, she shot an amazed glance towards the grumbling crowd.

"I wish they weren't quite so......so keen on us winning," she said to Mary Bonny, the home team's tall, red-haired centre-half. "At least, not so keen as to be prejudiced. The Villa are quite entitled to play the one-back game if they want to. It's our fault for letting them."

"We've got two goals to get and ten minutes to get 'em in," said Mary. "That is, if we're going to win. You've got to find your shooting boots, Bess, lass."

But from the ensuing free kick the Villa made a spirited raid on the Bees' citadel. Their outside-right sent in a long, swinging centre, and it was Sally Soper, the Bees' clever little goalie, who saved the situation by running right out and snatching the ball off the opposing centre-forward's toe.

"Now then the Bees. Book Up! Where's your sting today?"

It certainly looked very much as though Bessie Booth's team's unbeaten home record was to go by the board that afternoon, but a moment later the crowd was cheering and shouting for all they were worth.

It was Connie Tree, the Bees' slight, fair-haired outside-right, who caught a long pass from Mary Bonny and set the forward line in motion. With her eye on the opposing backs, Bessie Booth purposely hung back, only dashing in at the last instant, taking the ball on the volley and slamming it into the back of the net from thirty yards range.

It was a wonderful goal and the spectators cheered themselves hoarse. Two goals all, and four minutes to go!

But there was no holding the Bees now. They played up as if the game had only just started, and veritably swept their opponents off their feet. Down the field they tore, flashing the ball deftly from foot to foot. Mary Bonny sent in a tremendous shot which struck the crossbar with a crash and rebounded into the midst of a swarm of players in yellow-and-black and red-and-white shirts.

It was more like a rugby scrum than anything else. The Villa's left-back fell on the ball and gripped it firmly between her knees whilst she crawled away from the goal amidst a roar of laughter. Four players were on the ground at once, and with a glance at his watch the referee stopped play, picked up the ball and threw it down.

Quick as thought, Bessie Booth got her toe to the leather and scooped it clean over her shoulder – over the unprepared goalkeeper's head – and into the back of the net.

Pandemonium broke loose, drowning the final whistle, and amid a storm of delighted cheers the victorious Bees fled from the ground to the pavilion. They had snatched the game out of the fire with the last kick of the match, and strengthened their position at the head of the league table.

Bessie Booth's hazel eyes were sparkling and her cheeks flushed with delight as she ran swiftly from the field. She was the best-known girl footballer in all of Blacktown – probably in all Lancashire.

"By gum, Ah thought we were in for it this afternoon," said Sally Soper as the victorious team fled into their well-equipped dressing room. "Ah thought the Villa were going to beat us fair and square."

Meanwhile the delighted crowd were steadily streaming out of the little ground, until there were only two left – two men who were seated on a bench outside the pavilion.

"Well, I've seen some first-class professional football matches in my time," said Dick Trueman as he watched the last of the crowd leave the ground. "But I've never enjoyed a match more. Those two last goals were regular corkers. Bessie......Miss Booth was simply splendid."

"Ay, she's a gradely player......a gradely lass in every way is our Bess," declared Ned Bromley proudly. "Ah congratulate you, Trueman. You're the luckiest fellow in the world."

"Eh, why what d'you mean, Ned?" stammered Dick Trueman confusedly, flushing up to the roots of his hair.

"Reckon you know, lad, without me telling you," replied the overlooker drily. "Ah've got eyes in my head, and when a lass looks at a lad the way our Bess looks at you, and a lad looking at a lass the way you look at her, well......."

Further conversation was prevented by the opening of the pavilion door and the appearance of Bessie Booth herself, looking more charming than ever in a neat tweed coat and skirt and green tammy hat. She blushed prettily at the sight of her sweetheart as she came towards him.

"Well, we managed to win," she said happily. "And I hear that Henneker's won as well, so that now they are second to us in the league table."

"They'll never get any higher than that," declared Dick Trueman stoutly.

The team formed out of sheer spite by Peter Henneker was indeed a strong one, and they were running Bessie Booth's eleven very close for championship honours.

"Well, reckon Ah must be getting along," said Ned Bromley, scrambling to his feet. "Got an appointment down the town. So-long, Bess. So-long, Dick, lad."

Bessie Booth and Dick Trueman made an ideal, well-matched couple as they left the football field and passed through

Further conversation was stopped by the opening of the pavilion door and the appearance of Bessie Booth herself, looking more charming than ever in a neat tweed coat and skirt and green tammy

the mill yard. The mill itself was empty and silent till the following Monday morning, but Bessie unlocked the door leading into the general office, and looked into the letter box to see if there was any post.

There was only one letter, and as the girl ripped the envelope open her cheeks paled and she uttered a little cry of dismay.

Dick Trueman's arm was around her shoulders in an instant.

"Why, Bessie, dear, what's the matter?" he asked anxiously.

"This letter," replied the girl, nervously. "See, it's from Mr Chaddon, poor Mr Browell's lawyer, and it begins 'Dear Miss Booth, I have heard from young Mr Browell'......oh I daren't read it!"

There was a strange expression on Dick Trueman's face as he stood by his sweetheart's side. He knew exactly the reason for Bessie Booth's alarm and agitation. He knew that any arrangement made between Bess and the old Josh Browell was not in writing, and Mr Chaddon the lawyer had as good as told her that she would probably have to give up possession as soon as young Mr Browell put in an appearance to claim his inheritance.

"Oh, Dick, what shall we do?" she faltered.

Dick Trueman did an extraordinary thing. He grinned slyly behind his sweetheart's back, and deliberately winked at the tall chimney stack that towered over the Bee-Hive Mill.

"I suggest you read Mr Chaddon's letter before you do anything else," he said encouragingly. "It may not be bad news after all. Here, let me read it for you. 'Dear Miss Booth, I have heard from young Mr Browell, my late client's only son, and heir to all his property, and am more than delighted to tell you that he is perfectly agreeable for you to continue your tenancy of his mill on the same terms as those agreed with his late father.....'"

Bessie Booth's cheeks were flaming, and her eyes blazing with excitement as she snatched the letter out of Dick's hand.

"Dick, I can't believe it!" she exclaimed. "You're joking! It's cruel of you....oh!"

With her own eyes the girl read the lawyer's type-written screed, and a sob of joy welled up in her throat.

"Oh Dick...Dick! Isn't it wonderful?" she half sobbed. "Young Mr Browell says we can have the mill for as long as we want, and on the same terms. And I thought he'd want to turn us out."

"What, after he'd seen you?" smiled Dick Trueman.

"But he hasn't seen me," cried Bessie Booth. "How I wish I could see him to thank him. The dear.....I feel I could kiss him."

"Look here, if there's any kissing to be done there's only one person in it," declared Dick with assumed indignation. "And that's me."

Bessie rested her tiny hands on his broad shoulders, raised herself on tiptoe and offered him her fresh young lips.

She did not dream that she was kissing Richard Trueman Browell, only son of the late Joshua Browell, and owner of the Bee-Hive Mill!

And Dick winked again at the chimney stack as he gathered the girl in his arms. The time was not yet ripe for him to admit his true identity to Bessie Booth, and explain the reason for him having kept it a secret up to now!

Dick in Trouble

Henneker's Crusaders had been playing at home against Rigan Rovers on the same afternoon as the Busy Bees had met Hitchdale Villa. Peter Henneker himself had no interest whatever in football, but he was present at the match and saw his team win, for if he could not damage Bessie Booth in any other way, he knew that it would be a bitter disappointment to her if he could prevent the Busy Bees from carrying off the league championship.

The success of the Bee-Hive Mill spelt Henneker's ruin. His own mill was losing money hand over fist, and it was only a matter of a few weeks before he would be compelled to admit defeat and close down his business.

Having been sent away from his meeting in Liverpool, Henneker knew he had only one hope left.

Henneker's manager, Smith, had been watching the game with his boss and now turned to him as they left the ground.

"Henneker, my friend, you have been a fool," said John Smith stolidly. "All this trouble could have been avoided. The worst day's work you ever did was when you forbade Bessie Booth and her friends to play football."

"Confound it, don't I know it!" snarled the mill owner. "But who would have thought things would have worked out as they have done? That girl has the luck of the devil."

The two men passed through the yard into the mill and Henneker made his way straight to his outer office. There a clerk approached him carrying a yellow envelope.

"A cablegram for you, sir," he said. "It came just after you left this morning."

Peter Henneker snatched at the missive with a hoarse cry of excitement.

"From America!" he exclaimed. "Then it must be from Carl Hart, my New York agent, who has been searching for young Browell. Perhaps he has found him? Quick, Smith. The code book."

Henneker sat down at his desk and spread the flimsy sheet of paper out in front of him. As he swiftly decoded the cable a growing look of utter amazement took shape on his sallow face.

"By heavens, Smith, listen to this," he gasped at length. "This is what Hart says – 'Have traced your man. Richard T Browell is the president of the Top Notch Cotton Company. He sailed for England three weeks ago to open an office in Liverpool. Instruct me further.'"

For a long minute the rascally mill owner and his manager stared blankly at one another! Old Josh Browell's son, owner of the Bee-Hive Mill, was supplying Bessie Booth with all her raw material.

"Thunder and Lightning!" Peter Henneker exploded at length. "No wonder that confounded girl's order was accepted! This is the last straw, Smith!"

"But where is young Browell?" rasped John Smith excitedly. "He must have landed in England a fortnight ago. Why hasn't he shown himself in Blacktown, to claim his inheritance?"

"Ada Miller to see you, sir," announced a clerk who had knocked at the door, and admitted the thin girl with peculiar green eyes, a shawl wrapped around her head.

"Gaffer, I've got some news for you," she said in a low, tense voice. "Ah've found something out, something that'll interest you. You know Bessie Booth's new business manager, him as calls himself Dick Trueman?"

"Know him...of course I know him, the....the hound," snarled Henneker, with vivid memories of the punch on the nose from Trueman for insulting Bessie Booth. "What of him? Quick, I'm busy."

"You've got to to listen to what Ah've got to tell you," declared Ada Miller. "Ah've always been suspicious of young Trueman, and this morning, when he hung his coat up in the cloakroom, I went through his pockets and I found this."

She produced what looked like a flat wallet from beneath her shawl, and smacked it down in front of Peter Henneker. It was no wallet, as Henneker soon found when he examined it. It was a passport, issued to one Richard T Browell, traveller from New York to Liverpool.

"Great Scott, young Browell's passport," gasped Peter Henneker amazedly. "How did it come into that cub of a manager's possession?"

Then he happened to glance at the photograph affixed to the passport, and a great light of understanding burst upon him! The photograph was that of Dick Trueman....he and Richard T. Browell were one and the same!

"Here, take this, clear out and keep your mouth shut," bade Henneker suddenly, taking some notes from his desk and handling them to his girl-spy. "You have done very well."

Ada Miller tucked the money away inside her shawl and hurried out of the room. John Smith stretched out his short, podgy legs and glanced curiously at his companion.

"Well, this is the end, Henneker," he said grimly. "You might as well throw up the sponge now as any other time. You're beaten."

"Beaten, by heaven, I'm not beaten yet!" snarled the mill owner, waving his clenched fists above his head. "There's still one chance left, and I mean to take it."

"And what is that?"

"I mean to buy the Bee-Hive Mill from Richard Browell," declared Peter Henneker. "If he won't sell willingly, I shall use means to make him sell! This is no time for half measures, Smith. It must be one thing or the other."

John Smith repressed a little shudder. There was a light in Peter Henneker's eyes that was not good to see.

Good News

Meanwhile, across the town, The Bee-Hive Mill, big and square with many windows, was silent and deserted. But it was Saturday evening, and the little town was a bustle of busy shoppers and chattering throngs of workers and operatives who were out to enjoy themselves after a hard day's work. There was little enjoyment to be found in Blacktown, save a third-rate music hall and two cinemas, and all were well patronised, as were the noisy little trams that bore courting couples out to the open country that lay beyond the outskirts of the town.

But though the Bee-Hive Mill stood silent and deserted, with motionless engines and looms, there was plenty of life and jollity to be found in the cosy little club-house attached to the football ground at the back of the mill.

The Busy Bees – having won their home match that afternoon – were now entertaining their vanquished opponents to a substantial tea before they piled into the motor char-a-banc that was waiting outside to drive them back to the neighbouring town of Hitchdale.

Even though Hitchdale had been narrowly beaten by three goals to two, it had been a close game, and they took their defeat all in good part.

"Girls," cried Jenny Shields, the flaxen-haired captain of the visiting eleven, rising to her feet with a cup of tea in one hand and a slice of cake in the other. "Ah propose the health of Bessie Booth and the Busy Bees. They gave us a good licking, but they've given us a rare tuck-in as well. Here's to the next time we meet, and may we treat them the same as they've treated us.....licking, tea and all!"

A chorus of laughter greeted this brief speech, and Bessie Booth jumped up from her chair, her pretty face flushed and her big brown eyes sparkling like twin stars.

"Bees, I give you the Villa," she smiled. "A rattling good team, and sports every one of them. All I can say is that it's a pity we can't both win.....but just the same we're coming over to Hitchdale next Saturday to take another two points off you!"

"Hear, hear!" cried Mary Bonny the centre-back. "As you say, Bess, we can't both win, so here's luck to all of us."

The toast was drunk enthusiastically, and a few minutes later the smiling girl footballers from Hitchdale donned their hats and coats, and picking up their kit-bags, streamed out to the waiting char-a-banc. Waving and cheering they went bowling away down the hill, and Bessie Booth and her companions turned back into the club-house.

"Don't hurry off for a moment, girls," standing at the head of the long table with a mysterious smile playing around the corners of her pretty mouth. "I've got something to tell you all.....a piece of news that you'll be glad to hear."

There was an instant silence, and every eye was fixed eagerly on Bess.

"What's that you say, Bess.....you've got some good news for us?" asked Mary Bonny. "You don't mean to say Peter Henneker's thrown in the towel and cleared out of Blacktown? That's the best news Ah can think of."

Bess smiled and shook her curly head.

"No, but I don't think it will be long before he does," she replied with meaning. "I've had a letter from Mr Chaddon, the lawyer, and he tells me that he has received a communication from young Mr Browell."

A gasp of surprise burst from the little group of mill girls and they stared at each other in dismay. So Richard Browell had finally come back to claim his inheritance. And now, according to Bessie's announcement, it appears that the long-expected notice to quit had arrived! But Bessie was smiling happily, and it was good news that she had promised them.

"Cheer up girls," she said reassuringly. "I know what you're thinking, and it's the same as I thought at first. But the lawyer states that he has heard from his client and he is quite agreeable for us to continue our tenancy of the mill on the same terms as agreed by his late father. And......"

But the remainder of Bessie Booth's words were drowned in a tremendous outburst of cheering that threatened to lift the roof off the club-house and into the air.

"Hooray! Three cheers for young Mr Browell!" roared Mary Bonny, cavorting wildly amid the cups and saucers. "He's a great sport, like his old dad was before him."

"Girls, this means we've got Peter Henneker beaten," cried Sally Soper, as soon as the pandemonium of excitement had died down.

"Henneker won't give in until he's absolutely compelled to," vowed Bessie. "He'll last the football season out if only in the hope that his team'll top the league."

The pretty captain of the Bees started as she glanced at the strap-watch on her wrist, and hurriedly commenced to put on her coat and hat.

"I must be slipping off. I didn't know it was so late," she said a trifle lamely. I've got...."

"Ay, don't miss your appointment, Bess," said Mary Bonny with a sly wink at her companion. "It wouldn't do to keep young Trueman waiting.....not that he wouldn't wait all night for you!"

Bess flushed up to the roots of her curly hair as she scampered out of the club-house. Bessie had suspected for some time that her girl chums had guessed her secret – that she and the young business manager of the Bee-Hive Mill were in love with each other.

Bessie glanced at her watch again as she hurried down the hill into the town. She had promised to meet her sweetheart at half-past seven outside the Royal Cinema in the High Street, and it was then just on time.

But though she was a couple of minutes late, Dick Trueman was still later, for there was no sign of the upright figure when she arrived at her tryst. There were plenty of other people streaming into the picture palace, and many a cheery greeting was flung to the pretty girl as she stood in the brilliantly lit entrance.

Bessie tapped her foot impatiently on the ground, and frowned as she glanced at her watch again. Ten minutes to eight, and still Dick had not put in an appearance. It was not like him...he was usually punctual to the moment. In fact, he had always been there waiting when she had arrived.

Vague doubts crept into the girl's mind as a neighbouring clock boomed out the hour of eight. But she was more annoyed than alarmed at her sweetheart's prolonged absence. Perhaps now that he had won her love some of the glamour of courtship had faded. He was not so eager to make the most of every minute of the time he could spend in her company.

A quarter past eight. With a little sigh of disappointment Bessie bought her ticket and passed into the cinema.

"You know Mr Trueman," she said with a slight flush to the commissionaire who stood at the door. "If you see him will you please tell him that I am inside?"

"Ay, that Ah will, lass," he replied heartily. "And Ah'll give 'im a piece of my mind for keeping you waiting."

The pictures held no interest for Bessie Booth that night. There were tears of disappointment in her brown eyes as she sat staring listlessly at the flickering silver screen. It was the first time that Dick had failed her.

Nine o'clock......ten o'clock.......half past ten came, but no Dick Trueman. The lights flashed up, and the people commenced to file out into the street, and with them went Bessie Booth, feeling sick at heart and strangely sad as she hurried home with one burning question on her mind.

Why had Dick Trueman failed to keep his promise?

Dick Browell whistled cheerily as he shaved, changed his clothes and donned his hat and coat. He was to meet Bessie Booth seven-thirty to take her to one of the local picture palaces, and the young man had made up his mind to tell her who he really was.

It was dark when Dick Browell left the house where he lodged, and a grey mist hung over the town. Even as he turned towards the High Street a voice called him, and someone beckoned from a closed car that was drawn up alongside the kerb.

"Excuse me.......you Mr Trueman?" said a gruff voice from the interior of the motor. "You know me, don't you?"

Quite unsuspecting Dick approached the stationary vehicle and peered through the open window. Instantly some blunt instrument descended upon his head with crushing force, his heels were whipped up from behind, and he was thrown roughly into the waiting car.

"Got him!" muttered Peter Henneker evilly as he bent over his helpless captive, and signalled to the chauffeur to drive on. "Now, Mr Richard Browell, there's to be a reckoning between you and I, and if you don't choose to consent to my terms, Heaven help you!"

At this point it was half past seven and Bessie Booth was waiting outside the Royal Cinema in the High Street – waiting anxiously for the man she loved. But she was destined to wait in vain, for Dick Browell was not to keep his appointment that night!

Henneker's Revenge

Henneker's Mill was enshrouded in darkness, but behind the closely-drawn blinds a light was burning in the mill-owner's private office.

Peter Henneker himself was striding restlessly up and down the floor, his hands clasped behind his back and a gloating expression of triumph on his sallow countenance. But he was not alone. John Smith, his manager, square-headed with a fleshy nose, watched Henneker with short-sighted eyes bulging behind thick-lensed spectacles.

The third man sat huddled in a chair to which he was tightly lashed with stout cords, which rendered it impossible for him to move as much as a finger. But he was not capable of attempting to move at that moment. His head lolled back limply on his shoulders, his eyes were closed, and his handsome, clean-cut face was deathly white.

Peter Henneker halted in his restless pacing and glowered down at the helpless figure.

A fluttering sigh escaped Dick Browell's lips, a tinge of colour crept back into his pallid cheeks and he opened his eyes.

For a moment he stared dazedly at his surroundings, at Peter Henneker and the other man who stood leering down at him.

"What.....what does this mean? Where am I?" he gasped, attempting to sit up, only to fall back with a wince of pain. "Henneker, you villain, what foul game is this?"

Peter Henneker folded his arms and sneered as Dick's memory of his abduction in the car came flooding back to him, right up to the sickening dizziness he still felt from the blow that had struck him down.

"What's the meaning of this, you scoundrel?" he demanded fiercely, straining helplessly at the cords that pinioned him. "I knew you for a villain, Henneker, but I never thought you were such a fool as to resort to this kind of thing."

"A fool! We shall soon see who is a fool, my friend," sneered the mill-owner. "I've got you where I want you now, Mr Richard......Browell!"

Dick gave a violent start of surprise and his face hardened.

"Ah, so you've found out who I am," he said quietly.

"Yes, I've found out who you are," snarled Henneker with a sudden burst of fury. "You're Richard Browell, old Josh Browell's son and the real owner of the Bee-Hive Mill. Now I know who has been bolstering up that brat of a girl, Bessie Booth. Now I know where she gets all her supplies of cotton. You dog, but for you I should have crushed her and driven her out of Blacktown long ago."

"And, as it is, you're the one to be crushed and kicked out," said Dick.

Peter Henneker uttered a violent oath, and struck the helpless man savagely across the face. Dick Browell's eyes gleamed like chilled steel as he tasted the blood on his lip.

"You spineless dog!" he said hoarsely. "I'll make you pay for that blow one of these days. Like all of your kind, you're a coward and a bully at heart!"

"Hold your tongue, curse you!" rasped Henneker in a growing rage. "I'm in no mood to brook any impudence from you. You're in my power, and you don't leave this place until you've done as I wish."

"And what might that be," said Dick defiantly.

Henneker ground his teeth and the veins bulged on his sallow forehead.

"You don't leave this place," he said grimly, "until you've sold the Bee-Hive Mill to me, lock, stock and barrel and given me a receipt for it."

Dick Browell stared amazedly at the man, staggered by his cool effrontery.

"You're mad," he said shortly. "I wouldn't sell you the mill for a thousand pounds."

"You'll sell me the mill for just eight thousand pounds," said Henneker softly. "I'm a desperate man, Browell, and I'll stop at nothing to get hold of that mill. You don't seem to realise your position. You are my prisoner for as long as I choose to keep you, and no one will have the vaguest idea what has become of you. They may search and search, but they will never find you....and they would never think of searching here. And even if they did they would not find you. There on the table is a written-out agreement for the sale of the Bee-Hive Mill from you to me for the sum of eight thousand pounds, which I am willing to pay you. There is pen and ink. All you have to do is to sign. If you won't sign willingly I will find other ways of making you do so."

"Why, my dear fellow, you must be as mad as a hatter," jerked Dick Browell scornfully. "If I signed that agreement under compulsion it wouldn't be worth the paper it is written on."

"Ah!" leered Henneker cunningly. "But I should require you to sign another little document to the effect that you were a willing agent in the sale of the mill, and guaranteeing that you would take no action against me in any shape or form to contest my claim to it."

"Well, you might just as well tear that agreement up now and stuff it in the fire," said Dick Browell emphatically. "I wouldn't sign it if you kept me here for the rest of my life."

John Smith shook his big head as if to say 'I told you so'. In vain Peter Henneker ranted and raved, stormed, threatened and cajoled. Dick Browell was adamant.

"You've had my answer," he declared, "and that's the only one you'll get."

"Very well. We'll see if you'll have altered your mind in another twenty-four hours," snarled Henneker, his face black with baffled rage. He thumped heavily on the floor with his heel and the door opened to admit two roughly dressed hang-dog looking ruffians whom, to the best of his knowledge, Dick Browell had never set eyes on before.

"Take this stubborn dog away," ordered Henneker. "You know where to put him, and see that he doesn't escape. Bread and water and nothing else. See if that'll bring him to his senses."

Without question the two men lifted Dick Browell, chair and all, and carried him out of the room. The door closed and John Smith stared at his employer with a shrug of his heavy shoulders.

"I knew he wouldn't sign," he grunted. "I know the type....stubborn as a pig. You're wasting your time, Henneker. You'll never get him to give in to you."

"I can force him to....through somebody else," persisted Henneker. "Do you think Browell would refuse to sign if it came to a question of protecting, not himself, but......Bessie Booth?"

John Smith started, and his eyes glinted behind his thick spectacles.

"Heavens, you're a cunning dog, Henneker!" he said with grudging admiration. "What, would you kidnap the girl as well, and use her as a lever to force young Browell to give in to you?"

"No, I would not kidnap the girl," declared Henneker with a sly smile. "I have got a better plan than that, a much safer plan. Listen, Smith, and I will tell you how Bessie Booth will deliver herself into my hands."

Ned Bromley made his usual morning tour of the spinning-rooms, and clattered down the stone steps to the ground floor. The big-hearted overlooker of the mill squared his big broad shoulders, knocked gently on the door of the general office, and stepped inside. Then he froze on the threshold with a little gasp of alarmed surprise.

Bessie Booth was alone in the big room. She sat at her desk, with her face hidden on her crossed arms, and her slender shoulders heaving conspicuously.

"Why, Bess lass, what's the matter?" cried Ned, running across to the girl's side. "Damn me, you're crying! Lass.... lass, what is it?"

Bessie lifted her tear-stained face with a wan, pathetic attempt at a smile.

"Oh, Ned, it's Dick....Dick Trueman!" she said brokenly. "I can't understand......I don't know what's happened to him!"

"Happened to him?" echoed Ned Bromley, glaring around the office."Why...where is he?"

"That's just it......I don't know, Ned. He's not here. I haven't seen him since Saturday afternoon, after the match. He promised to meet me in the evening, but he never turned up. And on Sunday he never came round, and now today he hasn't come to the office."

"He may be ill in bed," said Ned, soothingly. Don't worry, lass, I'll run down to his lodgings and see if there's anything wrong."

Ned Bromley hurried away out of the office, and Bessie Booth wiped her eyes and strove to allay her vague fears. What could have happened to her sweetheart? Even if he was ill, why had he sent her no word?

Half an hour later Ned returned, a puzzled look in his blue eyes.

"Bess, lass, there's something funny here," he said gently. "Ah went to Dick's lodgings and his landlady said that he went out at seven o'clock on Saturday evening, an' she hasn't seen him since."

Bessie Booth uttered a low cry of dismay, and the tears started afresh in her eyes.

"Maybe he's gone to Liverpool to see about more cotton?" suggested the overlooker. He did say as he'd be going one day this week. Ah'm not believing anything's happened to him. Ah know Dick. He can look after himself."

But the hours dragged along, and there was no sign of the missing manager, or no word from him. It was the most miserable day Bessie Booth had ever spent, and when the evening came and the engines ceased their roar, she was one of the first to don her coat and hat and creep away home, white-faced and sick at heart.

As she opened the door the first thing she saw was a letter lying on the mat.

There was nothing inside save a soiled scrap of paper, and on this was written the following brief, bewildering sentence – '*Richard Trueman is a prisoner at Henneker's Mill*'.

Bessie Booth sank into a chair, her heart throbbing till it almost seemed to suffocate her. Could it be true.....Dick, a prisoner at Henneker's Mill?

Bessie's first idea was to fly to the police with the mysterious message, but she soon abandoned that. She knew she would only be laughed at. It was not even yet established that Dick Trueman *had* vanished.

But the more she thought about it the more convinced Bessie grew, that in some way or other Henneker was connected with her sweetheart's disappearance, and a bold, reckless idea gradually took shape in her mind.

She would find out for herself if there was any truth in the mysterious message.

It was just on eleven o'clock when Bessie wrapped a shawl around her head and shoulders, and slipped out of the house. Her aunt was long since in bed and asleep, and the streets of Blacktown were practically deserted.

Having worked at Henneker's, Bessie knew every inch of the place, and she had no difficulty in scaling the wall at the back of the mill and dropping down into the stone-cobbled yard. Like a shadow she slipped across to the main building, and here again her previous experience of the place served her in good stead. She knew that one of the windows leading into the general office had a faulty catch, and in a trice she had scrambled up on to the broad sill. With a narrow screw-driver she had brought with her she easily succeeded in forcing the catch, and cautiously pushed up the window.

The next instant she had wriggled over into the darkness beyond, and closed the window again behind her. For a moment the girl stood mentally locating her exact position, and then without warning every light in the room was suddenly

Dazed and dismayed, Bessie Booth
shrank back

switched on, and she found herself confronted by Peter Henneker and his manager, John Smith.

Together they stood, three or four yards away, Henneker with a revolver clenched in his right hand.

"Ah, I thought so!" rasped the mill-owner. "A burglar! I told you I heard a noise, Smith. Hands up my man, you're.....why it's a woman! Good heavens it's the Booth girl!"

Dazed and dismayed Bessie Booth shrank back, her hands clutching at her quickly beating heart, her face pale as a ghost. Instinctively she realised she was in a very awkward position, and that Peter Henneker would not fail to make the most of it.

"Ho, ho, Miss Bessie Booth! So this is your latest game is it?" cried the mill-owner. "Burglary, eh, Smith? There's a police-whistle in my desk. Go outside and blow it."

A moment later a shrill blast split the night air, and in surprisingly quick time John Smith returned, accompanied by a blue-uniformed constable.

"Officer, we caught this woman breaking into these premises," said Henneker grimly. "Take her away. I'll come down to the station and charge her."

Bessie shivered as the constable laid a heavy hand on her shoulder. She realised it was useless saying anything at the moment. Appearances were against her.

With a sob in her throat she turned away and walked steadily out of the room by the policeman's side.

"Trapped! Trapped her like a rat!" hissed Henneker gleefully, rubbing his lean, yellow hands together. "I knew she'd bite, Smith. I knew she'd fall for that note. And now I've got the hussy where I want her. Wait till I show Richard Browell the report in the paper of his sweetheart's arrest on a charge of attempted burglary."

"What good will that do?" asked Smith stolidly

"Do?" echoed Henneker. "When I tell him I'll only withdraw the charge on condition that he signs the agreement to sell me the Bee-Hive Mill, I'm willing to wager you a hundred to one that he signs. The mill is as good as mine. We've saved ourselves at the eleventh hour."

John Smith glanced admiringly at his employer. With Bessie Booth under arrest on a serious charge on which she seemed bound to be convicted, and Richard Browell helpless in their clutches, it certainly seemed that Henneker's triumph was complete.

At the Court

Bessie Booth arrested for breaking into Peter Henneker's Mill!

Scarcely had the dawn broken than the staggering news commenced to run through Blacktown like wildfire, creating such a sensation as had never been known before in the little Lancashire mill-town. Amazed, incredulous people stood around in the narrow streets discussing it instead of going straight on to their work at the looms.

Anger succeeded amazement. Faces grew heated and voices shrill with indignation, for Bessie Booth was the most popular girl in Blacktown, loved and respected by all.

And now she was in the custody of the police, charged with having broken into the mill of Peter Henneker, her rival and deadly enemy.

Ned Bromley heard the news when the knocker-up came along to wake him in the morning. He rapped vigorously on the window with the long pole he carried, and instead of passing on as usual, rapped again and again.

Ned scrambled out of bed and poked his head out of the window.

"What's the matter with you, Tom?" he demanded drowsily. "D'you think I'm deaf that I can't hear you?"

"Ned, lad, Ah've got some bad news for you," cried the knocker-up. "The police 'ave taken our Bess. She's been arrested for breaking into Henneker's Mill."

Ned Bromley positively staggered, and nearly pitched headfirst through the window.

"Damn it, Tom, are you mad!" he gasped. "What fool's yarn is this?"

"It's true," vowed the knocker-up. "Ah got it from Sergeant Brown himself. He says they caught Bess in the act and she's being brought up before the magistrate this morning."

Ned's head was in a whirl and he scarcely knew whether he was standing on his head or his heels as he flung on his clothes, and without waiting for any breakfast dashed out into the street. Instead of making for the mill as his duty demanded he hurried straight to the police station, and the moment he turned the corner he realised that the alarming news must be true.

The narrow street was packed chock-a-block with a murmuring, jostling crowd of mill-operatives – men, women, lads and girls. A policeman stood at the top of the station steps haranguing them not unkindly, and evidently trying to persuade them to disperse.

"Where's our Bess? We want our Bess!" they chanted.

"It's a damn put-up job. Henneker's at the bottom of this," cried one.

"Bess has done nothing. Let her go!" called another.

Ned Bromley had no sooner turned the corner than half a dozen mill-girls with clogs on their feet and shawls on their heads made a rush at him. They were all members of the Busy Bees Football Club – Sally Soper, the goalkeeper; Mary Bonny, the centre-half; Amy Olroyd and Enid Foster, the full-backs; and Connie Tree, the slender outside-right.

"Oh, Ned. 'ave you heard what they've done with our Bess?" cried Sally Soper tearfully. "The police 'ave got 'er. They've locked 'er up in a cell and won't let her go."

"By gum. This is more of Peter Henneker's dirty work," roared Mary Bonny, her red hair literally bristling. "Wait till Ah see 'im. Ah'll ring 'is neck for 'im."

"Steady on, lasses, steady on," said Ned Bromley soothingly. "Kicking up a rumpus won't do no good. Let's hear the whole yarn. Of course, there's a mistake somewhere, and the police will find it out."

It was Ned Bromley who forced himself through the angry, indignant crowd and approached the constable who stood in the entrance to the police station.

"What's all this, Jack Snelling? Is it true you've got our poor Bess in there?"

"Ay, it's true, Ned," replied the policeman gruffly. "But it's nothing to do with us. We can't help it. We had to take the charge, and as it was a serious one, we had to keep the lass here."

"And who charged her?" demanded Ned, his eyes flashing.

"Peter Henneker himself. And the charge is all right, Ned. Ah can't tell you anything about it. Best wait till the charge is brought up at the court at ten o'clock, and you'll hear everything."

Ned clenched his great fists, and his rugged features were set and grim. His heart bled at the thought of Bessie Booth confined in a cold, lonely police-cell. He worshipped the very ground the pretty girl walked on but as he knew he could never be anything more to her than a friend he meant to fulfil every duty that true friendship entailed.

"Peter Henneker!" he muttered under his breath. "So he charged her, the skunk. There's foul play here. Ah'll stake my life on it!"

It was common knowledge that Peter Henneker was on the verge of ruin......and now Bessie Booth was under arrest on a charge of felony, and Henneker was the man who had charged her!"

"By gum, there's dirty work 'ere," muttered Ned huskily, as he turned away from the police station. "It's a false charge....it must be a false charge, and Ah'll see that Henneker suffers for it!"

He made his way to where the group of girl footballers stood talking anxiously amongst themselves.

"You'll do no good standing here, girls," he said kindly. "Best thing you can do is go up to the mill and get on with your work, for there's work got to be done. Reckon that's as Bess'd want it."

"Ay, but we can't leave Bess in the lurch," cried Sally Soper, dabbing her tear-stained eyes.

"We shan't be leaving Bess in the lurch," said Ned. "Ah'll see to 'er. You leave it to me. Ah shall be in court when the case comes in."

It was sound advice, and with considerable reluctance the little band of girl footballers drifted away towards the Bee-Hive Mill. As Ned Bromley had said, there was work to be done, and they would only make things worse for Bessie Booth by neglecting it.

The next two hours were a nerve-racking ordeal for Ned Bromley. The suspense and uncertainty were almost more than he could bear, and a vision of Bessie Booth, desolate, miserable and worried was continually before him.

He repaired to a local coffee-shop for some breakfast, but he couldn't eat anything. The food seemed to choke him.

"If only Dick Trueman was here," he muttered gloomily.

Long before the opening of the police-court there was a big crowd assembled outside, but way was made willingly for Ned Bromley to force himself to the front. He was the first in when the doors opened and got a position of vantage at the front of the public seats.

A moment later everyone rose with a scraping of feet as the magistrate entered and took his place at the bench.

The first case was one of street-betting and was soon disposed of, and then a tense hush fell over the court as a door was flung open and Bessie Booth stepped into view.

The girl's pretty face was pale, but her brown eyes were shining and she carried her trim figure proudly and confidently as she stepped up into the dock and flashed a quick, eager glance around the big room.

A sympathetic murmur swelled to an enthusiastic cheer.

"Silence in court!" rapped the magistrate sternly.

The charge was read out, that of 'forcing a way into the premises of Mr Peter Henneker with intent to steal', and the usual question put to the pretty girl in the ugly dock.

"Not guilty!" replied Bessie Booth in a firm, ringing voice.

A police constable immediately stepped into the witness-box and gave evidence of the arrest.

"Do you wish to ask the officer any questions?" queried the magistrate, peering over the top of his glasses.

"No, sir," replied Bessie Booth quietly.

"Where is the prosecutor?"

There was a rustle, a drawing of many breaths as Peter Henneker rose to his feet in the well of the court.

"I am here to charge this woman in the dock of breaking into my premises with intent to commit a felony," he said harshly, and Ned Bromley clenched his fists and bit his lower lip. "I and my manager, Mr Smith, were working late at the mill last night," continued Peter Henneker. "We were in the inner-office, and just about eleven o'clock I heard a slight noise in the adjoining room. I thought it sounded like a window being pushed open and, switching off the lights, I opened the communicating doors. Then I switched on the lights again and discovered the prisoner standing in the room, the window open behind her. I summoned a policeman and gave her in charge."

A gasp ran through the crowded court, and the people in the public seats stared wonderingly at one another. Things were beginning to look black against the pretty, pale-faced girl in the dock.

Henneker's manager, John Smith, was the next to step into the witness-box. He corroborated his employer's evidence in every detail, and stepped down with a smug smile of satisfaction.

"Do you wish to question the two witnesses?" asked the magistrate smoothly.

"No," replied Bessie Booth scornfully. "But I should like to speak a few words on my own behalf, sir. I have pleaded 'not guilty' to breaking into Henneker's Mill with a felonious intent, but I admit that I was caught on his premises."

Again a gasp of amazement, and the magistrate and the magistrate raised his eyebrows in surprise.

"Do you wish to go into the witness-box and give evidence?" he asked.

"Yes," said Bessie.

"I broke into the mill, said Bessie Booth, when she had taken her place," because I had reason to believe my manager, Mr Richard Trueman, was being forcibly detained there by Peter Henneker."

There was now quite a sensation in court.

"That is a startling statement to make, Miss Booth," said the magistrate gravely. "Perhaps you would be a little more explicit. Remember, this is your defence to a serious charge."

"Mr Trueman has been missing since last Saturday," said Bessie Booth, and her voice broke a trifle. "And....."

"Did you report his disappearance to the police?"

"No, I thought he might turn up at any moment. But yesterday I received a message informing me that he was a prisoner in Henneker's Mill. I decided to go and find out the truth for myself. This is how I came to be caught."

"And, by gum, that's the truth," declared Ned Bromley loudly.

The magistrate flashed an angry glance in his direction.

"Where is the message you received?"

Bessie Booth passed a slip of paper up to the bench, and the magistrate raised his eyebrows again as he glanced at it.

"Hmmph, anonymous!" he said shortly. "And why should you be so quick to believe that Mr Henneker was forcibly detaining your manager at his mill?"

"Because he has threatened time and time again to ruin me and the Bee-Hive Mill," said Bessie boldly.

A roar of approval went up, which was instantly checked by the clerk of the court.

"Who is this Richard Trueman?" asked the clerk of the court.

"He is my business-manager"

"Where does he live....where does he come from?"

"He lives here in Blacktown, but I don't know where he originally came from. He applied to me for a situation one day and I engaged him."

"What references did he supply?"

Bessie Booth flushed.

"I did not ask for any references," she said in a low voice.

"Did any money from your mill pass through your manager's hands, Miss Booth?" he asked.

A flame of crimson flashed up into Bessie Booth's cheeks, and her brown eyes flashed fire as she drew herself up in the box.

"You are suggesting that Mr Trueman has absconded....and that he is an embezzler!" she cried indignantly. "I should like to inform you that not a penny-piece is missing from the mill. In fact, it is the other way round.....there is a week's wages owing to Mr Trueman. Dick Trueman is as straight as a die. I would trust him with my life. In fact, I intend to do so....we are engaged to be married."

A roar of delight burst from the irrepressible public at these strong words, and Peter Henneker scowled savagely.

"All this is beside the point," said the magistrate. "On the evidence I have no option but to remand the prisoner for a week."

Bessie Booth clutched convulsively at the edge of the box.

"The question of....bail?" she faltered.

The magistrate hesitated and glanced at his clerk.

"I think so, sir," whispered the latter. "This girl is very well known and very popular in Blacktown. I fear there will be a very strong public protest unless you grant bail."

"Very well," said the magistrate, and bail was allowed.

Bessie managed to stammer a few broken words of thanks to the people who staunchly supported her, and it was Ned who eventually managed to get her away from the well-meaning crowd and up the hill to the Bee-Hive Mill.

There, roars of cheering greeted her appearance, and the delighted girl footballers swarmed around her in the true manner of their team's name.

Top Dog

Once in the office alone with Ned Bromley, Mary Bonny and Sally Soper, Bess sank into a chair with a grave expression on her pale face. She flashed a quick glance round the room.

"No....no news of Dick....Mr Trueman yet?"

Tears sprang to Bessie's eyes as she spoke, but she dashed them away quickly as there came a solid knock on the door and an elderly, white-haired man in a black frock coat and top hat entered the office.

"I hope I'm not disturbing you, Miss Booth," said Mr Chaddon, solicitor to the Browell family. "I have just heard that you have been in trouble with Peter Henneker," said the old solicitor. "If there is anything I can do for you, you only have to command me, Miss Booth. As a solicitor I might be able to be of some service to you. What is all this talk about you having been arrested?"

Briefly, the pretty mill-girl related exactly what had happened, and as he listened the solicitor suddenly caught his breath sharply, and an anxious expression crept into his cold, grey eyes.

"What? Your manager, Mr Trueman, has disappeared?" he exclaimed. "You haven't seen him since last Saturday, and you suspect foul play?"

"I feel certain Peter Henneker knows what has become of Dick...Mr Trueman," replied Bess. "I know he hates him for the thrashing he gave him, and he would stop at nothing to injure me in any way he could."

There was a strange expression on the old man's withered face as he took his departure a few minutes later. He alone – as he supposed – knew the real identity of 'Dick Trueman', and now the young man had vanished. Had he gone away of his own free will, tired of Bessie Booth and the double part he had been playing? Or could it be that Peter Henneker had discovered the young man's true identity and kidnapped him to further his own ends and aid him to wreak his revenge on Bessie Booth?

Meanwhile Peter Henneker and his manager, John Smith, had left the police-court by a side door and stepped into the motor car that was waiting for them.

"By thunder, I'm top-dog now, Smith!" he chuckled as the car swirled up the hill towards his mill. "I've got that hussy of a girl where I want her this time. I told you my plan would succeed."

John Smith shrugged his shoulders and adjusted his thick-lensed spectacles on his fleshy nose.

"Yes. You certainly seem to hold the whip-hand now, Henneker," he said in his deep, guttural voice. "It rests with you whether the girl gets convicted or not. She can't get out of the net you've thrown around her."

Peter Henneker did but little work that day. He walked up and down his office, chuckling to himself, and gloating over the manner he had turned the tables on Bessie Booth. It was dusk before John Smith entered with a copy of the local paper which contained a verbatim report on the police-court proceedings of that morning.

An hour later, when the looms had ceased to roar and rattle and all the operatives had departed, Henneker tucked a couple of folded documents into his pocket and, accompanied by his manager, descended the iron staircase into the engine room. He walked right through to the farther end and lifted a heavy metal trapdoor set in the stone floor.

Cautiously he descended a narrow steel ladder and found himself in a low-ceilinged cellar that was cold and damp and mouldy, Switching on an electric torch he walked twenty paces to the right and halted, flashing a beam of light upon the figure of a man that lay huddled upon a couple of old sacks.

"Well, Mr Richard Browell. How do you find yourself today?" jeered Henneker.

"None the better for seeing you, you swine," replied Dick Browell, struggling to a sitting position. His wrists and ankles were tightly bound together, and he was chained to a stout staple embedded in the brick wall. He presented a sorry spectacle with his dishevelled clothes, tousled hair and unshaven face, but there was a defiant light in his blue eyes.

"I trust I find you in a more tractable frame of mind," went on Henneker. "Are you prepared now to sign these documents which make me the sole owner of the Bee-Hive Mill?"

"You had my answer last night," retorted Dick Browell. "And that is the only one you will get if you keep me here for the next ten years."

"I think not....I think not," chuckled Peter Henneker. "I fancy I have the means to make you alter your mind, my friend. Supposing you read that, and then we will re-open the discussion."

He spread out the copy of the local paper in front of the helpless prisoner's face, and there was a long, tense silence as Dick Browell ran his eyes over the printed report of the police-court proceedings against his sweetheart, Bessie Booth. Gradually, the colour drained from his cheeks and a hunted, dismayed look crept into his eyes.

Dick Trueman lay on the ground, his hands manacled, feet bound together and chained to the wall. His eyes wore a determined expression

"What you read there is perfectly true," chuckled Henneker. "Bessie Booth is in my power. I set a trap for her and she walked into it. How would you like to think of your sweetheart serving a sentence of three months for felony? And you are the only one who can save her, if you care for her, as she believes you do."

Dick Browell drew a deep breath.

"I? How can *I* save her?" he demanded firmly.

""By signing this document and giving me a receipt for the Bee-Hive Mill. Then, and only then, will I withdraw the charge against Bessie Booth."

"You cunning fiend!" muttered Dick Browell huskily. He hung his head for a moment and bit his lip till the blood came. Then he looked up with a resigned shrug of his shoulders.

"You win this time, Henneker," he said grimly. "Loosen my hand and give me a pen. I'll sign. The mill is yours."

Peter Henneker threw back his head with a sinister laugh of triumph and relief. He was saved, and the girls of the Bee-Hive Mill were ruined.

And the best part of his revenge was yet to come, when he should claim possession of the mill and turn Bessie Booth and the Busy Bees out into the street!

Henneker's Trump Card

"Bess, lass. Ah don't like to see you looking so white and peaky. You've got to book up, or you'll 'ave the whole crowd of us down in the dumps."

There was a keen note of anxiety in Ned Bromley's gruff voice as he stood in the centre of the general office of the Bee-Hive Mill and gazed down at the seated figure of Bessie Booth.

Bessie's pretty face was pale and wan, her eyes were heavy and tired-looking, and it was with a listless air that she was running through the pile of letters that lay on her desk. She looked up with a start when Ned spoke to her and summoned up a wan attempt at a smile.

"I'm quite all right, Ned," she said quickly, "just....just a bit of a headache, that's all."

Ned turned away with a sigh. He knew it was more heartache than headache that was troubling the pretty mill-girl, that had stolen all the roses from her cheeks and silenced the happy laugh that all had known so well.

Dick Trueman had now not been seen for nearly a week.

"Ah'm thinking," said Ned slowly, "that you'd best not play today, Bess. You don't look up to it."

Instantly Bessie Booth's back straightened and a flush of colour crept up into her cheeks. The Busy Bees were down to play an important league match on their home ground that afternoon, and it was all important they should win if they were to retain their proud position at the top of the league table.

"Not play?" echoed the girl indignantly. "Of course I'm going to play, Ned. I wouldn't miss today's match for anything!"

"That's better! I thought that would put some fire in you!" chuckled the big, bluff, kindly overlooker. "Of course you're going to play, lass. It'll do you good and take your mind off......off what you're worrying about. You mustn't worry. Worrying never did no one any good."

The big overlooker lumbered away to make one of his tours of the noisy, clattering spinning rooms, and Bessie Booth dropped her head dejectedly into her hands. It was all very well for Ned Bromley to say 'Don't worry', but how could she help worrying when the man she loved had utterly disappeared? They had parted on good terms the previous Saturday afternoon, and since then no one had set eyes on him, nor had he sent any word to account for his absence.

The tears sprang to Bessie's eyes as the amazing events of the last four or five months raced through her mind – the Busy Bees fighting for their right to play football, sacked by Henneker, given a chance by Old Josh Browell and starting up the Bee-Hive Mill, Henneker's attempts to ruin them, the success of the team and, finally, finding the love of her life in her new business manager, Dick Trueman. But this last thought only made her sigh deeply as she felt deep sorrow and despair at how it had all come to this.

She stared at the pile of letters on the desk before her, but that which she sought was not there. There was no word from Dick.

"Ada!" She steadied her voice and turned to a thin, pasty-faced girl who sat at the farther end of the office busily engaged in addressing envelopes. "Are you......are you sure these are all the letters that came this morning?"

Ada Miller raised her sly, green eyes and nodded her small head.

"Yes, that's every one Ah 'ave seen, Bess," she lied deliberately, and instinctively her hand closed over a crumpled envelope that lay tucked away in her pocket at that moment. It had come by that morning's post, and it was the very letter Bessie Booth had been expecting.....the letter that would have put all her doubts and fears at rest, and set her heart beating for joy.

In her capacity as spy for Peter Henneker, Ada Miller had deliberately withheld the letter. It was under his orders that she should look out for a letter in Dick Trueman's handwriting and intercept it so that it should not reach Bessie Booth.

Ada Miller had opened the letter to make certain it was the one she sought, and she knew every word of it by heart.

'Darling Bess' it read, ***'Don't worry, and don't pay any attention to anything that happens. Everything is all right, and I shall be with you in the next twenty-four hours. Explanations when I see you. All my love – Dick'***

"Huh, what wouldn't she give to have a look at this?" muttered Ada Miller maliciously, as she crumpled the piece of paper in her pocket and shot a sly glance across at Bessie Booth. "I wonder what Peter Henneker's game is? He's got something up his sleeve, an' he's going to produce it this afternoon by what he says."

At twelve o'clock the hooter blared out its welcome note, and the roar and clatter of the busy looms lapsed into silence. With a rattle of their clogs on the stone stairs the operatives came swarming down from the spinning-room and Bessie Booth closed her book and left the office.

The Busy Bees were in a high state of excitement, and all looking forward to the football match that was to be played that afternoon on the trim little ground at the back of the mill.

Holton Ramblers was the name of the visiting team, and the Bees knew that they would have to give their best to take two league points off of them, for the Ramblers stood high in the table and had scored some remarkable victories that season.

Big, red-haired Mary Bonny, the Bees' centre-half, linked her arm through that of Bess and drew her away towards the well-equipped canteen where the mill workers had their midday meal.

"Our colours are black and yellow, as you well know, Bess," said Mary half-jokingly, "and yet here you are. Looking as blue as a blue bug. 'Ave you lost all interest in football, lass?"

The words brought a flush of colour to Bessie's cheeks and she threw a look of reproach at her companion.

"Don't be so silly, Mary!" she replied indignantly. "You know I'm keener than anyone for the Bees to win this afternoon. We must win to make certain of carrying off the championship of the league. I......I've got a bit of a headache, but the fresh air will soon blow that away."

Mary Bonny squeezed he chum's arm affectionately. She was no more deceived by the excuse than had been Ned Bromley.

A quarter of an hour before the kick-off the visiting team drove up in a motor charabanc and repaired to their dressing room. By this time quite a goodly crowd of spectators had gathered on all sides of the ground. There were few people in Blacktown who did not take a keen interest in the clever local team of girl footballers.

A roar of cheering greeted the twenty-two bright, healthy-looking girls as they came running out onto the well-kept expanse of green turf.

The rival captain's kissed each other heartily, and a coin was spun in the air. Bessie lost the toss, but there was no advantage to be gained from the wind, and a moment later the referee's whistle shrilled, and the ball was set in motion.

The Busy Bees immediately initiated a dashing attack. Swinging the ball from wing to wing, they made a determined raid on the visitors' goal, and Connie Tree, the Bees' outside-right, almost scored in the first moment with a rasping shot that just grazed the upright and went behind.

Bess through herself heart and soul into the game, but even she herself knew that she was not playing up to her proper form. There was a distinct lack of the customary fire and vim that marked her usual game. Her attention wandered, and she could not concentrate all her thoughts on the varying stages of the play.

"Play up, Bess! On the ball, lass!"

Bessie crimsoned and choked back a big lump in her throat. The rebuke from the crowd was well-deserved. A sudden blur of tears had obscured her vision, and she had missed a splendid opening that Mary Bonny had made for her.

And a moment later the Ramblers took the lead. It was a somewhat fluky, long-range shot that found Sally Soper unsighted, and the ball went into the net without her having as much as seen it.

Heartened by their early success, the visitors attacked with redoubled vigour. For quite ten minutes the Busy Bees were continually hemmed in their own half of the field, and had it not been for the dour defence of Amy Olroyd and Enid Foster, the two backs, the Ramblers must have increased their score.

It was left to Mary Bonny to put the Bees on level terms. Within a few minutes of half-time she suddenly dashed across to dispossess the Ramblers' inside-right, and with the ball at her toe went charging down the field like a bull at a gate.

There was no stopping the wild, impetuous rush. A vigorous but perfectly fair shoulder-charge sent the opposing right-back spinning, and though the goalkeeper came running out, waving her arms excitedly, Marry Bonny dodged her cleverly and slammed the ball into the yawning net.

Scarcely had the teams lined up again than the whistle sounded for half-time, and the panting girls left the field.

There was a dejected look on Bessie Booth's pretty face as she entered the dressing room. She knew that she had not played up to her proper form, and though no word of criticism was uttered, she sensed the silent reproach of her companions.

She set her even white teeth fiercely in a slice of lemon, and threw back her shoulders. Nothing should be allowed to upset her play in the second half. She would play till she dropped. The Bees must win this match!

Bessie's eyes were sparkling and her red lips were firmly compressed as she led her team out for the resumption of the game.

But Bessie Booth's sudden change of attitude and new-born determination to give of her best and lead her team to victory had come too late. The match with the Ramblers was not destined to be finished that afternoon!

Even as the girls filed out of their dressing room they found their way barred by three individuals who had been standing waiting outside, and Bessie's heart leaped with surprise.

Bessie's heart leaped with surprise as she found herself confronted by Henneker. "I am here to tell you to clear out as fast as you can," he said. "This property belongs to me!"

She found herself staring into the lean, sallow countenance and cunning dark eyes of Peter Henneker!

With the mill-owner were his manager, John Smith, and an elderly, crafty-looking man in a well-worn silk hat and frock-coat.

"Gaffer Henneker!" gasped Mary Bonny. "What's this dirty skunk doing 'ere?"

"I'll soon show you what I'm doing here," rasped Peter Henneker, a savage note of exultation in his voice. "I'm here to tell you to pack up and clear out of this place as quick as you can!"

Bessie Booth positively staggered, and a bewildered, anxious look crept into her brown eyes.

"Clear out of here?" she echoed. "Are you mad? Do you know what you are talking about? It's you who have no right here without my permission!"

"Your permission," jeered the unscrupulous mill-owner. "You don't own this mill, and the land it stands upon, do you?"

"No, but it has been leased to me."

"Leased to you!" Peter Henneker threw back his head and showed his yellow teeth in a hoarse laugh. "And where is your lease, eh? Can you show it to me?"

Bessie Booth's breath was coming quickly and her face had paled. She sensed trouble of some kind. What was Peter Henneker driving at? What lay behind this unexpected visit, and his gloating air of confidence?

"I have no.......no signed and stamped lease," she replied. "And I don't need one. The owner of this property is Mr Richard Browell, the son of the late Joshua Browell, and I have his special permission to occupy this mill for as long as I please."

"Then that's just where you're wrong," cried Peter Henneker gleefully. "This mill and all this land belong to me now, and I am within my legal rights in demanding you to give up possession forthwith!"

A gasp of amazement burst from the little group of girl footballers, and Bessie Booth's hand trembled as she grasped Mary Bonny's shoulder for support.

"I....I don't understand," she faltered. "What do you mean? How can this mill possibly belong to you?"

"Because I have bought it!" almost shouted Peter Henneker. "My lawyer, Mr Crane here, can tell you the same I hold the title-deeds of this property, and Richard Browell's receipt for the purchase money."

A low cry of alarm burst from Bessie Booth's lips, and she staggered and would have fallen had it not been for the support of Mary Bonny's strong right arm. The pretty mill-girl felt stunned and sickened by this unexpected announcement. If it were true it spelt utter ruin for herself and her girl chums, and certain disaster for the Busy Bees!

She could scarcely credit that Richard Browell had sold the place over their heads without a single word of previous warning. And now Peter Henneker claimed that he had purchased the entire mill property from Richard Browell, and there seemed no reason to doubt his word.

A low sob welled up in Bessie's throat and the tears came to her eyes. Peter Henneker rubbed his lean hands together and glared triumphantly at the girl.

"You dirty skunk!" cried Ned Bromley, elbowing his way through the rapidly gathering crowd, his face white with scorn and anger. "This is more of your danged villainy, Peter Henneker. If you've bought this mill, you never did it by fair means. For two pins Ah'd tan the hide off you!"

Henneker jumped back quickly.

"I'll give you in charge for using threatening language if you talk like that to me," he threatened. "I've a right to possession of this mill, and I demand it!"

White-faced and anxious-eyed, the little group of girl footballers stood staring miserably at one another. All their bright hopes for the future were levelled to the ground. Black ruin and disaster stared them in the face. They would be thrown out of employment....the team would have to be disbanded. It was a grim, hopeless outlook.

"As a legal man, I can only tell you I am here to enforce my client's claim," croaked Samuel Crane, the solicitor. "Everything's in order. I can assure you on that point."

With a great effort Bessie Booth pulled herself together, though her lips were trembling and her heart was throbbing violently.

"Girls we must face this out," she said firmly. Mary, you'd better go and tell the Ramblers that we cannot continue the game. We shall have to give them the points. Explain what has happened. And you, Ned, run and get on the telephone to Mr Chaddon, Mr Browell's lawyer, and find out if it is true that he has sold the mill to Peter Henneker."

Ned Bromley was off like a shot, and a moment later the wondering, disappointed crowd commenced to file out of the ground. Ned Bromley came running back, a puzzled look in his blue eyes.

"Mr Chaddon knows nothing about it," he declared. "He's coming along here at once."

James Chaddon was as good as his word. He must have run all the way from his office in the town, for he was panting for breath as he came hurrying onto the ground.

"What's this I hear?" he queried, throwing a glance of disfavour at Peter Henneker and his companions. "Do you mean to tell me that Richard Browell has sold the property to.....YOU?"

"Quite correct," jerked Samuel Crane, stepping forward. "As a legal man you will appreciate these documents, Mr Chaddon."

He produced a sheaf of papers from his pocket and James Chaddon took them and adjusted his glasses. A troubled look gradually took possession of his face as he commenced to read. He shook his head bewilderedly, and Bessie's heart sank as she clenched her little hands until the nails bit deep into her flesh.

"Well, do you doubt those deeds?" sneered Peter Henneker. "Do you dare to say that that is not Richard Browell's signature?"

"No," replied James Chaddon quietly, and he threw a sympathetic glance at Bessie Booth and her companions. "These deeds are perfectly in order, and there is not the slightest doubt that they are signed by Mr Browell. I am amazed....I can scarcely believe it. I should have thought you were the last man on earth Mr Browell would have sold his mill to."

Bessie uttered a little groan of despair. It was true then. The Bee-Hive Mill was now the property of Peter Henneker!

"Where did this transaction take place?" queried Mr Chaddon.

"In my private office, at the mill, and there were witnesses there."

"So I see. And how did you get into communication with Mr Browell in the first place?"

"That's my business!" snapped Henneker pompously. "It has nothing whatever to do with you."

James Chaddon sighed and shook his head again.

"Miss Booth, I am very sorry," he said sincerely. "But there is not the slightest doubt Mr Browell has sold this property. I can't understand it.......I am frankly amazed. And now I am going to tell you something. It is the nature of a secret, but under the circumstances I think I am justified in revealing a surprising truth!"

"I know what you are going to say," chuckled Peter Henneker. "You are about to tell this girl here that Richard Browell and Richard Trueman are one and the same person!"

Bessie Booth's hands flew to her heart, and she uttered a low cry of amazement.

"Yes, that is the truth, Miss Booth," said James Chaddon gravely. "Richard Browell and the man you know as Richard Trueman are the same person! Mr Browell didn't willingly deceive you, Miss Booth," he assured her. "He came back to Blacktown intending to open the mill himself, but when he saw you and realised the plucky fight you were putting up he couldn't bring himself to disappoint you of your ambition. On the spur of the moment he said he had come to apply for a position, and he was utterly flabbergasted when you engaged him as manager. But he was determined to go through with it, and he swore me to secrecy regarding his true identity. What I can't understand is why he has sold the mill to this man here, and what has become of him. I know that it was his intention to make the mill over to you as a deed of gift. There is some mystery here. Leave it to me, Miss Booth. I will find out what has become of Mr Browell, and what induced him to part with this property. In the meantime I very much fear that you cannot remain here. The mill indisputably belongs to Peter Henneker, and the conditions of sale give him the right of immediate possession."

"Which I mean to enforce," snarled Henneker maliciously. "Out into the gutter the lot of you, and don't come cringing to me for employment, for you won't get it."

Dazed and stupefied at the disaster that had befallen them, Bessie Booth and her companions returned to the club house to change out of their football kit. Their cup of misery was full to overflowing.

Bessie's grief was beyond tears. She had lost everything that she had to live for. The mill had been taken away from her, and there were penalties for broken contracts to be faced. The Busy Bees would have to disband, and the man she loved had deceived her and left her. It was he who was responsible for all her misfortunes.

He had won her love, only to spurn her and deliver her into the hands of her greatest enemy.

Outside, Peter Henneker was chuckling as he read the letter from Dick Browell to Bessie Booth that his paid spy, Ada Miller, had brought him that morning.

"Let him come back now, as soon as he likes," muttered the unscrupulous mill-owner. "He can't cheat me out of my revenge! I told you I'd break you, Bessie Booth, and by thunder I have!"

It was Peter Henneker's day of days, and little did he dream of the tomorrow that was to come, and the grim reckoning that it held in store!

The Strike

It was long-acquired habit that brought Bessie Booth leaping out of bed at seven o'clock in the morning, and it was some minutes after she had scrambled into her clothes that she realised, with a dull sense of misery, that there was no particular need for any hurry.

There was a lump in her throat as she went across to the window, and resting her elbows on the sill, gazed over the forest of chimney pots and the narrow streets of Blacktown, to the big mill on the top of the hill, crowned by towering smoke-stacks.

In the past twenty-four hours Bess had lost everything that made her life worth living. The loss of the mill meant ruin to her, and to all of her girl chums, who were better known perhaps for their connection with the football team, the Busy Bees, which now stood at the top of the Lancashire Girls' Football League.

The strident note of a hooter echoing over the little town brought the tears flooding to Bessie Brown's eyes. The summons was not for her, or any of her girl chums. There were only two mills in Blacktown, and now both were under Peter Henneker's control. There was no work, no employment of any kind for anyone associated in any way with Bess and her Busy Bees.

It was a dreary, hopeless outlook, but Bess bravely choked back the tears, and donning her clogs and winding her shawl around her head and shoulders, she slipped out of the house.

She was not the only one who could not lie abed that morning. At the corner of the High Street there was gathered quite a little bunch of dejected-looking girls, amongst whom Bess was quick to recognise most of the Busy Bess F.C. – Mary Bonny, Sally Soper, Amy Olroyd and Enid Foster, and Connie Tree. And there was one man, a big broad-shouldered giant of a fellow with rugged features and kindly, sheepish blue eyes – the now former head overlooker at the Bee-Hive Mill, Ned Bromley.

"Here's our Bess!" cried Mary Bonny, twining an arm around Bessie's slender waist and drawing her close with an encouraging squeeze. "Ah guessed you couldn't lie abed this morning, Bess, lass. Now then, are we down-hearted?"

A cheer went up, but it was sadly lacking in spirit, and Ned Bromley's eyes flashed fiercely as he shook his fists at the chimney stacks of Peter Henneker's mills.

"Damn you, Henneker! You're top dog now, but we'll find a way to beat you," he muttered under his breath. "It's against human nature for a scoundrel like you to prosper at our expense. You've robbed us of our mill, but you haven't beaten us down yet, and you never will!"

"That's the talk Ned!" cried Amy Olroyd sturdily. "What's the use of crying over spilt milk? We're up against it, and we've got to find a way out."

"But how? What can we do?" queried Connie Tree forlornly. "Where are we going to find employment? Not here in Blacktown, that's a certainty, with Henneker owning all the mills. And we can't even play football. We've no ground!"

"We've only got three more matches to play, and we'll have to find a ground," said Mary Bonny grimly. "And if we can't find work in Blacktown we'll have to go somewhere else and find it. We're not whacked yet by a long way. How much brass is there in the bank, Bess?"

"Not very much, and what there is we daren't touch," replied Bessie Booth. "It'll all have to go to pay the forfeits on the contracts we can't complete."

"By gum, what Ah can't understand is why young Mr Browell sold the mill to Peter Henneker, without giving us any warning!" burst out Amy Olroyd impetuously. 'Twas a dirty underhand trick......Oh, Ah say, Ah'm sorry, Bess!"

Bessie Booth had flushed up, and her lips trembled as she tried to smile reassuringly at her companions. Amy Olroyd's careless words had touched upon an aching wound in her heart.

"Never.......never mind about Dick......Mr Browell," said Bess bravely. "After all, it was his mill, and he had a perfect right to sell it to anyone he liked. I......I don't suppose we shall see him again."

"Dang me if Ah believe that!" cried Ned Bromley, slapping his thigh vehemently. "I'll not believe Dick Browell is an out-and-out rotter until Ah hears it from his own lips. There's summat funny about the whole business. Look how he's helped us get the better of Henneker time after time."

That was true enough. As Dick Trueman the Bee-Hive Mill business manager he had saved Bessie Booth and her chums on several occasions. It made it all the more inexplicable why he should suddenly have disappeared from Blacktown, having sold the mill lock stock and barrel to his greatest rival.

"Here comes Meg Ryan. What's the matter with her?" suddenly exclaimed Mary Bonny. "She seems mighty excited about summat or other."

Meg Ryan was the dark-haired girl who played inside-left for the Busy Bees. Holding her shawl together with one hand she came clattering along the street in her clogs, her face flushed, and her eyes blazing with excitement.

" 'Ave you 'eard the news, girls?" she panted as she reached the little group of mill-lasses. "My word, there isn't half a to-do. There's a strike up at Henneker's. There's not a man, woman, gal or boy in Blacktown but what hasn't refused to go to work out of sympathy with us. Henneker may 'ave both mills now, but he ain't doing no good with 'em. There's not a loom working."

It was soon discovered that Meg Ryan's piece of information was no mere rumour. Peter Henneker's two mills stood empty and desolate; no engine running...... no looms clattering and whirling. Outside was grouped an enormous crowd of people, whilst Henneker himself stood by the entrance gates, his bowler hat on the back of his head, a sullen scowl of fury and chagrin in his dark, close-set eyes.

"What's all this nonsense about?" he shouted harshly. "Has everyone in Blacktown taken leave of their senses. If you idiots don't come in and get on with your work, I'll declare a lock-out!"

"Yer can do what yer like," declared a burly, bearded operative stubbornly. "Yer've played a danged dirty trick on Bessie Booth and her chums, an' we're on their side. Yer'll get no work done till that matter is set right."

A murmur of approval came from the crowd.

"Confound your impudence," shrieked Henneker. "Do you expect me to make that hussy of a girl and her football-playing rabble a present of a mill I have paid good money for? Let them starve, curse them. They've nearly ruined me during the past six months."

He suddenly caught a glimpse of the very person he was discussing, standing at the back of the crowd, and a spasm of hatred flickered across his sallow face.

"This is some of your work, I suppose," he snarled. "Inciting my own workpeople against me. I'll have the law on you for this."

"Shut yer gob!" shouted Ned Bromley angrily. "Our Bess has nothing to do with this at all. She's opposed to a strike, and so am Ah. But not on your account, you dirty skunk!"

Ned Bromley stepped out into the centre of the road and faced the assembly of would-be strikers.

"Listen to me, mates!" he cried in a voice that could be heard by all. "Reckon you think you're doing the right thing by refusing to work for Henneker. But our Bess says that you're not to strike. You won't be doing us no real good, and you'll be doing yourselves a heap of harm. An' the union won't stand for you under the circumstances. Take my advice....or rather take Bess's advice.....an' go back to your work."

The crowd of operatives stared wonderingly at each other, and Peter Henneker himself looked frankly dumbfounded.

"Why should we work for Henneker?" shouted a sturdy spinner. "He's a rotten dog!"

"Granted. But you've got your bread and butter to earn," said Ned. "Don't you worry about Bess and all the rest of us. We can fend for ourselves. But we don't want the whole town wandering around without graft."

"By gum, Ned's right!" declared the big, bearded man, with a resigned shrug of his broad shoulders. "Our place is at the looms. We can do Bess a heap more good by working than we could by striking. We'll see that she don't go short."

For a moment the crowd hesitated, and then, somewhat reluctantly, they commenced to file through the gates into the mill. Peter Henneker heaved a fervent sigh of relief. A strike at that juncture in his fortunes would have utterly ruined him. He had spent every penny of his available capital in the purchase of the Bee-Hive Mill, and if it were to stand idle for only a week it would put him out of business.

But there was a sneer on his face as he stared across to where Bessie Booth, Ned Bromley and the others stood.

"Don't think you can get over me with that kind of soft-soap," he rasped. "I'm not having any. Want me to thank you for advising my operatives to go back to work, I suppose? Think I'm going to offer you a job...eh?"

Ned Bromley laughed scornfully.

"I wasn't thinking of you when I gave the folk that advice, Peter Henneker," he retorted. "An' as for working for you, Ah wouldn't do it if you owned every mill in Lancashire, an' offered me fifty pounds a week!"

"Bah! You'll come to heel soon enough," sneered Henneker. "As a matter of fact, I don't want to be too hard on you folk. You were led away by that girl Bessie Booth, and now you see what she has brought you to. You can all go back to work at the Bee-Hive Mill if you want to.......all except Bessie Booth of course."

It was a cunning move on Peter Henneker's part. He was really anxious for the former workers of the Bee-Hive Mill to go back to their jobs. He wanted to get the mill working again as soon as possible, and he knew that he would have difficulty in securing sufficient labour.

"And you can keep your football club going as usual," he added slyly.

"Dang you for a smooth-tongued villain, Henneker!" cried Ned Bromley hoarsely. "We'll have nothing to do with your offer. We're standing by our Bess through thick and thin."

"Hear, hear!" chorused the Busy Bees. "That's the talk Ned!"

Peter Henneker turned away with a careless shrug of his shoulders.

"Very well," he jerked. "But you've heard my offer, and it's still open to you. Better think it over."

He vanished through the gates into the mill and Bessie Booth turned to her companions. Her face was pale but her eyes were bright.

"Girls, you can't do this," she said firmly. "The best thing you can do is accept Henneker's offer and go back to work. It isn't fair that you should sacrifice yourselves for me. I can look after myself. I shall be able to find work somewhere else......"

A roar of indignation cut her short.

The tears crept into Bessie's eyes. She was touched to the heart by this show of loyalty......but she knew it was all wrong. It was too great a sacrifice to expect her chums to make, and she had already decided that, for their own sakes, they must be compelled to accept Henneker's offer.

And there was only one way to do it. She would have to leave Blacktown....forever! Once she had gone, the Busy Bees would have no option but to go back to their duties at the Bee-Hive Mill!

Foiled!

Peter Henneker rubbed his lean hands gleefully together as he sat in his office at the mill, listening to the busy rumble and clatter of the looms. In a few days time he hoped to have the Bee-Hive Mill going full steam ahead again. He had no doubt that the tempting offer he had made would eventually be accepted by Bessie Booth's companions.

He raised his eyes and glanced through the office window, as the roar of a motor caught his ears, and was just in time to see a big limousine-bodied car swerve through the gates into the mill yard. A moment later his manager, John Smith, entered the room, a peculiar look etched into his heavy features.

"Henneker, young Browell has arrived," he said nervously. "He wants to see you."

Peter Henneker frowned, and then threw himself back in his chair with a careless laugh.

"Show him in," he said with a casual flick of his hand. "I'm not frightened of Richard Browell. He can't do me any harm...now"

Tall, well-built and handsome, Dick Browell strode briskly into the room, and coolly flung himself into a chair.

"Well, Henneker, we meet again," he said shortly, a frosty smile in his blue eyes.

"By no wish of mine," snarled Henneker aggressively. "What do you want here?"

"A few words with you. You have taken possession of the Bee-Hive Mill?"

"Of course I have. It's my property, isn't it?"

"And Miss Booth and the others.....what of them?"

"How do I know? Walking the streets looking for work, I suppose."

Dick Browell's teeth came together with a snap.

"Henneker, you're the biggest scoundrel of all!" he said grimly. "You gained possession of the Bee-Hive Mill by foul and illegal methods. You kidnapped me, kept me prisoner, and forced me against my will to sell the mill to you."

"Yes," sneered Henneker. "And you also signed another document declaring you sold the mill of your own free will, and that you would take no future action against me."

"Perhaps so. But all the same, I mean to have the Bee-Hive back."

"You can't do it. It can't be done."

"Oh yes it can, and I'll show you how!" replied Dick with a confident smile. "I've been pretty busy these last few days, Henneker. That's why I haven't been in Blacktown. And I've made a few interesting discoveries. For one thing, I understand there is a heavy mortgage on this mill."

Peter Henneker started, and then an uneasy look crept into his eyes.

""Well.....and what of it? What has that got to do with you?"

"Everything," retorted Browell. "Considering that I have purchased the mortgage. I have the deeds in my pocket now. The mortgage is due in two days' time, and I know that you haven't the money to pay it. Therefore I shall seize this property, or I will give you the deeds in return for the Bee-Hive Mill."

Peter Henneker fell back in his chair with a choking cry of baffled fury, and beads of perspiration suddenly burst out on his pallid forehead.

"How....how did you get hold of that mortgage?" he gasped. "That villain Chard at the bank, he's sold me out, curse him! He promised to renew the mortgage."

"Well, they'll be no renewal now," declared Dick Browell. "I don't mind telling you that I had to pay Chard a pretty stiff sum to transfer the deeds. The game's up, Henneker. What's it to be? Pay up or hand back the Bee-Hive Mill?"

"Neither, curse you!" spluttered Peter Henneker, springing to his feet.

Leaving Henneker trembling with fury and dismay, the wealthy young mill-owner returned to the waiting car.

"Now to see my darling Bess, bless her heart!" he muttered, his pulses leaping with anticipation as he gave the chauffeur the address to Bessie Booth's lodgings. "By Jove, I've got a lot of explanations to give her. She's sure to be expecting me after the letter I sent her."

But Dick Browell had no idea that his letter had been intercepted by Henneker's spy within the Bee-Hive Mill, and had in fact never reached Bess.

Bessie's aunt opened the door to him gave him a peculiar stare.

"You want Bess? She's gone," she informed him.

"Gone?" echoed Dick. "Where's she gone, and when will she be back?"

"She won't be back at all, and Ah don't know where she's gone," replied the woman, sadly. "She packed up her things and left this afternoon."

"You mean to tell me she left no message of any kind?"

"She said nothing, save that she was leaving Blacktown for good. Poor lass, she seemed fair broken up. I wonder why?"

Dick Browell felt the sting in the woman's tone and turned dazedly away, sick with disappointment and dismay. Bessie Booth had left Blacktown! What did it mean? Passing through the gate he collided violently with a man coming in the opposite direction.

It was Ned Bromley, panting, white-faced and wild-eyed, and Dick Browell seized him fiercely by the arm.

"Ned, where's Bess!" he demanded. "What's happened? I hear she's left Blacktown? What does it mean?"

Ned Bromley wrenched himself away and stared scornfully at the young man.

"This is your doing, Dick Browell," he said thickly. "An' you dare to ask me questions like that. You've driven our Bess away. You deceived her, left her, and sold the mill over her head."

"Good Heavens! What are you talking about man?" gasped Dick. "Do you mean to say you don't know the truth? Didn't Bess tell you? I wrote to her...."

"Wrote to her? She's had no letter from you..... that I'll swear."

"I wrote to her two days ago."

Volubly, excitedly, Dick Browell burst into a flow of explanation. He told how he had been kidnapped and held by prisoner by Peter Henneker, and how he had come to sell the Bee-Hive Mill, and when he had finished Ned Bromley sprang forward and gripped him warmly by the hand.

"Dick, Ah knew there was summat wrong. Ah knew you were a good'un," he cried. "If only we'd known this before! Bess was fair breaking her heart over you. And now she's gone. Ah've just received a letter from her. She says she's left Blacktown in order that the rest of us will be free to go back to work for Peter Henneker. Dang it, as though we would do that!"

"But where's she gone Ned?" cried Dick Browell frenziedly.

"Ah don't know lad. She didn't say. She don't want us to know where she's gone."

"Ned, Bess has to be found!" cried the young mill-owner hoarsely. "I shan't rest a minute until I find her. I don't care what it costs, if it is every penny I possess."

Meanwhile, Peter Henneker was striding up and down his office like a caged lion. His face was the face of a madman, and his heart was black with hatred. The day's work was over, and the looms had ceased their rumble. The place was deserted, save for Henneker himself and his manager, John Smith, who sat staring phlegmatically at his employer.

"There's no getting away from it, Henneker, we're beat," said Smith. "Browell has proved one too many for us. You've no money to pay off that mortgage. If he seizes this mill the Bee-Hive will be of no use to you, even if you had the capital to run it. Best sell it back to Browell and we'll get out of Blacktown."

"Never!" raved Henneker. "By Heaven, I'm not beaten yet! I'm going to fight to the end. I can see a way out, Smith. It's dashed risky, but it's worth the risk. Listen, and I'll tell you how I'm going to turn the tables on Dick Browell."

John Smith listened patiently for several minutes, and a light of hope kindled in his short-sighted eyes.

"By thunder, I should think it is risky, Henneker! He breathed. "But it might succeed."

In a little back room, in a cheap lodging house, in a quiet street in Rigan, thirty miles away from Blacktown, Bessie

Booth lay sobbing her heart out against a coarse pillow. To her it seemed that all interest in life had gone. She had lost everything.

And the greatest wrench of all had been to tear herself away from Blacktown. It had been the supreme sacrifice.....made for the sake of her loyal chums.

"I've got to live it down," she whispered bravely to herself, dashing her tears away. "Tomorrow I shall look for work, and make a fresh start in life,"

A Scoundrel's Reward

"Sorry, Mr Browell, no news as yet, but don't you worry. We'll find the girl for you. She can't have gone very far, and we've wired her description to every police station in Lancashire and Yorkshire."

The big police inspector spoke kindly, but stolidly, and his words brought a faint gleam of hope to Dick Browell's blue eyes.

"You really think you'll be able to trace her, then?"

"Ay, sure. Ah don't say we be able to make her come back. But we'll find out for you where she is and what she's doing."

The disappearance of the captain of the Busy Bees F.C. and controller of the Bee-Hive Mill had caused a tremendous sensation in Blacktown, and none had been hit harder than the man who had been intended to become her husband, Dick Browell.

Dick picked up his hat and strode heavily out of the police station. It was the second time he had called there that day to inquire if there was any news of the girl he loved, and he was not the only interested party. There was a little group of mill-girls, clad in clogs and shawls, standing at the corner of the street, and Dick Browell recognised them instantly as members of the Busy Bees football team and Bess's former team mates.

The big, brawny, red-headed centre-half Mary Bonny came rushing towards him. All the girls now knew the truth behind Dick's mysterious disappearance, and how unjustified their previously bad opinion of him had been. Little did they know, however, that Bess herself was still completely in the dark as to the real events.

"Oh, Mr Browell, is there any news of our Bess?"

"No, no news as yet," replied the young man with a kindly smile, "but we'll soon find her, Mary, if it means spending every penny I've got in the world. None of you has heard, I suppose? Not even a postcard?"

"Not a line," replied the girl, her lips trembling with disappointment. "Oh, if only she'd waited another few hours, everything would have been all right, wouldn't it, Mr Browell?"

"Yes, everything would have been all right!" echoed the young mill-owner, "and everything *will* be all right very shortly, Mary."

He passed on up the street, busy with his thoughts. It had been by pure villainy and underhand dealing that Henneker had taken the Bee-Hive Mill away from him, from Bess, and the football team. Now that he owned the mortgage on Henneker's own mill he was set for a little harsh punishment of his own. When the mortgage came due the next day he would foreclose and, unable to support his own mill or the Bee-Hive, that would be that as far as Mr Peter Henneker was concerned, a ruined man.

Turning into the High Street Dick made his way up the steps and into the marbled interior of the town's main bank. Here he would find Mr Chard from whom he had purchased the mortgage on Henneker's Mill and begun his downfall. The old bank manager greeted the young man warmly as he stepped through into the large wood panelled office.

"Everything in order for tomorrow, Mr Chard?" asked Dick. "I wanted you to rub it into Henneker as hard as you can, the scoundrel. I've got him in a corner from which he can't escape. He must realise that the only thing he can do is hand me back the Bee-Hive Mill and clear out of Blacktown while he has a safe skin."

Henry Chard looked up over the rim of his glasses.

"But supposing he allows you to seize his own mill and retains possession of the Bee-Hive?" he queried.

"What would be the use of it to him? I shall set up in opposition to him in the other mill and put him out of business in less than a week."

"Ah, true enough," assented the old man, "and what of Miss Booth? Is there any news of her as yet?"

"No, not as yet," replied Dick gloomily. "It drives me almost mad to think of the unnecessary worry and hardship she is probably causing herself. Do you think it would be of any use advertising in all the big Lancashire daily papers?"

Henry Chard was silent for a moment.

"Yes, if you advertise in the right way," he said at length.

"What do you mean, in the right way?"

The old bank manager leaned forward and spoke a few brief, pointed sentences that brought a gleam of excitement to Dick Browell's eyes.

"By Jingo, that's a splendid idea!" he cried, slapping the old man vigorously on the back. "What a cunning and helpful man you are! I shall get it arranged straight away......ring up a big agency and see that advert appears in all the daily papers in Lancashire. If it doesn't get me in touch with Bess, then nothing will!"

Up on a hill above the outskirts of Blacktown stood Peter Henneker's Mill, and like a caged animal Peter Henneker himself sat in his private office scribbling, scribbling on his blotting pad, or else pacing restlessly up and down the floor.

He had never dreamed that Dick Browell knew anything about the mortgage on his mill and he had felt certain he could easily renew when the time came. It had come as a devastating shock to him to learn that Browell had purchased the debt from the bank and intended to foreclose the following day.

Over by the fireplace was Henneker's manager and confidante, John Smith, his squat heavy features illuminated in the glow of the flames as he blinked at his employer through thick spectacles.

"I'm not beaten yet, Smith. I don't mean to allow myself to be beaten. There is still one way I can win through and take the wind out of that cursed cub Browell's sails."

John Smith gave a slight shudder and nervously rubbed his hands together in front of the fire.

"What...the....the way you mentioned last night," he croaked hoarsely. "No, that is too risky, Henneker......far too risky."

"Nothing is too risky at this stage of the game," declared the mill-owner. "People may suspect me, but they would never be able to prove anything, Smith. Why, it is the simplest scheme in all the world. This mill is insured right up to the hilt, and the premium is fully paid. A fire in the cellars, where the raw cotton is stored...spontaneous combustion we will call it.....and the whole place is raised to the ground. Out of the insurance money I shall be able to pay off the mortgage and have enough to give me a good set up in the Bee-Hive Mill, and it will be the only mill in Blacktown. I will have beaten Dick Browell and Bessie Booth at their own game."

John Smith shook his big head again.

Half an hour later Peter Henneker switched out the lights in his private office, locked all the doors, and left the mill by the main gate, locking that behind him as well.

He said 'Goodnight' genially – and deliberately – to a police constable who stood on the other side of the road, and turned the corner in the direction of the town, but he did not proceed very far on that way.

A quick, keen glance around to see that he was not observed, and he dived into a narrow turning that brought him round to the back of the mill he had just left. With an agile spring Henneker clutched the top of the high brick wall, drew himself up and dropped down on the farther side. Keeping to the shadows, he darted across the stone-paved yard and pushed open a little door leading to the engineer's quarters that he had purposefully left unlocked ten minutes before.

Closing it behind him he switched on a pocket electric torch and unlocked a cupboard, set beneath the stone stairs that led up to the spinning rooms. Here, where he had concealed them earlier in the day, were a couple of two-gallon cans of petrol.

Passing a short length of steel rod through the handles, Henneker was able to carry the two cans in one hand and, holding the electric torch in the other, he passed down a flight of stone steps and through the engine room.

Right at the farther end he set the cans of petrol down and bent over a heavy iron trap-door set in the floor. It took all his strength to lift it and prop it up with a steel bar attached for that purpose.

Fully laden again he felt his way gingerly down a short length of ladder and found himself in a big, stone-walled cellar, where vast quantities of raw cotton were stored away.

There was a gleam almost of madness in Peter Henneker's eyes as he strode to the farther end of the cellar. He dragged out a couple of bales of cotton, broke them, and saturated them with the contents of the two petrol cans.

The crucial moment had come. Peter Henneker was risking everything in one last desperate throw of the dice to save himself from utter ruin. Surely he was more insane than sane as,

with a peculiar grating chuckle, he tore off a lump of the petrol-saturated cotton and retired to a safe distance.

Wrapping the cotton around one end of a short piece of wood he struck a match and, igniting the inflammable substance, tossed it into the midst of the piled-up bales.

They immediately caught with a roar and a blinding burst of flame that scorched the very hair on Henneker's head, despite the intervening distance, but Henneker didn't mind. He laughed aloud and jigged with glee at sight of the leaping tongues of fire and then turned and raced back to the ladder that led to safety.

He scrambled up the steel rungs two at a time, and then a shower of sparks flashed before his eyes as he struck his head against some immovable substance. It was a nasty shock, and for a moment the rascally mill-owner hung dazedly to the ladder, scarcely able to realise what had happened.

Then, as he gazed upwards, he saw that the iron rod supporting the heavy trap-door had slipped allowing the heavy door to fall back down on its hinges.

With a muttered curse of annoyance Henneker placed a hand beneath the lower side of the trap-door and pushed upwards with all his might. But the trap-door was heavy and he could not shift it. He climbed up another two rungs and applied both hands, but the result was the same.

A withering blast of scorching hot air almost took his breath away and he realised he had no time to waste. Higher still he went until he had his shoulders set beneath the trap-door, and he heaved until his muscles cracked and the veins bulged on his forehead.

But the trap-door was immovable. He could not move it an inch and a hoarse scream of horror burst from the scoundrel's bloodless lips as he realised he was caught like a rat in a trap of his own making.

Something seemed to crack in his brain and he howled and foamed at the mouth like a mad dog as he pounded and scratched and tore at the steel trap-door, until his nails were broken and the blood spurted from his fingers' ends.

A gush of searing flame licked around him like a fiery serpent, and with one last terrible cry of despair Peter Henneker lost his balance and toppled backwards to be swallowed by the flames...... a doom that he himself had wrought.

The End

"Sorry, lass, we're full up. There's no job going here."

The grey-bearded timekeeper of the mill spoke gruffly, but there was a distinct note of sympathy in his voice, as he glanced at the pretty, pale-faced girl who had approached him.

Tears of disappointment welled in Bessie Booth's sorrowful brown eyes as she drew her shawl closer around her head and shoulders and turned listlessly away.

A week had elapsed since Bessie Booth had left Blacktown and made her way to Rigan, hoping to find employment there. In a strange town, amongst strange people, she felt utterly friendless and alone in the world, and all the happy days at the Bee-Hive Mill seemed like nothing more than a dream to her.

Her feeling of despair had deepened upon reading of her good friends and former work colleagues the Busy Bees girls' football team and a report of their recent draw with Richdale Rovers. It was a good result against a strong side, and part of Bess's heart was filled with praise for her former team mates. But a large part of her was overwhelmed with sadness; sad that she was not there with them to help, to once again be part of the great things they had achieved to become one of the most respected women's football teams in Lancashire, if not the whole of the North of England.

And there was misery, even dread, at the thought of what the draw with Richdale actually meant....the Bees equal on points at the top of the league with the team they would face in the last game of the season....Henneker's Mill! Bess wiped away a tear as she reflected on how that villain seemed destined to have the final say, over their lives, over their work, and over their football.

"I have to live it all down and make a fresh start," she muttered, dashing the blinding tears from her eyes as she commenced to trudge back through the town towards the cheap lodging house where she had secured a tiny room.

Two more mills Bessie applied at, but the result was the same in each case. There was no work for her it seemed and footsore and heavy-hearted she wandered back to her lonely lodgings.

Seated on a small uncomfortable bed, facing a grimy window that gave onto a dreary vista of smoky chimney pots, she counted her small store of money. She had exactly thirty-five shillings left. She did not dare to think what might happen to her when that had gone.

Unable to help the heavy sigh of despair that escaped her lips, Bess listlessly opened the newspaper she had bought and automatically turned to the small adverts section in the hope that something, just something might change her fortunes. Almost instantly her eyes were drawn to the words ***'Girl footballer wanted'*** and a tinge of colour crept into her pale cheeks as she read what was underneath. ***'Wanted, a capable girl footballer – good player – to take charge of team of mill-girls. Good pay and excellent prospects. Apply personally to B.Wells, 12a Durham St, Liverpool'.***

Bessie Booth drew a deep breath and fresh hope sprang up in her heart. Here was the very kind of situation she had been looking for. If only she could be fortunate enough to secure it.

Quickly she packed her few belongings together, donned a neat outfit and her best hat and, settling her bill, hurried away to the railway station.

She arrived at Liverpool late in the afternoon and, leaving her bag in the cloakroom at the station, set out in search of 12a Durham Street. It was a block of offices in the heart of the business district and the lift-man, to whom she stated her business, whisked her up to a room on the second floor.

Bessie's heart was beating fast as she pushed open the indicated door and entered a plainly furnished office, where a dark-haired young man sat at a desk reading a newspaper. He glanced up quickly, and a light of approval leapt to his eyes as he stared at the pretty, neatly dressed girl.

"Are.....are you Mr Wells?" faltered Bess nervously. "I've come in answer to your advertisement in the Rigan Advertiser."

"I'm not Mr Wells, but I'm acting for him," replied the young man. "Will you give me a few particulars? Your name please?"

Bessie hesitated. There was no reason why she should not give her real name.

"Booth.....Bessie Booth."

She did not notice the perceptible start that the young man gave that sent his pen spluttering across the paper.

"If you will wait one minute?" said the young man, and vanished through a door into an adjoining office. He was back again almost at once.

"Mr....Wells will see you if you will go straight in," he said with a peculiar smile.

Bessie Booth was trembling as she stepped over the threshold and closed the door behind her. A tall, well-built man stood with his back turned, staring out of a window. He swung round quickly as Bess entered and she fell back, her head swimming, her heart beating like a drum as she found herself gazing into the eager face of the man she had loved and lost.....Dick Browell!

"Dick!"

"Bessie, my darling! So I have found you at last!"

In two strides Dick Browell was across the room and swept the bewildered girl into his strong arms.

"Bess! Oh, Bess! Why did you run away?" cried the young man huskily. "If you only knew the anxiety you have caused me and all your friends. It has all been a mistake. Why couldn't you trust me? You knew that I loved you. I wrote to you...."

"I had no letter...."

"My darling.... let me explain."

In a few brief sentences Dick Browell related all that had happened, and with a sob of joy Bessie Booth crept into her sweetheart's arms and laid her curly head on his broad chest. She was frightened....frightened that her new-found happiness was all a dream, from which she might awaken at any minute.

"But......but what are you doing here, Dick? That advertisement...."

"I had one put in every paper in Lancashire," smiled Dick Browell. "I felt certain that if you saw it you would answer it, and I was right."

"But the Bee-Hive Mill, Dick, and Peter Henneker?"

"Peter Henneker is dead," said the young man in a grave voice. "He was burnt to death last night whilst attempting to set his own mill on fire in order to get the insurance money. I have no sympathy for him.....he deserved it, and the Bee-Hive Mill is yours again, Bess."

Tears of happiness streamed down Bessie Booth's cheeks as she clung to her sweetheart.

"Come, Bessie darling," said Dick. "My car is waiting outside. We are going back...back to Blacktown, to the Bee-Hive Mill, and the Busy Bees. There's a match to play and a trophy to win!"

"Ten Minutes!"

Bess couldn't hear the words, but there was no mistaking what Ned was saying, just as if they were mouthing one of their lip reading conversations surrounded by the deafening clatter of looms in the Bee-Hive Mill.

She looked around to see who else had picked up the message and it was obvious from the deeply anxious looks on the faces of those closest to her... they had. But all of them were really looking to Bess for what they should do next.

They had been pounding the opposition goalmouth for nearly the entire second half with almost no effect. Seemingly content with their two-nil lead at half time - and obviously confident of victory – Henneker's Ramblers had yet again reverted to the simplest and bluntest of defensive tactics, with the entire team encamped in their own half and every one of them behind the ball when the Bees had possession, save for one solitary striker who paced the half way line, like a prowling cat, in the hope of getting a lucky break away.

It was not pretty, but it was proving very effective. The Busy Bees had laid siege to a seemingly impregnable wall of red and white shirts and only once had they managed to find a way through -an inspired solo effort from Connie Tree, having dummied a cross only to slip through between two defenders to slot the ball in with the goal mouth - and the goalie's mouth - left wide open.

That had made it two-one and the Bees had dared to believe there was a glimmer of hope. But as Connie once again crossed the ball into the deep red sea that was Henneker's penalty area, that goal seemed a long time ago and, as the ball was yet again smothered into the safety of the opposition keeper's hands, any chance of levelling the score now seemed to be rapidly fading, and the chance of actually *winning* nothing more than a foolish, distant dream. The precious minutes evaporated into the crisp winter's air along with their exhausted breath.

"FOUL REF!" screamed Mary Bonny as Meg Ryan, by far the smallest and youngest on the field, crumpled to the floor following a vicious and rather clumsy 'sandwich' from two Henneker's defenders, each twice her size. It was just outside the penalty area and as the referee's whistle blew sharply for the Bees' free kick Bessie's brain immediately went into overdrive.

"Don't let Meg get up too quickly" she said to Mary. "I know she's made of stern stuff but we can buy ourselves a couple more minutes of injury time".

Mary nodded and trotted over to where two of the others were kneeling beside the young player as she desperately tried to rub away the pain from her calf muscle.

Bess studied Henneker's defensive wall as it formed, forced reluctantly backwards to the correct distance from the ball by the impatient waving of his arm by the referee who had quickly paced out the correct number of yards.

Standing over the ball Bess could not see many options around it, and beyond it the goalkeeper appeared and then disappeared, first at one end and then the other, shuffling sideways up and down her goal line, checking for the best view of the kicker and the ball from around her defenders and screaming instructions to them over the incessant rumble of the crowd.

By now the referee had turned his impatient attention on Meg, gesturing for her to get to her feet and for the game to restart. Bess thought quickly.

"Who's got the strongest kick?"

Mary looked puzzled.

"Well, Connie can put the ball pretty much where she....".

"No, no" interrupted Bess. "Not the most accurate. Who can kick it the *hardest*"?

"Oh. Well. Sally in goal, I suppose. She can kick it to the half way line no problem".

"Right then" said Bess, a determined plan hatching in her head. "Sally it is then".

To the great surprise of the bemused Mary, her friend turned and waved frantically for Sally the goalkeeper to come up the field. An equally puzzled Sally first trotted and then sprinted up to them as fast as she could as she realised the urgency in Bessie's vigorous gestures.

A mystified murmur rippled through the crowd with the odd jeering comment of a Henneker's supporter clearly heard above the low rumble of anticipation. Bess rested her hand reassuringly on Sally's shoulder and smiled.

"Okay Sally. We know you can kick like a mule, so that's exactly what I want you to do. Kick it as hard as you can".

Sally's expression turned blank and inside her head her thoughts were whirling around like water down a plughole, bringing a sinking feeling to her legs.

"But I'll never get it around the wall" protested the goalie. "I can kick it hard, no problem, but I can't be sure where it will *go*".

"Straight at the wall!" hissed Bess through her teeth, desperately making her point but trying not to be heard. "You can do it Sally. *You can do it*. Straight at the wall as hard as you can!"

"C'mon the Bees!" shouted the referee, obviously irritated by the delay, and blew his whistle for the game to restart. Sally shrugged, gave a brief nervous smile, and trotted off to take up position several yards behind the ball, all the while repeating over and over in her mind that this was no different from kicking it out from her own goalmouth.

There was now some distinct laughter from parts of the crowd and Mary could not disguise the look of disbelief she gave Bess, who in turn smiled nervously and shrugged her shoulders.

"Perhaps we're trying to be too clever" she said. "Let's see what happens".

Sally's full concentration was now focussed on the ball and nothing else, as if by sheer power of the mind she could send it flying effortlessly into the goal. She seemed to be taking an age to prepare herself, and the rest of the Bees dotted around on either side of her started to shuffle nervously, uncomfortable that there was now no one in their own half of the field, as well as unsure of when they should start their run into their opponents' penalty area.

The opposition's wall stood frozen to the spot, mesmerised and mystified by the unfolding events and unsure as to what to expect. Behind them the goalkeeper shimmied even more anxiously left and right along her goal line as the tension mounted and she tried to second guess what Sally was going to do.

After a deep intake of breath Sally raced towards the ball like a charging bull and with all the strength she could muster struck the hard heavy leather full on with the solid toe of her boot.

The ball rocketed towards the Henneker's defensive wall, as straight as a die and dead centre. Before she could realise what was happening, or take any action in her defence, the tall Henneker's centre half was struck full on the chest, instantly punching all the air from her lungs and she keeled over onto her back like a falling tree.

What followed was utter confusion and blind panic. The other players in the wall were caught in two minds as to whether they should clear the ball or help their fallen team mate. Some of them looked to the referee to blow his whistle for an injury whilst others looked for the ball amidst a confused tangle of legs and boots as several Busy Bees players piled into the penalty area.

With so many bodies crammed into a small space - and all fighting for possession of the ball - every time one of the panicking Henneker's players managed to desperately try and clear it away the ball merely ricocheted off another pair of legs, and then another, bouncing erratically around like a pinball.

The bellowing of the crowd was now deafening as the supporters of each side roared encouragement for their players in what had become a desperate and frantic fight for survival.

True to her word, Bess stood a little way off from the crowd of players, waiting to see what would happen. One of the Henneker's defenders lunged at the ball in panic, but her boot made more contact with the air than with the leather and she executed a strange off-balance pirouette, unable to stop herself slamming down onto the hard ground with a *thud*.

The miss-kick had turned the ball into a spinning top and it now came whirling crazily out of the pack of players and towards Bessie's general direction.

Seizing her moment she dashed forward and carefully took the ball under control with both feet, conscious that she only had seconds before the Henneker's players would be on to her. She skilfully dribbled around the mêlée to be faced with an open goal. But the Henneker's goalie was quick to see the danger. She had been looking in completely the wrong direction, but as Bess appeared from around the pack to her left, the keeper was across the goalmouth like a greyhound and diving to smother the ball at Bessie's feet.

Before she knew what had hit her, Bess felt her legs snatched from under her and she was sailing through the air towards the open goal. She collided into the hard winter ground with a sickening crunch and for a second she saw nothing but a blur as her whole brain seemed to rattle inside her head. Then, as it quickly cleared, she looked up in time to see the dark brown of the leather ball trundling almost sedately over the goal line and into the open net.

Somehow, she had managed to instinctively slot the ball under the goalkeeper's body before the crunching challenge could stop her and now - before the crowd realised fully what had happened - there was a split second of stunned hush, like witnessing the silent flash of an explosion before the deafening sound of the *bang* reaches your ears.

The ground erupted into an ear splitting mix of euphoria from the Busy Bees supporters and cries of disgruntled disbelief from the Henneker's crowd.

GOAL! Was the single word that came ringing around the ground and in seconds Bess felt herself being lifted back to her feet and hugged in turn by every member of the Busy Bees. Surrounded by beaming smiles there was little point, or need, to say anything. She was still a little stunned, even shocked, at how she had managed to turn their fortunes around. It hadn't been the neatest or most skilful of goals she had ever scored, but it was a goal nevertheless and now, with the score at two-two it had become a very different game indeed. Although, there was still the small matter of how much time there was left.

Bess trotted up to the referee as she made her way back to the centre spot for the restart and as if reading her mind he glanced again at his watch.

"Six minutes of injury time and then extra time if you're still level" he said bluntly, holding up six fingers to Bess so as to make his point perfectly clear.

Her heart plummeted into her boots from the dizzy heights of just a few short seconds before. She felt her legs still had quite a bit of life left in them but for most, if not all, of the others the match had been a long hard slog and they were visibly drained, exhausted by the physical and mental strain of the whole occasion. Extra time would bring them, literally, to their knees.

Bess resolved that the result had to be in the next six minutes or not at all, one way or the other. With the new wave of hope the equaliser had brought there would be renewed energy for the Bees, revitalising tired legs and boots that felt like lead weights, but it wouldn't...it couldn't, last.

It had to be now or never if they were to win and it would be an enormous gamble. But as she put on a brave and spirited smile for the rest of the team, clapping her hands and shouting words of encouragement, Bess knew it would take nothing short of a miracle.

The single sharp blast of the referee's whistle to restart the game made Mary's heart jump and she sensed that this was really it, the final chapter in their long and breathtaking adventure. It was no surprise to her that from the kick off the Henneker's centre half, now recovered from her battering by Sally's dynamite kick at the defensive wall, sent a long high arching ball deep into the heart of the Bees' defence. She, like Bess, was very aware of the greater physical strength of the Henneker's players and of the almost overwhelming exhaustion she now felt in her own legs, the gulping of the crisp cold air into her lungs now almost painful with every breath.

Henneker's had been on the back foot for most if not the entire second half, but extra time for them was more an opportunity than a disaster. They would keep the ball in the Busy Bees' half, merely kicking it down field and making no real attempt to score. They would sit back....and wait. The Busy Bees would have to keep bringing the ball from deep in their own half every time, sapping vital energy from already tired legs. Henneker's would simply wait until their opponents literally ran themselves into the ground, and then seize their moment to snatch the victory.

Time and time again the ball sailed over the Bees' heads, deep into their own half. The kicks themselves were never threatening and each time were gathered quite easily by one of the Bees, only for her to then start the long race against time and exhaustion, back towards the Henneker's goal and a solid shield of red and white shirts.

Vital minutes ticked by and the hardness of the ground, the heavy leather ball and sheer fatigue had by now robbed most of the Busy Bees' legs of any strength or skill. Whatever ground they gained was easily lost as yet another easy tackle lost them possession, leaving them to then helplessly crane their necks upwards and follow the path of yet another long high kick downfield behind them.

Three minutes of the six had already passed and by now two of the Busy Bees had collapsed to the ground with cramp, followed quickly by a third. Bess looked around her in despair, boiling with anger and frustration. She had the fresher legs, but she could not be everywhere at once and she was an obvious danger to Henneker's and a target.

They had taken the precaution of having two of their larger players stick to Bess like glue, shadowing her every move no matter where she tried to go on the pitch and easily blocking any attempt for her to get the ball.

For the second or third time Connie lost the ball to a Henneker's defender, her weary legs unable to fend off the tackle, venting her despair with clenched fists and flinging her arms down hard against her sides. Bess could see she was close to tears and her heart went out to the young player, instead of fulfilling a dream she was living a nightmare. There were looks of anguish engrained on virtually every Busy Bees' face, including Mary's. They all looked completely spent; no energy, no ideas, no hope.

Surprisingly however, even the Henneker's spectators seemed to be growing tired of the lack of ambition and drive from *their* team and started to air their views. 'COME ON, GET ON WITH IT! ... DON'T JUST GIVE IT BACK! ....FINISH 'EM OFF HENNEKER'S! were some of the shouts from around the ground. Some even started to boo the time wasting tactics.

Bess noticed a flicker of unease at this on the face of the Henneker's captain and for a few brief moments, as she looked around her and heard the jeers, her look betrayed a lack of confidence and certainty as to what to do next.

The ball was at the Henneker's captain's feet and to the great surprise of the rest of her team she waved her arms for them to advance towards the Busy Bees' goal, urging them up the field. The instinctive response from the Bees was to fall back even deeper into their own half, caught off guard by the sudden change in attitude and tactics of their opponents and furiously back peddling to protect their penalty area.

Almost unseen by anyone other than Mary and Connie, Bess gestured for the three of them to stay where they were on the halfway line. Not only would it mean Henneker's having to keep at least two or three players back to defend but, if the Bees could just hang on, keep them out and win back the ball, it was also the slimmest of opportunities.

The three team mates eagerly followed the action in the Busy Bees' half, jogging nervously on the spot and feeling every lunging tackle a Bees player made, or missed. Already one of the Henneker's players, a very talented inside left, had swerved almost effortlessly past two of the Bees and was heading straight for goal.

Bess, Mary and Connie could only look on helplessly as first one challenge and then another was brushed aside by the player's fitness and strength. With great skill she had managed to make her way to the very edge of the Busy Bees' penalty area and seemed determined to take all the glory for herself. She steadied herself for a shot at goal, and time seemed to almost stand still as she gauged her moment carefully, waiting for the ball to stop bobbling on the hard winter ground. Her foot finally went back to strike the ball, but out of nowhere the yellow and black of a Busy Bees' sock flashed across her path, boot making solid contact with ball, pushing it harmlessly back to Sally in goal and sending the Henneker's attacker sprawling headlong into the penalty area.

"FOUL! PENALTY!" roared the Henneker's team with a single voice, their supporters joining in and leaping triumphantly into the air. But the referee would have none of it and shook his head vigorously.

"Fair tackle" he said pointedly. "Play on", and he waved for the game to continue as he dashed back up the field. Without hesitation Sally thumped the ball with her right boot as hard as she had ever done in her life, sending it sailing high over the heads of the Henneker's attack and into the midfield gap now occupied by Bess, Mary, Connie and two Henneker's defenders.

Immediately seizing the moment, Mary was onto the ball with a new spring in her step, bringing it under control before turning sharply and heading straight for the Henneker's goal. Bess and Connie each ran off at opposite angles, leaving the bemused defenders unsure as to who they should follow. One of them decided to take Mary on before she could get too far into the half and do any serious damage, but she did not bargain on Mary's raw grit and new found strength. Even though it was a crunching challenge it was the Henneker's player who was left stranded on the ground as Mary surged on.

By this time another Henneker's player had managed to sprint back to help her team mates and Mary realised her rush at goal was quickly running out of steam with the odds stacking up against her. There were now two defenders between her and glory, with the goalkeeper standing her ground and waiting for the right moment to pounce. Mary desperately tried to look as if she knew what she was doing, that there was a plan, but in truth it was all happening so fast she had no idea what to do or where her team mates were.

Instinctively she charged on and, as she had done so many times before, she ran straight at the defender, made an obvious glance to her left and then at the very last moment slotted the ball firmly to her right, tying herself up in knots and falling over in the process, but all the while hoping for the best.

As Mary hit the ground there was a huge cheer from the Henneker's supporters, but they almost instantly fell silent as Connie now skilfully collected Mary's pass at her feet and sprang towards the dead ball line with the speed of a player that had just come on the field. With Mary having drawn a defender there was now only one other red and white shirt and the goalkeeper to beat, with the rest of the Henneker's team desperately making ground back into their penalty area.

Connie swerved to her left and looked to be taking it all the way. The Henneker's goalie barked manic instructions to her team mate who hesitated, waiting for what she felt to be the right moment, before finally springing towards Connie. But the nippy winger was too quick and the defender too slow and in one almost seamless movement Connie deftly flipped the ball to the right around the defender's boot and sent a high looping ball across the face of the goal.

In the briefest of seconds, as the defender's legs whipped her own from under her, all Connie had seen to her left was a gathering mass of red and white shirts, and the cross was more last ditch desperation than well executed plan; one last chance with the last of her strength. She had put her all into the run and the cross and now lay sprawled on the side of the pitch anxiously looking back at the action through the side netting of the goal.

The ball was looping over the heads of a number of Henneker's players all jumping frantically to head it away. But then to her amazement Connie saw a Busy Bees shirt rise out of the crowd, head and shoulders above the rest.

In spite of her hatred for heading the ball Bess closed her eyes and hoped. She had timed her run and jump perfectly, giving the ball added power and speed as it flew off her head, straight as an arrow, and giving Connie a grandstand view as it hit the back of the net, dead centre.

From the roar that followed it was as if the entire ground had turned instantly into Busy Bees supporters, the very air rippling like a shock wave that almost knocked the players off their feet. Connie leapt up and raced into the penalty area towards Bess, leaping over the sprawling figure of the goalkeeper and dodging Henneker's players who now stood motionless, strewn around like statues, dejected, hands on hips in disbelief.

All the Busy Bees had now, somehow, found extra fire in their legs to race down the field to join in the celebrations. The Henneker's captain had grabbed the ball from the back of the net and started to run towards the centre spot, urging her players up the field for the restart. But they merely trotted half heartedly. This sudden blow had taken all the wind from their sails, aware that the referee was already looking at his watch and sensing that there would be barely time for even one more kick of the ball.

Sure enough, no sooner had the Bees reformed in their own half and the ball passed back by the Henneker's centre forward than the referee gave a long undulating blast on his whistle for the end of the game.

Immediately the Bees were drawn to each other in a single huddle, riding on the crest of the moment before some of them collapsed into an exhausted heap onto the hard winter ground, unable to fight the exhaustion any longer. Fans raced onto the pitch, a surging wave that completely surrounded and engulfed the players and carried them along towards the touchline, with Bess raised aloft on two pairs of strong shoulders and punching the air with both fists in sheer delight.

So what did the future hold for Bess and the team?

It was as Mrs Bessie Browell that their captain, centre forward and top goal scorer started the following season.

For Ned and all their fellow workers at the Bee-Hive Mill there was success and security.

For Mary, Connie, Enid, Sally, Amy and the rest of the Busy Bees, their bond of friendship, belief in each other, their strength and their determination to play the game they loved was never to fade. And as the most successful team in the Lancashire Girls' Football League their adventures were far from over.

In fact, with a whole world to conquer, they had only just begun!

Bess and the Busy Bees will be back!

For more great items on the first golden age

of women's football visit

www.womensoccershirts.com

Like us on Facebook/womensoccerbooks

and follow us on Twitter

wsoccershirts1